MW01063618

Not
QUITE
SCARAMOUCHE

Tor Books by Joel Rosenberg

Not Exactly the Three Musketeers
Not Quite Scaramouche

Not
QUITE
SCARAMOUCHE

JOEL ROSENBERG

TOR®

A TOM DOHERTY ASSOCIATES BOOK
NEW YORK

This is a work of fiction. All the characters and events portrayed in this novel are either fictitious or are used fictitiously.

NOT QUITE SCARAMOUCHE

A Tor Book
Published by Tom Doherty Associates, LLC
175 Fifth Avenue
New York, NY 10010

www.tor.com

Tor® is a registered trademark of Tom Doherty Associates, LLC.

Library of Congress Cataloging-in-Publication Data

Rosenberg, Joel.
    Not quite Scaramouche / Joel Rosenberg.—1st ed.
        p. cm.
    "A Tom Doherty Associates books."
    ISBN 0-312-86897-9 (alk. paper)
    I .Title.

PS3568.O786 N65 2001
813'.54—dc21

00-047918

First edition: January 2001

Printed in the United States of America

0 9 8 7 6 5 4 3 2 1

for Harry and Spring
always missed; never forgotten

Not
QUITE
SCARAMOUCHE

Prologue:

✠ A Night in Biemestren

Pirojil liked the night.

Yes, in part it was that the darkness hid his face—in large part—but there was more to it than that. After all, a mask could hide his face—although, under most circumstances, that would draw more attention than even his ugliness did—and a beard and mustache did just that at the moment.

No, it wasn't just that it concealed his ugly face. Darkness was a comforting thing, a blanket of shadows and grayness that warmed him like a distant fire. With a quick motion of cloak and body, you could disappear into that darkness, or reach out from it with the steely finger of a sharp blade, darkened with lampblack.

Darkness offered detachment, both physical and emotional.

And detachment was a good thing in his line of work.

Nights in Biemestren were brighter than most; by edict of the lord warden, oil lamps flared brightly from just after sunset until just before sunrise in front of every commercial establishment along most streets, including the one that was officially named the Street of Pirondael's Treachery—the new emperor, or more likely his mother, had gone in for some serious renaming—but which, for reasons nobody seemed to be able to remember, was called Dog Street by all the natives. It was filled with lower-class establishments—taverns and bordellos that catered to the soldier trade, mainly.

Loud, drunken singing and a quartet of staggering Tyrnaelians poured out through the open door of the Tavern of the Broken Mug—at least, that was what Pirojil thought it was called, given that the emblem mounted at the edge of the roof was a mug fit for a mythical giant, with a jagged crack sawed down the side, still dripping water from the earlier rainstorm.

He took a battered leather eyepatch from his pouch and adjusted it about his left eye, tightening the thong hard behind his head to prevent any light from leaking in, then shrugged his cloak up to hide the Cullinane green and gold stitching on his collar and epaulets, and shouldered his way in, his left hand automatically going to the hilt of his sword to pull it vertical so that the tip didn't brush against anybody.

It made sense to be careful about that sort of thing. It would be easy to start a fight, and at times when he had nothing better to do he might do just that—he had, in the past, and he would again, some night where he needed to feel blood on his knuckles even if that meant tasting his own blood in his mouth—but he didn't want to do so accidentally, and for no purpose. If he wanted a fight this night, it would be easy to find a purpose.

The Broken Mug was a raucous and manically happy place. Over in the corner three drummers maintained a rhythmic beat that reminded Pirojil of a galloping horse, while a dozen Tyrnaelians belched out a song whose words Pirojil probably could have made out, if he had ever acquired a taste for porcine Tyrnaelian drinking songs, which he hadn't.

And wasn't bloody likely to. There wasn't enough beer in the world . . .

The line of men in front of a curtained doorway moved quickly enough that Pirojil was sure there were at least three whores in the back room, and hoped it was at least four or five.

A quartet of imperials in the black-and-white of the House Guard kept dour watch over their mugs from a darkened far corner, carefully ignored by all and sundry. Baronial soldiers saw duty in the capital as an opportunity to drink and swive away their pay.

Imperials lived there and expected—and demanded—better prices on everything.

Pirojil was sympathetic—in principle, but in practice you didn't save up enough money for your retirement by getting four-for-three on beers or whores. There were, however, ways to put aside a few coins here and there . . .

He slid a copper quartermark coin across the bar and accepted a large mug of sour beer in return. He had had worse and he had had better. Good enough to get drunk on, and that would be fine for lonely men, late at night, and more than enough to boost the spirits of the four men in peasant's tunics who sat in front of a low table in the darkened corner farthest away from the fireplace.

Reading people came naturally to Pirojil. These four had come to the capital to sell something—and given that the harvest was many tendays away, it would be livestock, and a fair amount of it, or four men could not have been spared from their crofts long enough to make a trip to Biemestren and back. Pirojil could practically have counted the coin in their pouches.

Drinking and whoring up a bit of their profits was only natural, and as one blocky man rose to take his place in line in front of the curtain to the back rooms, an imperial soldier pushed out through the curtains and beckoned to his companions, who, despite a few grumbled complaints, quickly drained the last of their tankards, rose, and left.

Pirojil nodded to himself. Midnight was fast approaching, and while baronial soldiers would not likely have to put up with a nightly head count in the barracks, the imperials would be on duty the next morning or the next afternoon at the latest, and neither imperial decurions nor officers were noted for their understanding and sympathy at lateness. Or at anything else, for that matter.

As the imperials exited into the night, raucous laughter followed them. One started to turn back—putting up with mockery from Tyrnaelians was probably not something any of them cared for— but desisted when one of his fellows grabbed his arm and pulled him along. There were times to fight—and times not to be late.

With the last of the imperials through the door and out into the night, the speed and volume of the singing and drumming picked up instantly, as though the Tyrnaelians had been holding back out of respect for the stodginess of the departed soldiers. Pirojil muffled a grin.

One Tyrnaelian laughed loudly, raucously, and the cackling was picked up by the rest, as though to emphasize for the imperials that the real fun only began when local soldiers had to report back to their barracks.

A civilian, a well-muscled young man whose clean, well-tailored white linen tunic spoke of wealth, joined in the laughter, too loudly.

"A round of beer for my Tyrnaelian friends, if you please," he called to the innkeeper, his voice too loud still, his tone too familiar by half. At least.

"Friends, are we?" a thick-set Tyrnaelian answered, quietly. He was a big man, half a head taller than his companions.

The silver bars on his collar points proclaimed him a decurion; the untarnished shine on them and the empty pitchers stacked on the table suggested that he was busy drinking up his promotion pay with some friends. This was, quite possibly, the last time he would be able to do that; that was one of the troubles with rank. After the first or fifth or thirty-fifth time he put his former drinking friends on extra duty, he would have to find himself new friends to do his drinking with. He would have to find himself some higher-class establishment to do his drinking in, as well: flashing his rank off-duty would turn out to be more trouble than it was worth, and he wouldn't be able to rub elbows with ordinary soldiers in this sort of dive without having to do that.

But let him enjoy tonight, at least for the moment. There was no possible harm in that. The lot of them were in well-worn but clean uniforms, and from that and the rate at which they were drinking and swiving up their pay, Pirojil guessed that they were being rotated out of the capital, and back to their barony. It didn't do to keep baronial troops too long away from home, and that was something that both the barons and the emperor agreed on, although likely for entirely different reasons.

The decurion more staggered than walked over to where the merchant sat, and plopped himself down in a chair. "Friends, you say," he said from around a sneer, his voice thick and slurred. "You will forgive me not recognizing the old companion you surely must be."

"No offense was intended, Decurion," the merchant said, quietly. "I've had a bit of luck in the markets of late, and I've always thought that to share the good luck is to plant more." He raised his tankard. "This good beer comes from grain that was planted— scattered across plowed fields as though it was simply thrown away—only to come back twenty- and thirty-fold.

"Why should it not be that way for a round of beer bought for soldiers of Baron Tyrnael? We're all in the same empire now. Yes, I'm a Holt, fealty-bound to Barony Keranahan, and you're part of the same army that raped and pillaged and burned its way across all of Holtun in general and Keranahan in particular," he said. "But that's all over now."

He smoothed a hand down the front of his tunic, as though emphasizing that he was dressed in fine linen, rather than the rough cotton and raw wool of their uniforms. "It's my pleasure to share with you just a small, a tiny, an unimportant portion of the wealth that my wise trading and good fortune have brought me." He spread his arms wide, as though he was about to embrace them all. "Could anything be more reasonable?"

The Tyrnaelian muttered something under his breath. Pirojil wouldn't have bet against the decurion throwing a punch or the beer tankard at the merchant—Pirojil didn't particularly care for his smarminess, himself—but perhaps the decurion's new rank had brought some caution with it: Instead, he rose, and taking away the merchant's tankard with a broad sweep of his arm, returned to his place, accompanied by the drunken, mocking comments of several of the soldiers in various parts of the tavern.

One of the decurion's companions muttered something about how he wouldn't have taken that shit, not off a nose-high Holt, not last tenday, and if the decurion's bars made him go this soft, well, shit, they were all in for some easy duty, and wasn't that grand.

The decurion just glared at his friends and at the merchant as the merchant shrugged at the wet circle on the table where his tankard had rested, and rose.

The merchant settled his debt with a flip of a coin to the tavern keeper and headed out the door into the night, pausing only to give the decurion a quick salute that was more than mildly insolent under the circumstances.

That did it. The decurion pulled one of his fellows close and whispered in his ear. The soldier rose, and Pirojil quietly drained the last of his own beer and followed him out into the night.

Pirojil switched the eyepatch from his left eye to his right, which brightened the night considerably. It would be less than ideal in a fight, of course, but being night-blind would be worse, in or out of a fight, and his right eye would adjust to the darkness soon enough.

The Tyrnaelian whistled a drunken ditty as he followed the merchant, as though to entertain himself. Pirojil took to the shadows, his cloak reversed, the taupe side out, as he followed the two down to the corner. The merchant and his follower continued up Dog Street, while Pirojil moved swiftly into an alley between two wattle-and-daub buildings, and broke into a fast walk intended to eat up distance without drawing attention to himself by running. He pulled a soft cap from his belt and pulled it down over his ears, hiding the sloping forehead that added to his ugliness. From any distance at all, he would no longer be recognizable; he was just another bearded man in a cloak and a cap and, if you looked particularly closely, an eyepatch. Hardly uncommon in Biemestren, or anywhere else.

By the time his quick steps took him up the street then back across, the whistling had stopped, and a quartet of dark shapes had joined the single Tyrnaelian soldier.

The street—Pirojil didn't remember the name—was quiet hereabouts; the merchant had led his pursuers into a largely residential area, mainly consisting of two-story buildings housing lower-class laborers in conditions worse than even the roughest barracks. It was the sort of neighborhood where doors were barred from sunset to sunrise, and wise people avoided the night. Biemestren was the capital of the empire, and while there were benefits that came with empire, the constant flow of people in and out of the capital brought not just trade and wealth—although it certainly brought plenty of that—but crime and misfortune. You could sentence all the thieves you wanted to a tour of the copper mines, and dangle murderers from the gibbet like crabapples on a tree, and others would come to take their place, or be driven to.

Pirojil understood the temptation, after all.

The merchant threw a glance over his shoulder, and Pirojil didn't have to see the expression of alarm on his face to understand what the quickening of his pace meant, and as he broke into a trot, and then ducked into an alley, with a communal laugh the Tyrnaelian soldiers followed him.

The alley was barely lit by a lantern on a pole across the street, the flickering light reducing everything to shades of dark gray and black.

Pirojil removed his eyepatch. It was dark, but he had made his way through—and fought in—darker.

No windows opened on the alley, save for the shuttered ones on the second story. The ground was littered with detritus—a broken wagon wheel here, a jagged scrap of broken stone there. A carefully stacked pile of wood laths spoke of some construction project going on in one of the neighboring buildings—probably some landlord partitioning an already tiny apartment into two smaller ones.

But the alley terminated with a high fence, shards of glass plastered into its surface to prevent climbing.

Cornered, nowhere to go, the terrified merchant turned to face his pursuers, one arm outstretched, palm out, as though he could hold them all at arm's length if only he wished hard enough.

The decurion stood silently for a moment. "Not quite so bold with your language, are you now, my old, dear companion, are you? Not quite so eager to rub a few coppers together under our noses, eh?"

The soldiers shuffled forward slowly.

"Truly, I meant no harm," the merchant said. "I just wanted to, to—"

"You just wanted to ask for a beating," the decurion said. "You just wanted to show disrespect for Baron Tyrnael, and his house. You just wanted to—"

It was at that moment that he lunged at the merchant.

In principle, Pirojil approved. No matter how little you respected an adversary, it would make no sense to give him a chance to, say, get a small, hidden knife out and into play, and surely a merchant who carried money would have a knife on him somewhere.

They would just beat him thoroughly, strip him of his money and valuables, and then be gone in the morning, leaving behind nothing but bruises and empty accusations to fall on imperial ears. Armsmen had seen losers of fights before, and this fellow was well-muscled enough that it would be at least credible that he had involved himself in a fight, rather than been the victim of a simple robbery.

And the bragging merchant was a Holt, to boot. While there were certainly a few notable exceptions, most of the imperial troops and armsmen were either native-born Biemish or immigrants, and there was more than enough long-term hatred of Holtun and Holts to go around.

The only trouble with the decurion's lunge was that he went right through the merchant, as though the merchant simply wasn't there.

Things happened quickly after that.

A dark shape dropped down a line from the nearest roof, just after a silent explosion of light shone brightly, even though Pirojil had his hands firmly over his tightly closed eyes. It was more like the light was in his brain then in his eyes, although he was only barely dazzled as he dropped his cloak to one shoulder, and moved swiftly into the alley.

The silence was almost deafening: he could no more hear the shouts of the Tyrnaelians than he could his own breathing, or the pounding of his own heart that had always been the rhythmic accompaniment to a fight.

Coming from behind, he threw his cloak over the head of the nearest Tyrnaelian, then kicked the man next to him hard, up against the wall, slamming his elbow into the ribs of each in turn. The breath of the second man was warm and fetid in Pirojil's nostrils, but soundless.

Kethol had already made his way down his rope, had kicked the decurion once, hard, in passing, and in a move that Pirojil hadn't seen since Durine died, had grabbed hold of the hair of the two remaining men and brought their heads together so hard that they bounced.

That was when a shadow in a dark corner of the alley brightened momentarily, resolving itself into the shape of Erenor. Daintily, delicately, he looped a cord over the decurion's neck, then drew it tight with a quick snap of the wrist, securing the other end of the cord to the soldier's thumbs before proceeding on to the next man, and giving him the same treatment.

Pirojil was already trussing up his own opponents, and quickly had them bound, with their own cloaks tied around their heads. Kethol was only a little slower.

Erenor's fingers worked quickly in the dark as he moved from one man to another, quickly stripping each not just of pouch, but of other valuables: one man's silver belt buckle; another's bone-hilted belt knife; a third's bootheel, which turned out to be a cache for several leather-wrapped coins.

Pirojil smiled. Erenor had a taste for this sort of theft—something that Pirojil had never doubted any more than Kethol had—but he also had a talent for it. Not just the setting up part, but the cashing in, as well.

It wouldn't do to leave the Tyrnaelians trussed up until morning—that would announce robbery, rather than fight.

Kethol beckoned to Erenor and Pirojil to get going, and Pirojil backed slowly out of the alley while Erenor set off at a brisk pace.

By the time the three of them returned to the rooms they rented just down the hill from the imperial barracks, the patch and soft cap had been returned to Pirojil's pouch and belt, as had the false beard; Kethol and Erenor were out of their disguises and dressed as soldiers, as well.

They passed through the common room in company, singing in off-key, drunken harmony a song about a captain and a mule. It drew glances and glares from all and sundry, but it was far better to be seen coming back from a night of drinking than to be re-membered as skulking in, as though they were trying to hide some-thing.

That entrance had been Erenor's idea, and Erenor did have his uses. Which probably had a lot to do with why he was still a simple soldier of Barony Cullinane—although not as much so as the fact that Pirojil still had most of his spell books safely hidden away.

Singing and weaving, they made their way down the hall to their rooms, where a wrought-iron pot of thick, meaty-smelling soup burbled quietly on the small brazier in front of the empty fireplace. A half-dozen wooden bowls and spoons were stacked on the mantelpiece above the fireplace, and the dirty ones had been taken away.

The wall lantern lit, the door shut and the bar dropped, Erenor and Kethol donned leather gloves and carefully, silently, lifted the cauldron of soup and set it aside, then did the same with the brazier.

Pirojil quickly removed the cover to their hiding place, and sketchily sorted through the collection of coins and jewels and the odd, irregular lump of gold or silver. He would trust Kethol with his life, but Erenor was, at best, an only partly known quantity. Yes, Erenor had saved all their lives in Keranahan, but he had been part of that all—self-preservation and loyalty were two different things. Right now, Pirojil would trust more to the fact that he had the most important of Erenor's spell books quite safely hidden away than he would to any protestations of personal loyalty.

He actually had gotten to like Erenor, if only a little—but trust him? No. He could trust Erenor to do what Erenor thought was in his own best interest, and that was good enough, all things considered.

The cache was re-covered, and Pirojil ladled out a bowl full of soup for each of them, himself last. He raised his own bowl in a toast, then sipped at the soup, not bothering with the spoon. It was thick and salty, the vegetables reduced by endless hours of cooking to an indistinct, but tasty, mush.

In the flickering light of the wall lantern, the three set their weapons and accoutrements aside, and more collapsed than lay down on their sleeping pallets.

You didn't get rich on an ordinary soldier's pay, and it made sense to keep an eye to the future. It was, after all, entirely possible that Pirojil would make it to old age, as unlikely as that had seemed at times. It would be nice to have something to count on, preferably to stack high on a table and count.

Yes, there always would be a place for loyal retainers with the baron, but as raw and unpleasant as a soldier's life could easily be, neither Pirojil nor Kethol would ever be of a mind to trade that for the lot of a household servant.

It was one thing to put your sword and your body between those you were sworn to protect and danger, and it would be another thing entirely to haul slop buckets up and down stairs at the command of some old woman, or, worse, some man who had never set foot on blood-soaked ground.

But a little bit of money put away here and there could add up, and if the source of a fraction of it was Tyrnaelian soldiers who had been looking to beat and rob somebody, that wouldn't bother Pirojil any.

Yes, money was money—but it did matter how you got it. He would no more steal from the baron than he would from Kethol—if you had no personal loyalty, then you had nothing—but the decurion and his friends had been fair game.

And, besides, it wasn't quite stealing—just a not-quite-fair application of deception, with an illusion or two thrown in.

Kethol, only one of his boots off, was already fast asleep, his snoring regular and reassuring. That was a strange thing about the rawboned redhead: he would snore and stir all night long when they were quartered in the city, or in the barracks at the baron's keep—but put him on cold ground, wrapped in blankets, just out of sight of a road, and he would sleep silently, waking at the slightest touch or out-of-place sound.

Erenor sipped quietly at his soup. He was a good-looking, well-muscled man, with his smile that was often too easy and rarely sincere, but Pirojil had long since given up hating handsome men simply for being handsome, as most of the time they gave him additional reason, anyway.

The trouble was that he wasn't Durine.

Durine was dead, and Erenor was only his replacement in title, not in function. His swordsmanship was coming along quickly—too quickly; Pirojil suspected that Erenor's background included some work with the sword, despite the wizard's protestations to the contrary—and he had a steady hand and a good eye with a cross-bow, although he would never be a longbowman. And even though most of the spells Erenor had mastered were illusions—seemings, mostly trivial ones—there were advantages to be had for Pirojil and Kethol to be partnered with a wizard who was not known to be a wizard.

But Pirojil ate his soup slowly, and waited until he was sure that Erenor was asleep before he set his bowl down carefully on the packed-dirt floor, and lay back, covering himself with his cloak, and then pillowing the back of his head on his hands.

Pirojil wouldn't have traded a hundred like Erenor for two-thirds of a Durine, but, then again, that hadn't been his choice. Durine was dead, and Erenor was of some value, and there was a distinct advantage for Pirojil and Kethol to be partnered with a wizard, even if the wizard was, like Erenor, not much of one except when it came to illusions.

He lay there a long time thinking about that.

He was never sure whether he had actually slept or not when there was a loud knock on the door, followed by three short knocks, then two more.

Kethol was on his feet a fraction of a heartbeat before Pirojil, with Erenor lagging far behind.

"Who is it?" Kethol asked, at Pirojil's nod.

"Messenger," came back through the door. "From the imperial proctor. You are summoned to his presence; he said to tell you that he has an idea."

Pirojil frowned. There were worse things in the world than Walter Slovotsky with an idea, but not many.

But there was only one possible answer, and Kethol beat him to it: "We're on our way."

Part I

BIEMESTREN

1

Earlier: the Proctor and the Emperor

Life is a series of unplanned accidents—largely
because nobody asked my opinion. Me, I'd
rather it was a series of planned accidents, and
I can think of a few people I'd very much like
to plan some for.

—Walter Slovotsky

I t would be infuriating to a lesser man that the emperor didn't
see things his way all the time.

But Walter Slovotsky wasn't, at least in his own opinion, a
lesser man. Besides, life would get boring if everything was easy.
Life wasn't boring. Life was, sometimes, far too much the contrary.

"My point, do you think?" the emperor more said than asked,
lowering his practice sword, his voice level and even, although
maybe there was a hint of a challenge in it. Slovotsky wasn't sure.

But the emperor's point? That would depend on what rules
they were using, if any. By standard practice rules, no point had
been scored—Slovotsky's springy practice sword had touched the
emperor's leather chest plate within a heartbeat of when the emperor's own sword had scored on Slovotsky's left biceps. Had it been
a real fight, Slovotsky would have come out with a painful if not
disabling wound, and Thomen Furnael, Emperor of Holtun-Bieme,
would have had his belly pierced deeply and would not be wondering at all whose point it was.

This style of sparring encouraged defense, and waiting for an opportunity to score a touch, some disabling wound to the arm or leg that would, in a real fight, slow an opponent down enough so that you could go in for the kill safely. Slovotsky's personal preference for that sort of thing was to anchor a foot or leg with a thrown knife from a bit more distance.

If he had to engage in a sword fight at all.

That wouldn't be anything close to Walter Slovotsky's preferred method of settling a serious argument. A well-sighted rifle at one hundred yards was far preferable, and if the opponent was missing a leg, blindfolded, hobbled, and tied to a stake with a nice circular target pinned over his heart, that would make it all the better.

But in life, enemies were rarely considerate enough to arrange things so conveniently, alas. Sometimes—too often—they weren't even considerate enough to identify themselves. Even to themselves.

It made for more complication than one would like; it made the dowager empress's naked hatred almost refreshing, by contrast. Almost.

"Perhaps you didn't hear me," the emperor said, irritated. "I said, that I thought it was my point."

"No, I don't think so," Walter Slovotsky said. He raised his practice sword again in salute. "Or perhaps you're changing the rules on me here when you allow me to change them on more important things?"

He couldn't make out Thomen's facial expression through his mask, but a stiffness in the shoulders and posture said that he caught the emperor by surprise. That was a good thing, in moderation. Moderation had its virtues; there was a reason that the term in Dwarvish for dwarves meant "the Moderate People," and Walter Slovotsky liked dwarves, generally.

Not that Walter Slovotsky was a big believer in moderation for himself. Nor even a moderate believer in moderation, come to think of it.

Thomen didn't answer, at first, then: "Very well. Your point it is." His breath was coming in audible pants, and he removed his mask for a moment as he walked to a side table and poured himself a goblet of water and drank it in one large gulp before setting it back down.

He was, for all his flaws, a handsome man, strength of will showing in the bones of his face, and in the too rarely blinking eyes that seemed to miss nothing. His hair was black, jet black, the black of a raven's wing, but his close-cropped beard was shot with gray, as though he was only giving in by stages to the pressures of the Silver Crown and throne of Holtun-Bieme.

But as he returned from the side table, there was still that spring in his step that had been too long absent, and Walter Slovotsky wondered if the cause was the program of rest and recreation that Walter and Bren Adahan had talked him into, or whether it was the admittedly lovely Lady Leria that Kethol had brought back from Barony Keranahan.

No reason it couldn't be both, of course.

"Have at it, shall we?" Thomen asked, replacing his mask.

He was loosening up some, granted, Slovotsky decided, but somebody really ought to do something to remove that metaphorical broomstick he had stuck up his butt.

The throne room was empty, well, as empty as it got.

The Kiaran tapestries still covered the walls; if you squinted, you could almost have believed that you were in a green glen, surrounded by capering fawns frozen in mid-leap by some artistic wizard.

The throne itself and the smaller one next to it for the dowager empress—the old, and mean, vicious one, not Andrea Cullinane—remained on their podium, and the long banquet table had been separated into component parts, smaller tables that interlocked at their ends like jigsaw puzzles, and stacked in pairs, top-to-top, in the corner farthest from the great hearth. The thick carpets had been rolled up and carried away to be beaten in the open air, and replaced before Parliament met.

But there were no guards or servants, although the latter were as close as the pull of a bell-rope, and the former as close as a loud yell for help.

But Walter Slovotsky was one of the few people allowed to come into the emperor's presence either armed or unescorted, and one of the *very* few allowed into the presence both armed and unescorted—that came with the job of imperial proctor—and neither he nor Thomen particularly wanted House troops to see the emperor lose a point in an embarrassing way.

Or, for that matter, to see Slovotsky himself do so. For the emperor, it would be undignified, and Slovotsky had his own legend—read: unwarranted reputation—to maintain.

Besides, as much as such a thing was possible under the circumstances, Slovotsky and the emperor were friends, and friends could always use some time to themselves.

Straw had been scattered over the bare stone floor, to make the footing more treacherous. In a real fight, you could never count on having good footing beneath you, and Murphy—who, Walter Slovotsky explained to the locals, was the Spirit of Fighting and Battles on the Other Side, which was more true than not—would make sure you never did.

Thomen raised his sword in salute, which Slovotsky echoed, and they closed again. This time, Slovotsky tried to draw an attack, but Thomen read the spacing between the two of them better than Slovotsky had, and closed with a quick bounce that led him parry Slovotsky's counter, and then score easily on Slovotsky's sword arm before bouncing back out of range.

"Not bad." Walter Slovotsky stepped back and pulled off his mask. There had to be something more comfortable than this boiled-leather hood, ventilated with barely enough slits. An Other Side fencing mask would be ideal, but that would require stiff wire mesh, and New Pittsburgh was far too busy with more important production.

Eventually. There were other uses for wire mesh, after all. It would be nice to have all the windows of the castle unshuttered on a hot afternoon, and let the breeze blow through without turning it into a refuge for every bloodsucking bug in the Middle Lands.

Slovotsky had to force himself not to scratch at the maddeningly itching cluster at the base of the back of his neck. The fencing mask had been rubbing at the bites, making them worse than usual.

It had all been much worse last night than usual, and Slovotsky and Aiea had spent too much of it alternately unshuttering their window when it got too hot and stuffy, and then closing it when the mosquitoes took the open window as an open invitation.

Well, if nobody else was going to do it, Slovotsky didn't mind confronting the wizard. Walter and Henrad went way back, after all.

"Again," the Emperor commanded, lowering his own mask. "Have at you," he said, in English, the words slurred.

"Gesundheit."

"Eh?"

"Oh. That's English for 'As you would have it, my Emperor.' "

"A compact language, this Englits of yours. I should make it a point to learn more of it."

"It has its virtues," Walter said, moving in. "Baron Minister Adahan has noted that one, on more than one occasion."

They were well into a complicated sequence of counter, riposte, and counter-riposte that was, Slovotsky thought, destined to end with the emperor's blade just enough out of line for Slovotsky to beat it to one side, when the door creaked open behind him.

That was enough of a distraction that Thomen was able to judge the distance better than Slovotsky could, and ended the point with a well-judged stop-thrust that actually stung.

Slovotsky managed a too late parry, and spun around in annoyance, prepared to give whoever it was a few choice words about interrupting.

He was only slightly surprised and vaguely disappointed to see that it was the dowager empress herself, a thin smile on her pinched face as she silently tapped her fingertips together in applause.

Well, *a* dowager empress, at least: Beralyn Furnael, the Emperor's mother. It would have been a lot nicer to see Andrea Cullinane, the late emperor's widow. It wasn't just that Andrea was as lovely from skin to bone as Beralyn was ugly, although that certainly helped things.

"Well struck," she said. "Well struck, indeed."

Thomen had his mask off and his sword tucked under his arm as he walked swiftly to her for a quick and dutiful kiss.

"Good afternoon, Mother," he said. "You're looking well today."

She chuckled thinly. "Bieme and the whole Empire are fortunate that you can lie so easily and so well, Thomen. Truth is only an occasional tool of statecraft."

Actually, she looked about the same way she usually did, a collection of lumpy flesh covered in black muslin, topped by a sagging-jawed face that was itself framed by a tight helmet of gray hair fastened in a severe bun, small, piggish eyes softening only for a moment when she looked at her son, but hardening into an unconcealed look of hatred when she turned to Slovotsky.

Truth was an occasional tool of statecraft, after all.

"Good afternoon, Beralyn," he said.

"And to you, too, Lord Proctor," she said, ignoring the familiarity. "Are you not going to compliment me on my appearance, as well?"

Damned if I do, and damned if I don't. Slovotsky gave a slight bow of admiration. "I don't recall ever having seen you look healthier and more vigorous," he said.

Let her make what she would of that.

She barely sniffed. "I have some matters I wish to discuss with my son," she said, characteristically coming to the point right away. Beralyn was capable of subtlety, but she didn't waste it on the likes of Walter Slovotsky.

"Then I'll either beg leave to take my leave of the two of you—or maybe just go," Walter said.

He stripped off his fencing armor and mopped at his sweaty chest with a towel, tossing the armor and towel toward a far corner before he picked up his tunic and reclaimed his gear, his back to the emperor and his mother. That he was allowed to be armed in the Presence didn't mean that he wanted Beralyn and anybody else with a grudge against him to know just how well armed he was, or with what and where, after all.

One throwing knife went into the sheath in his sleeve, while another one went into a sheath hidden under the skirt of his tunic. As he belted his sword about his waist, he took the opportunity to check and be sure that his Therranji garrotes were still in his pouch. A brace of pistols completed his everyday armament—well, that and the other knives he had hidden, one sheath tucked just inside the waistband of his trousers, which he transferred invisibly (he hoped) to his boot as he bloused the legs of his bulky, loose trousers.

"You and Aiea will be at table tonight," Thomen said, as Walter pulled the door open. It was not a suggestion.

"Looking forward to it," he said, as he exited into the hall and closed the door behind him. Lying was an important tool of statecraft, after all.

With only two of the barons in residence, he had been hoping to skip it. There would be enough state dinners when Parliament convened, in just a few tendays.

A nice quiet dinner in their rooms would have been preferable. Aiea, having spent her morning as a member of the effete nobility, was spending her afternoon with her class of castle servant children, teaching them the rudiments of reading, writing, and arithmetic in the storeroom halfway up the southeast guard tower that she had converted to a classroom, although with her adopted mother due in Biemestren any day, she could probably lay that job off on Andrea, if she wanted to. Both of them liked to keep busy, and while both mother and daughter could and did handle themselves well among the nobility here for Parliament, both seemed to prefer teaching to that.

Understandable, really. Teach a kid to read and write and calculate, and you open up the world to him, even if it was a strange world.

The guard across the hall eyed him suspiciously; Walter headed down the long hall, toward daylight.

Not that Walter had seriously considered trying to eavesdrop on Beralyn and Thomen. Yes, there would be some advantages to being a fly on the wall at their conversation, but that was the only way he would hear something interesting. Beralyn played her hand closely, and Thomen was too loyal a son to tip her hand.

It would have been nice to have the room wired, but the technology for that was still, probably, years away—and talk about whisper channels and echoes and secret passages had long kept conspiratorial and private conversations in whispers, or out in the open air with no one about.

Walter Slovotsky rubbed at the back of his neck. It still itched, and he could either see the Spidersect healer about it first, and have the itching healed, or go brace the wizard about the bugs.

A lesser man would have picked the Spider, and Walter Slovotsky didn't mind passing for a lesser man.

Thomen knew what Mother was going to say before she said it, at least in general outline. There were times when he found it irritating, but this wasn't one of them.

"Well, Mother," he said, "what approach is it going to be today? Political: me marrying, and producing an heir, why that would make the Empire more stable, and bring peace to the land. Or personal: you want grandchildren, and it is my responsibility to produce them. Or philosophical: life does go on, but only for those whose line follows the past into the future. Or practical: if I keep—"

"Enough." Her lips pursed tightly. "You know how I feel, and we'll speak no more on that." Did she actually believe herself? "Actually, I was going to ask you about the seating at table tonight."

There was trouble on the border, more and more stories of orcs up in the hills of his—what had been his—barony, a baronial governor who had probably been involved in a conspiracy against the Crown . . . and Mother wanted him to worry about dinner seating.

He shook his head. It was strange, and he wished there was somebody he could talk about it with: he had had to manage most of the same problems when he was regent, waiting for Jason Cullinane to assume the Crown.

Keep the governors and barons honest; raise taxes and armies; judge and condemn; forgive if not forget—he had taken it all seriously, yes, but he had had the luxury of distance, of knowing that, finally, it was somebody else's responsibility, not his.

"Well," he said, "Niphael arrived just this morning, and Nerahan's party has been sighted on the Prince's Road—"

She interrupted him with a raised eyebrow.

"—as you well know, since you read the same telegraph message I did, probably before I did—so let's put them at the head, next to me."

She smiled slyly. "And Lady Leria Euar'den?"

He returned her smile, but didn't bother to dispute the family name. Whether or not Leria was the heir to the Euar'den dynasty that had ruled Tynear wasn't terribly relevant, save as that would soften the blow to the Biemish barons if he married a Holt.

If.

She was lovely, at that, but . . .

. . . but what? Forinel? He was long gone, and almost certainly dead. Could she still be pining after him? She seemed awfully comfortable in the presence of her three regular bodyguards—but she had been through much with them, and while one of them did sleep across her doorway each night, were there more than that going on it would have been reported to him, via Mother, if nobody else.

He shrugged it off. An emperor had more important things to worry about than why a lovely young woman seemed to harbor some dark secret.

It was all such a juggling act.

Back before the wars, back before it all fell apart, back when he was a boy, his father had brought him to the fair in Biemestren, once, and it was there that Thomen Furnael had seen his first juggler. He had thought, until his father corrected him—and Father was never wrong when he spoke so certainly—that it was some form of magic, but no: it had merely been skill that had kept a cascade of objects in the air.

An egg, a knife, two brightly colored juggling sticks, and at least in his memory, a full score other objects had flown through the air, seemingly more gently guided than carefully thrown by the bare-chested man whose eyes never left the stream as he continued his endless patter, in exchange for just a few coppers thrown into the wooden bowl at his feet.

But something had gone wrong, and the juggler had cried out, his finger flying to his mouth as everything that he had kept juggling fell about him in an absurd rain.

Thomen was willing to bet that the juggler's mother had never bothered *him* about seating plans . . .

2

Bats, Belfries, and Burnings

Meddle not in the affairs of wizards, for you are
not immune to itching, bolts of lightning, or being turned into a newt.
　　　　　　　　　　　—Walter Slovotsky

*T*here are some things man was not meant to know, Walter
Slovotsky thought as he climbed the seemingly endless steps
that wound up and around the tower.

One of which, for example, was why wizards, like owls, tended
to roost in the least accessible place available. Or maybe it made
sense, if you closed your eyes and looked at it sideways. The southwest tower was as far away as you could get from the donjon and
still have the protection of the castle walls, which kept Henrad
available, but not too nearby.

Normal folks didn't like to hang out around wizards, except, of
course, when they really needed one. Sort of like cops, except cops
couldn't issue lightning bolts from their fingers, and wizards didn't
eat doughnuts.

The wind blew, cool and dry, from the west, and Walter had
barely worked up a sweat by the time he reached the top.

The arched doorway was open, but light didn't seem to penetrate into the darkness beyond. Maybe there was some movement
off in the murk—darkest gray on black, shapelessness in motion—
but he wouldn't have wanted to swear to it.

"Henrad?" he called out. "Henrad?"

Meddle not in the affairs of wizards, Walter Slovotsky thought, *for your skin is thin and not invulnerable to lightning bolts.*

Well, at least that would be more understandable than his preferred version: *Meddle not in the affairs of wizards, for it makes them soggy and hard to light.*

Other Side jokes—even if they didn't involve such foreign things as cigarettes in a urinal—had a very small appreciative audience here, and most of that audience wasn't all that appreciative anyway.

It was a sad day when you couldn't get a laugh out of your own joke.

He didn't know what protections Henrad had in place, and he didn't have the genes to feel for them, and his reputation for recklessness was mainly for show, not for real; he would no more walk unannounced and uninvited into a wizard's residence than he would dance blindfolded along the ramparts, hoping for good luck and pure thoughts to protect him from falling and breaking his neck.

For one thing, his luck wasn't that good, and for another, his thoughts weren't that pure.

Stash and Emma Slovotsky's baby boy was only an idiot when absolutely necessary.

"Henrad? It's me, Walter Slovotsky."

Silence.

Then: "Come in," a distant, seemingly directionless voice whispered.

Slovotsky stepped forward into the dark, with the sensation of passing through a sheet of cold dryness that made his testicles tighten painfully, as though they wanted to climb back up into his body cavity.

The windows had stood open and unshuttered, but the only light that seemed to penetrate was a wan gray, apparently radiating from the juncture of curved wall and ceiling.

The air smelled of rotten meat and old sweat, leavened with a surprising hint of peppermint, and a deep, rank odor of something foul and unfamiliar.

Okay, Henrad, Walter Slovotsky thought. *Enough with the mystery of the wizard schtick. I've seen it before, I've liked it before, I've been impressed with it before, and I'll be impressed with it again, but I'm not here to be impressed.*

The tower was perhaps twenty feet in diameter, but it seemed to be a much farther distance off in the murk that gradually brightened, smoky shadows twisting and writhing silently, weaving themselves into a dim, gray skeleton. Wisps of flock rained out of the darkness in a silent, tiny tornado that whirled around and around the skeleton, little bits sticking first to the gray bones, and then to each other, as the tornado grew larger and larger until Walter Slovotsky had to close and shield his eyes and hold his breath to avoid inhaling the dust.

Soft, warm pieces of flock battered at him, filling his ears instantly, pounding themselves into creases in his face, filling his nostrils until he clapped his free hand over his mouth and nose and started to back up out of the wizard's workshop, forcing himself to maintain a clear picture in his mind of where the arched doorway was, hoping that his sense of direction, his almost inhuman sense of kinesthesia, wouldn't abandon him in his time of need—no, not hoping but *knowing* that it wouldn't because he was, after all, Walter Slovotsky, and he could no more be off-balance and disoriented than a tree could fail to be made of wood.

And then, suddenly, without any warning whatsoever, the flock storm was gone, and he stood, slapping at himself to clear the coat of flock and dust from his hair and clothes, Henrad standing in front of him, head cocked to one side, a twisted smile playing across his thin lips.

"Henrad, you look like shit," Slovotsky said.

Henrad was in his late twenties or early thirties, but between the thin, lifeless gray hair that drooped about his scalp, the gray pallor and deep lines of his face, and the obvious pain with which he stood, leaning on a crooked branch that he used as a staff, he looked decades older.

"Thank you so much, Walter Slovotsky," he said. "Now, having informed me, can you be on your way, if that's what you came here to say? I am rather busy."

Yes he was, but with what? Most of what Henrad was doing for the Crown was agricultural magic—sterilizing weeds, bewitching the corn and oats so that it frightened deer and crows, rainmaking, and like. But planting season was a memory, and the fields of green corn and golden wheat and rich, brown bitteroats were almost ready for harvest in the north, and were already being harvested in the southern baronies. This should be a time of relaxation for the wizard.

"Yes, apparently you have been busy," Walter Slovotsky said. "Too busy and too distracted to notice that every bug in the Eren Regions seems to have taken up residence outside my window, not to mention the rest of the city."

The wizard chuckled thinly. "I wouldn't say I haven't noticed; I would say that the time hasn't been right."

Walter Slovotsky rubbed at the back of his neck, where the Spider's balms and fingers and mutterings had relieved the itching and smoothed away the insect bites. "Well, what are you waiting for? Spring?"

"No." Henrad fingered his thin, gray beard. There were some men who shouldn't grow a beard, and Henrad was one of them. The hairs on his cheeks were thick enough, but the hair on his chin was too sparse, and the stringy strands of gray hairs were in bad need of untangling.

His thin, cracked lips parted enough so that Slovotsky could see that his yellowed teeth had more gaps then last time. "No," he said. "Bats."

"Bats?"

"Yes, bats. Those leather-winged creatures that flit from here to there and back again at night. You have heard of bats, haven't you?"

Slovotsky nodded. Yes, he had heard of bats. Pretty much the whole world had heard of bats, and of the crystallized potassium nitrate that could be found underneath sufficiently aged piles of feces, bat guano in particular. Grind it, grind it some more, then mix it—in the right proportions, and preferably wetted with wine or urine—with well-ground charcoal and sulfur, then mix that some more, and more, and what you had was gunpowder. Not the magical imitation that the Slavers Guild of Pandathaway had invented, but the real thing.

Slovotsky had had good reason at the time, so he had thought, to let the secret out, and so he had, but that had ended the shared monopoly that Home Guard and imperial troops had had on reliable rifles and pistols, and it was only a matter of time before every hedge-lord and farm-baron from here to the Cirric could, and would have to, equip his troops with guns and cannons.

The winter of the sword-slinging hero was in the air and the frost was nipping at Walter Slovotsky's nose.

Or his ass, depending on how you looked at things.

All men were created equal; Sam Colt had made them that way back on the Other Side. It took years of practice to become adept with a sword—absent a shortcut or two—or a longbow. Pike weapons took less time. And turning a peasant conscript into a crossbowman was more a matter of teaching discipline than marksmanship. And, yes, there was more to learn in order to be able to load and fire a flintlock rifle than a crossbow, but the range was longer, and bullets, particularly conoid bullets, bit harder and deeper and more frequently than crossbow bolts ever did.

And cannons could shatter castle walls, no matter how well-built and thick.

"So let me get this straight," Walter Slovotsky said. "You haven't killed off all the damn bugs because it might bother the bats."

"No. Not bother." He gestured clumsily, as though trying to take hold of something insubstantial and delicate.

Like a thought, maybe? Walter Slovotsky frowned.

Henrad *would* try to grip a thought in his fingers, wouldn't he?

"Balances," Henrad said, his voice a husky rasp, "balances are delicate things, Walter Slovotsky. A bat eats a bellyful of bugs daily."

The flapping of leathery wings and high-pitched squeaks filled the room. "Enough bugs, and she conceives a swarm of baby bats; no bugs, and she dies, lonely, of heartache."

The room fell silent. "No bats to eat bugs, and the bugs multiply, their numbers increasing geometrically, sucking the blood from legions of animals, human and other—" the chirping of crickets and the crunching of fidgetbugs grew louder and louder until Henrad had to shout to be heard "—chewing on the leaves of trees, covering the ground in a thick layer of insects that blankets field and farm, covers city and town, eating and reproducing and eating and reproducing until . . ."

Walter tried to take hold of him—a foolish move, in retrospect—but he couldn't. The air gave no resistance at first, but as his hands neared the wizard's robe, it wavered and thickened, slowing his hands before they could reach the wizard.

It was like trying to move through ever-hardening Jell-O. He gave up. There was no resistance as Walter dropped his hands to his sides.

The sound stopped. Henrad shook his head. "Touch a wizard? Walter Slovotsky, you have developed either a second sight or a death wish."

Slovotsky shrugged. "Maybe a little of both." He eyed the wizard closely. The mania was gone from Henrad's eyes, at least for the moment. But he still looked like he hadn't had a solid meal in a week, or a decent night's sleep in much longer than that.

"What is it, Henrad?" Slovotsky had seen this before, perhaps. Andrea Cullinane had developed a magical addiction, the need to learn and practice more magic, overloading herself until she threatened to burn out.

There are, indeed, some things that man is not meant to know, and at least some of those will drive men mad.

"Oh, it's nothing," Henrad said. "Just a feeling. I can, sometimes, detect banked fires nearby, trying to hide themselves from me." His voice lowered and his expression turned conspiratorial as he leaned closer to Slovotsky. "I think," he whispered hoarsely, "that there is another wizard about, trying to hide himself. Or herself."

Slovotsky kept his expression noncommittal. "Perhaps it's just one of your apprentices."

"No, no, no—I know their flame like I know my own. Francela and Chalres could not hide from me, even if they used none of their magic, or all of it. I'm not the young boy you used to know, Walter Slovotsky."

Well, that was certainly true. The years had not been kind to Henrad. Or, perhaps, more to the point, he had not been kind to himself over the years.

But right now, he was apparently working himself into a frenzy trying to find Erenor, and that would be good for nobody. Thomen wouldn't be happy if it came out that Walter had a wizard of his own tucked away, hidden as a Furnael soldier, and Beralyn would be sure to make him unhappier about it. Normally, there would be enough people in Biemestren who would look to put a metaphorical or real knife in the back of the imperial proctor—and with Parliament about to meet, there would be more.

Walter Slovotsky sighed. It would be nice to be elsewhere, just about now.

Time to get Erenor out of Biemestren, and away from Henrad, and since Erenor was mostly useless as a soldier and wasn't terribly trustworthy anyway, that meant sending Kethol and Pirojil along with him.

He could, of course, simply tell Henrad that he had a spare

wizard tucked away—and hope that Henrad would not mind, or would accept that Erenor was merely an illusionist, unable to work other than the simplest of other spells, and would keep his mouth shut about Erenor.

And you could, of course, play poker with all your cards face up on the table, and hope everybody would be too polite to peek. That didn't seem like a good idea, either.

Walter Slovotsky took his leave of the wizard without bringing up the matter of the mosquitoes again. A few bug bites could wait on more important matters, although it probably wouldn't feel that way in the middle of the night, when every mosquito, fidgetbug, gnat, and nameless insect was using Walter Slovotsky's skin as a combination parade ground and smorgasbord.

He walked carefully down the long, winding staircase, amusing himself with the image of Beralyn having climbed up to leave a wet bar of soap on one of the steps.

Well, she would, if she could. And he could tumble without that. It would be a shame to break his neck and disappoint so many women, after all.

Walter Slovotsky chuckled. He was always his own best audience.

3

Leria

If you're not at the poker table, you can't possibly win. Of course, if you're at the poker table
and the game is fixed, well, maybe you'd better
find another game.

—Walter Slovotsky

Life at court, Leria had quickly decided, was—at least for her—not an acquired taste. She had taken to it immediately. After all, what was there not to like?

She leaned back against the supporting ripples of the burnished copper tub, and toed the lever at the foot of the tub, rewarded by a delightful influx of hot water from the stone spigot, which had been carved into the shape of a dragon's head. Yes, two of the castle's maids waited in the outer chamber of the tiled bath, but privacy was an even rarer luxury than these endless streams of heated water, instantly available through the copper tubing that emerged from the juncture of wall and ceiling. She settled down beneath the water, careless of the way that motion sent soapy water splashing to the tiles.

After two long years under the all too watchful gaze of Baroness Elanee, constantly fending off the persistent attentions of her son, Miron, the respectful interest of the various lords of the imperial court was entirely refreshing. And with the dowager empress having taken her under her wing, the muted hostility of some of the ladies of the imperial court was quite easy to bear. Yes, and then there was the emperor himself. He regularly asked—and with a charming hesitancy that was far more boyish than imperial—for her company at table, and they had what had quickly become a standing riding date.

The heat soaked all stress from her shoulders, and more importantly relieved the irritation at the juncture of her thighs that always accompanied the end of her catamenia. It would have been preferable, if possible, to simply have skipped today's ride—and the Fedensday ride, as well, when her menstrual cramps had been at their worst—but she had learned from Elanee the necessity of seeming to do things effortlessly, and as much as she had hated the baroness, Leria was determined to follow her late father's advice and try to learn something from everybody she came in contact with.

She rose carefully, and by the time she was fully straightened, a pair of young maids—sisters, by the look of them—had bustled into the room, one with a stack of warm, fluffy towels, the other with fresh clothes from her rooms.

"We must hurry, Lady," the older one said, her eyes lowered. "They are already gathering at table, and it wouldn't do to arrive after the emperor."

Their averted eyes probably missed her smile.

Were they even more unsophisticated than Leria was? Yes, it wouldn't do to arrive after the emperor—but it would be impossible to arrive after the emperor. He simply would not arrive until the last lord and lady were gathered at table.

But, still, the point was well-taken. There were times when it would be amusing to make Thomen wait—men were so charming when they felt slightly put-upon but didn't want to show it—but this was probably not one of those times. Particularly with his mother in attendance. Leria had found herself in the dowager empress's favor without much effort, although she had spent much effort staying in that favor. Privately, she agreed with Kethol's eval-uation of Beralyn—mean, dangerous, and spiteful—but that argued for not offending the old woman, not without a very good reason.

She let her attendants groom and dress her quickly, not trying to help, as that would only hinder them.

That was another lesson she had learned from Elanee: let the experts do their work without bothering them. She had been raised in an outlying barony, and only rarely had had this kind of constant personal service. The house maids, even after her mother died, had always had far more to do than wait upon her every need, and her nanny was of the belief that a noble should reenact the climb from peasantry to nobility as a natural part of childhood, and her father had agreed.

That upbringing had left her far more comfortable currying a horse than sitting still for endless hours while attendants clucked and chittered and chattered, combing here, tucking there, their re-markably nimble fingers ripping apart a seam only to trim and resew it to a more flattering line.

She allowed herself a thin smile as she thought how Kethol would have reacted to such a declaration. After endless days on the road, hiding from pursuers and having little enough time for even a quick wash, much less a long bath and change of clothes, he would have shown great patience with such trivial complaints, and while he certainly would have thought less of her, he would have done the best he could to fail to let even a hint of that show on his face.

His best, at least in that, wouldn't have been nearly good enough. She couldn't have read his thoughts more easily if they had been written in Euar'den runes on his forehead.

There were some men, certainly, whom she couldn't read quite so easily. Most men, in fact, particularly nobility. Perhaps it was just that she had been raised too far out in the country, too rarely ex-posed to nobles.

Baroness Elanee had insisted on that, after she had taken over as Leria's guardian, and persuaded poor Forinel to go out into the world and win fame in his own name, not merely as the baronial heir.

She fondled the ring Forinel had given her, the night he had left.

Keep it until I return, to claim it, to claim my barony, and to claim you, he had said.

He had kissed her even more gently than usual, and taken her heart as well as her virginity that night, and ridden off toward the Katharhd in the morning . . .

Never to return.

It was getting difficult to remember his face these days. In her dreams, his soft but strong hands tended to become Kethol's big-knuckled ones without warning, and his smile and face would melt until it became Thomen's, all too often.

But Thomen's face, too, tended to melt into Kethol's.

She didn't need a witch reading her dreams to tell her what that meant.

Leria sighed. She was a descendant of the Euar'den rulers of Tynear, of Lerian the Red himself—a man who had gotten his nickname from the blood on his hands, not the red that legend had added to his hair—and hers were a practical people.

Still . . .

A distant bell chimed.

"The dowager empress should be ready to receive you for your afternoon visit with her."

Leria nodded and smiled.

She was doing a lot of nodding and smiling of late, and it was beginning to irritate her.

There were worse things than a little irritation.

"Then let us not keep her waiting, shall we?" she said.

4

The Proctor, Kethol, Pirojil, and Erenor

Y ou wanted to see us, Proctor?" Pirojil asked, as the imperial proctor stalked through the arch and into the office.

"Yes," Walter Slovotsky said. "That's why I sent for you," he added, deadpan, as though he didn't want to let on whether or not he was insulting them or having some sort of weak joke with them.

Pirojil and Kethol were standing, but Erenor was seated on the chair next to Walter Slovotsky's desk, leaning back, the very picture of a man at leisure. He either didn't notice—or, more likely, knowing Erenor, affected not to notice—the glare that Walter Slovotsky gave him.

Walter Slovotsky was dressed too elegantly by half. His doeskin tunic was soft and sun-bleached to a preposterous whiteness, particularly in contrast to the inky blackness of his undershirt, leggings, and boots. His long mustache and stylishly block-trimmed beard were shot with white, and he was silvery at the temples—and hair, mustache, and beard were all far more neatly trimmed and tightly combed than they had been in the old days.

The only visible reminder of the old days was the thick belt buckled tightly over his hips: it supported a short sword on the left-hand side, a plain one with a bell guard and leather grip, and a brace of pistols on his right hip. A knife with a highly polished, gold-encrusted hilt was strapped, angled for a quick draw with either hand, just in front of the sword. Of course, with the knife in that position, and not thonged into place, it would be easy for some-body else to snatch it out of its sheath and bury it in Walter Slov-otsky's gut.

Pirojil tried to spot where the trick release was, but couldn't. There had to be one, though; Walter Slovotsky had not gotten so far from his roots as to leave himself quite that vulnerable.

"We have a small problem," Walter Slovotsky said.

Pirojil's jaw twitched. A small problem? That was a silly idea to anybody who had been in the baron's service for a tenth the time Pirojil had. You could get killed every bit as dead over a small problem as you could over a major one.

Walter Slovotsky nodded in agreement with the unvoiced thought.

Ellegon? Pirojil thought, remembering not to move his lips. *Ellegon, can you hear me?*

But there was no answer.

So: the dragon wasn't around, reading Pirojil's thoughts and relaying them to Walter Slovotsky. That was too bad. Pirojil wished that the dragon had been doing that. It would be better to face some draconic mind reading than have Walter Slovotsky able to read his thoughts by human insight rather than magic.

Insight was a more dangerous resource, and Slovotsky was both devious and subtle.

"But it's not that kind of problem," Walter Slovotsky said.

"Fine," Kethol grunted. "Just tell us what you want, and let us get out of here. We're accompanying Lady Leria to dinner this evening."

Slovotsky cocked his head to one side. "Who do you think put you on duty as her guards?" He kicked Erenor's feet out of the way as he made his way to his desk and sat down.

Erenor gave Pirojil a quick, knowing glance.

It all went over Kethol's head. Which wasn't surprising, all things considered. Kethol had been far too grateful to be in Her Presence regularly once more to ask a lot of questions—which was fine with Pirojil—or to think about why the three of them had been selected—which wasn't.

That was always the trouble with Kethol. In or out of a fight, he was as reliable and steady as a stone wall. You could count him to do not necessarily the best thing—Pirojil couldn't count on himself to do the best thing, for that matter—but a useful thing, and his reflexes and instincts were quick and sure. And he wasn't stupid—but when his loyalty or affection was engaged, he refused to think ahead further than the next slash of a sword, pull of a trigger, or blow of a fist.

He hadn't even thought to ask why Leria had been given her own personal guards, much less why the three of them had been chosen for the job.

Not that that was something difficult to figure out: Leria's visibility around the emperor was not overly popular with any of the nobility with marriageable daughters and an eye on bettering themselves, which was to say: *any* of the nobility with marriageable daughters.

And particularly with Parliament in session, there were a lot of extra people around the castle.

Was it likely that somebody would hire an assassin to get Leria out of the way?

No; it was not likely at all.

But unlikely things had happened before and would again, and Walter Slovotsky had probably made a good decision in having three men that he could trust—Kethol and Pirojil because of their long and established loyalty to the Cullinane family; Erenor, because, like Kethol and Pirojil, Walter Slovotsky had the illusionist's balls in a vice—watching over her, supplementing them with hand-picked soldiers from the Home Guard.

"Very well, then: what does this problem have to do with our guarding Lady Leria?" Kethol asked, more of a challenge than a real question.

"Simple: you're relieved of guarding Lady Leria," he said. "I'll see that she's looked after."

Kethol bristled, but Slovotsky ignored him and forged on. "Draw mounts and spares from the imperial stables and get out of Biemestren as fast as you can without drawing attention to yourselves. There still a bit of an orc problem over the barony—if Doria doesn't have anything better for you to do, you can spot for the imperials. Or you can put yourselves on leave and go hunting dragon eggs, or go fishing, or just drop out of the service and get yourselves lost."

He picked up a pen and scribbled something, presumably his signature, on three sheets of parchment, not waiting for the ink to dry before setting each on his imprinting pad and embossing each signature with his personal seal.

Walter Slovotsky produced an envelope, unsealed, and handed that over to Pirojil along with the three parchment sheets. "Your orders, and a letter for Doria—or Jason, for that matter, on the off chance that he's warming his butt on his own baronial throne instead of gallivanting around somewhere, or heading here to be early for Parliament."

Kethol started to say something, but Pirojil touched him on the arm, and he desisted.

Slovotsky looked up from his desk. "Well? I'd ask what the three of you are still doing standing there, but there's no point in asking an illusion anything, and you must be illusion because I've just told the three of you to get out of here. Vanish, illusion, vanish."

As they walked away down the hall in silence—even Kethol knew better than to chatter openly in front of any guard or maid or servitor they happened to pass by—it occurred to Pirojil what had seemed so strange about the whole interview with Walter Slovotsky: not only had Walter Slovotsky not engaged Erenor in the conversation, but Erenor hadn't spoken as much as a word.

Pirojil shook his head. By the time they got to the barony, that surely would have long since ceased to be the case.

He was right, of course.

By the time they turned off the Prince's Road onto the dirt road that led across one last hill to Castle Cullinane, he would gladly have been dragging Erenor behind him, by a hook through the wizard's tongue.

Part Two:

Cullinane

5

⚜ Jason Cullinane

No, I don't want to go to Biemestren early," Jason Cullinane said. "We'll leave in another tenday, no sooner. I've got some business up around Kendall's Ridge—"

"You have some business in Biemestren, as well."

"—and I don't have to be early, and I really don't want to discuss it further. I'm the baron, remember?"

"It would be difficult to forget," his mother said, smiling sweetly across the breakfast table at him, "given that you remind me about it on a daily basis."

"If you'll stop nagging, then I'll stop reminding you," he said.

Janie Slovotsky hid a smile behind her mug, and U'len emitted a derisive sniff as she bustled in from the kitchen, her wooden serving tray piled high with slices of ham and pan-fried turnips, fist-sized loaves of bread fresh from the oven, and a steaming bowl of boiled, shredded cabbage, the smell of which made Jason's stomach shrivel to the size of a fist.

Cabbage.

When he was a little boy, U'len had told him that he would like it when he was grown. Wasn't twenty-three grown enough for her to admit that he never would like the disgusting stuff, no matter how often it appeared on the table?

"Just a baron, he is," she said, easily balancing the serving tray on one flipperlike hand as she removed plate after plate, setting the rolls down as far away from Toryn as possible—Toryn liked fresh-baked bread, but U'len didn't like Toryn—and, of course, putting the foul-smelling breakfast cabbage in front of Jason. "Just a baron. His father was an emperor; it appears to me that the family has fallen a long way."

She was an almost impossibly fat woman, old—but she had been old all of Jason's life—but apparently ageless, her flat, dull, gray hair neither more nor less gray than it had been last year, the wrinkles in her face and the creases in her many chins neither deeper nor shallower, and if her step was just a trifle less brisk, and her voice not quite so loud and booming as it used to be, well, then that couldn't be any sign of mortality, could it?

It was a silly thought. U'len was like the hills and valleys and trees. She had always been and would always be. He knew that was nonsense, but that's what it felt like.

Bang. Bang-*bang.* A trio of gunshots sounded from outside.

"What?" U'len almost dropped the now empty tray. Mother was already moving toward the sideboard where she had left her pistols, and Toryn was halfway out of his chair, while Jane Slovotsky simply sat and grinned at him.

"Sounds to me," she said, "like Erenor's shot was a little high, don't you think?"

Jason nodded soberly. "I think Kethol went wide. But it sounds like Pirojil hit the target fair squarely, as usual."

She shook her head. "Low and to the left, it sounded like to me."

Except for U'len's sniff as she stalked back from the morning room toward the kitchen, nobody rose to the bait, although Jason could see that Toryn was tempted to point out that you could no more hear a shot go low and wide than you could smell it, and knew without looking that Mother, still standing next to her pistols, was working hard at not saying anything.

He watched Janie watching Mother controlling herself. She was fun to watch.

From the smile you could tell that Janie Slovotsky was her father's daughter, although there was much more of Kirah in the slim build, high cheekbones, wide eyes, and full lips. She was starting to let her hair grow long—which he liked—and it was almost down to her shoulders. He made a mental note not to compliment her too often on it, or she would probably just cut it again, to show her independence. Janie would share his bed every now and then—she didn't like to sleep alone, either—but she was as independent in her way as her father was in his, and would show that independence in ways that were sometimes predictable.

Sometimes.

"Oh. Target practice this morning?" Andrea Cullinane sat back down at the table. "The guard decurion didn't mention it to me."

"Probably because he didn't know about it," Jason said, "until a little while ago. On my way down, I ducked out and told him that the three of them were going to be shooting this morning. Doria was pointing out to me just the other night that they missed the qualification shoot, and I thought that they ought to catch up."

"Never for a moment thinking that Doria likes to sleep in on Marketday, I take it."

He tried to look innocent. Doria had been nagging him, too. "Oh. I'm sorry—I forgot." He made as though to rise. "I should go up and apologize for them waking her, I guess."

"Sit down," his mother ordered. "It's bad enough to wake her once; worse to do it twice. She's been working hard while somebody has been off hunting."

His mother wasn't the only person who could decline to rise to the bait. Jason bit into the sausage. Too much pepper, and far too much garlic, but after a few swallows of milk, still warm from the cow, it settled nicely in his midsection.

Still, he was right and Mother was wrong, even if he didn't feel like arguing about it.

There was an orc infestation up north, and while it wasn't strictly necessary for the baron to go handle it himself—the baronial troops could handle it, under the direction of some wardens and woodsmen—he felt better about being involved in it himself.

Ruling wasn't just about setting taxes and settling disputes. It was, or at least his father had taught him that it should be, about protecting the people. Hunting down marauding orcs was, well, one of the more rewarding ways of doing that.

And, besides, the longer he could delay before leaving for Biemestren, the better the chances that Ellegon would drop in, and make it possible for him to fly over, rather than ride. It wasn't just that he liked to make an entrance—although there was something rather pleasant about the wide eyes and wide mouths that you saw when you arrived anywhere on dragonback—but it always felt strange to be going back to Biemestren, and the longer he put it off, the better.

Biemestren wasn't his, not anymore.

Visiting a place that had been your home was disconcerting. He was always tempted to run up the back stairs to what had been his bedroom suite—but it wasn't his, not anymore. It wasn't even a bedroom suite anymore—Thomen had turned it into single rooms, office and sleeping space for some of his clerks, to keep them nearby.

Hmpf. Thomen didn't visit here, either, and it wasn't just because the emperor did little traveling. This had been the Furnael ancestral home for something like eight generations, and while Jason didn't doubt for a moment that Thomen preferred being an emperor to being a simple country baron, it probably would have bothered him to see Jason at ease in the game room here.

People said that he looked a lot like his mother, but Jason didn't see it, except for the slightly aquiline nose—his had a more pronounced bend than hers did, from a recent break gotten in hand-to-hand practice, and he was trying to decide whether he wanted to keep the slight bump instead of having the Spider smooth it.

You didn't have to look like Pirojil, after all, just because you were going to let honestly won scars show a bit of character in your face.

Maybe with a few more breaks and scars, U'len and Mother would start treating him like something resembling an adult rather than a child.

Sure. And perhaps U'len would turn into an elven princess, and grant him a wish.

"You might have mentioned that they were going to be shooting this morning," Mother said. "So that poor Toryn and I didn't almost jump out of our skins."

"I was going to," he said, reaching his eating prong past the cabbage for another sausage. "But somebody decided to nag me about leaving for Parliament instead." He speared the sausage and returned it to his plate, then grabbed a couple of the hot rolls, tossing one across the table to Toryn, who wolfed it down in three quick bites.

He ate a lot for such a lath-slim man.

"Thank you much, Jason," Toryn said. He was quiet in the morning, typically, getting more talkative as the day went by. Probably out of caution that had become habit—an ex-slaver could too easily remind people of his former profession, which was none too popular, this side of Pandathaway.

There were a lot of people to thank for that. One of them was Jason's father.

Mother rose and went to the kitchen, calling out something about travel provisions, and Jason took the opportunity to give Janie a quick kiss—he felt awkward doing so in front of his mother—and made a patting signal to Toryn, telling him to finish his breakfast, before he grabbed up his own weapons belt and headed for the front entrance.

The watchmen were in their perches, high in the guardtowers at the corners of the squarish curtain wall, but Jason had given standing orders that they were to do nothing more formal than wave a hello to him. He had had his fill of ceremony while being heir to the empire, and, besides, any attention being drawn to him would make it easier for Mother and Doria to keep track of him.

Which wasn't what he wanted.

The gate was up, as usual, and he belted his sword around his waist as he walked through, waving a friendly good morning to the guard whose job it would have been, under the right set of circumstances, to either lower the outer, metal gate slowly and carefully or chop through the rope with one quick swipe of an always ready ax. He forced himself not to look up at the dagger points at the bottom of the gate—they just made him nervous.

Kethol, Pirojil, and Erenor were still reloading at the weathered shooting bench down the road at the range. An earthen berm had been built up in a semicircle, a good bowshot away, and a dozen thick posts, each more than a manheight, driven into the ground in front of it.

Years of shooting had chewed the posts to the point where the decurions' standing threat about them being used for firing squads was less believable all the time, but they worked just fine for the large plasterboard targets that were cheaper than paper.

"Good morning, Baron," Kethol said, not stopping for a moment in his reloading routine.

"Good morning," Jason said.

He was the tallest of the three, and the one Jason was most comfortable around. Redheaded and rawboned, with long fingers and knuckles that bulged like a dwarf's, he stood half a head taller than Pirojil.

Looks could be deceiving, but there was no deceiving that Pirojil was an ugly man. The massive, misshapen brow hung heavy with eyebrows that needed a trim, over sunken, piggish eyes and a nose that had been broken enough times to flatten in against the face. The receding jaw was barely covered by a spotty beard that never did quite seem to fill in, which was a pity. The more of the face it covered, the better it would be for all concerned.

But his thick hands had a certain delicate grace to them as he carefully tipped a measure of powder down the barrel of his rifle, then with no apparent effort or discomfort pushed a patched conical bullet into the muzzle with his thumb, not bothering with the short-starter that most everybody else, Jason included, used to save wear and tear on their fingers.

A few strokes from his ram, and Pirojil had his rifle loaded and primed, with hammer back, and raised to his shoulder, as Kethol was still priming his pan, and Erenor—who surely couldn't be as clumsy as he appeared to be—was still spilling gunpowder on the shooting table in an attempt to get a rounded measure.

Jason put his hands over his ears—there was no point in suffering loud sounds unnecessarily, and he nodded at Kethol and Erenor to do the same—as Pirojil raised the rifle to his shoulder. He barely seemed to set the stock of the gun against his shoulder before he pulled the trigger, and after a brief but infuriating hang-fire, the rifle went off with a teeth-rattling bang and a cloud of smoke that smelled of sulfur and worse.

Erenor shielded his eyes with his palm and looked downrange. "Low and right," he said. "By less than a palm's width."

Not bad at all. Jason could do little better with a careful rest.

Kethol was ready, but simply set the butt of his rifle on the table, resting, until Erenor finished loading. "You think you can better that?" Kethol asked.

"Oh, of a certainty," Erenor said. "Unless, of course, you'd rather I didn't." He touched a knuckle to his brow. "Master Kethol."

Kethol smiled. "Would you care to put a little coin on that? Just a few silver marks, perhaps?" He seemed to smell easy money, and perhaps he was right—that was an awfully good shot.

Erenor smiled as he sighted down the barrel. "Very well. Three silver quarters, shall it be?"

"Done." Kethol produced three silver quartermarks and slapped them down on the table.

Erenor raised his rifle—

"Not quite so fast, if you please," Pirojil said. He pushed the muzzle of the rifle up. "Kethol's coins look so lonely there, lying on the table, all by themselves. I think you'll want to produce some of your own, just to keep them company." He made a beckoning, come-on gesture.

Erenor didn't seem concerned. He produced an old silver mark—Jason could tell that it was old, although he couldn't tell where Erenor had produced it from; the coin had Father's face on it, rather than Thomen's—and set it down next to the quarters. Jason didn't quite see how he did it, but when Erenor resumed his grip on the rifle there were only two quarters on the table instead of three.

Erenor fidgeted as he wedged the butt of the rifle against his shoulder, and pressed his cheek firmly against the stock. He pulled back the hammer with a clumsy, two-fingered grip, then wiggled his fingers and took a shooting grip, his index finger stretched out straight, away from the trigger.

"Let this be a lesson to you, Master Kethol," Erenor said. He took a deep breath, let it out, then set his finger on the trigger, and slowly squeezed.

Wham. There had been a barely detectable hangfire, and when the smoke cleared, Erenor had set his rifle down on the battered surface of the rough-hewn shooting table and scooped up all three coins.

"Just one moment," Pirojil said. "Your target is unmarked—you missed."

"Ah. That, Master Pirojil, turns out not to be the case. I was not aiming at my target, but at Kethol's." He stretched his palm out, horizontally, toward the target. "And as you can plainly see, I got what I was aiming at: Kethol's mark. My bullet went right through the same hole as his."

Jason Cullinane cocked his head to one side. Did Erenor really expect anybody to believe this?

Pirojil made the same come-on gesture he had before. "That isn't even vaguely humorous, and I'm in no mood for a joke in any case." He shook his head. "If you had intended to shoot through the same hole that Kethol did—not that I believe it for a moment— you should have announced that in advance, and we could have plugged the hole. But as it is—"

"But as it is, when you examine the hole, you'll see that my bullet does not—quite—overlap with Kethol's. I invite you to look." He started to walk around the table. "Follow me, and I will show you."

"*Stop right there.*" Pirojil vaulted the table and squared off in front of Kethol. "I'll go look—you might be tempted to . . . improve the hole."

"Master Pirojil, you wound me deeply." He started to edge around the ugly man, his smile disarming.

But not disarming enough. "Not as deeply as I will if you don't stop moving."

"We will all go look," Jason Cullinane said. He walked across the hard-packed dirt toward the targets, the three soldiers half a pace behind.

Jason's mouth hung open, so he shut it. The hole should have been round, and about the size of the tip of his finger. But it was ovoid, as though two bullets had gone through.

Pirojil shook his head. "That happens every now and then, when a bullet tumbles, and hits the target side-on. I've seen it before."

Erenor crossed his arms over his chest. "So now you're claiming that I have good enough eyesight to see such a thing, and then the immediate foresight not only to accept a friendly wager, but to carefully miss the targets entirely, hoping to trap you into the false accusation that I would enlarge the hole, so that I could make you look foolish when you tried to change your story rather than simply permit Kethol to lose the bet with the good grace that you and I both know he has." He shook his head. "You seem to expect much complexity from a simple soldier such as myself," he said.

Pirojil didn't say anything.

Jason laughed. He wasn't sure what had really happened,

but . . . "If you're really that good a shot, Erenor, let's make a point to make a trip to Home sooner than later. There's been some noise from the Therranji elves, and it would be a lot of fun to show them what an average marksman from the barony can do."

He didn't know what he expected as a response, but it wasn't for Pirojil to jerk back as though he had been struck. His hands were at his side, formed into fists, the knuckles white, and there was blood at the corner of his mouth.

"What is it?"

It took a visible effort for Pirojil to calm himself. His fingers straightened themselves stiffly. "Your pardon, Baron," he said, his voice tight, his face pale. "But . . . I find myself angry at having been gulled so easily," he said.

"But—"

"Please, Baron," Kethol held up a hand. "Erenor has been winning far too many wagers lately, and Pirojil and I both tend to get angry about it." His smile seemed forced. "Perhaps it's just that we were partnered with Durine for so long, and it's difficult to fit in with somebody new."

That was a weak explanation, but maybe it was true. Not everything in life made sense to Jason Cullinane, after all. He could insist on a better explanation, but maybe all he would get would be a better lie. It wasn't as though he didn't trust Pirojil—Pirojil, Kethol, and Durine had been with Father on his Last Ride, and with the family both before and since, and . . .

"Jason." Mother's voice sounded from behind him. "Doria says that she wants to go over some of the accounts with you—she thinks that one of the village wardens may have sticky fingers, and—"

"Sorry, Mother," he said. "Erenor, here, was just telling me that word has come in of some orc trouble over at Findal's Folly, and we were just on our way to the stables to draw some horses and look into it."

Pirojil and Kethol stood silently, but Erenor spread his arms in a what-can-I-do apology. "Perhaps I shouldn't have mentioned it to the baron, my Lady," he said, "but it's my understanding that we are under orders to report all such things to him, and . . ."

Mother's mouth twitched. She looked from face to face. "I'm not sure I believe a word of this, but . . ."

"We'd better be off before the trail gets cold," he said, and broke into a trot, Pirojil and Kethol catching up with him while Erenor gathered the rifles together. "Would you ask Toryn to join us at the stables?" he called out to her.

"But—very well, Jason," she said. "I will."

"Thank you, Mother."

Riding off to kill a few orcs sounded like a much better way to spend a fine day than quizzing a loyal retainer about something he clearly didn't want to talk about, and a *lot* better than going over tax accounts.

6

Dinner Party

Maybe the Great Hall was just another battlefield in some sort of metaphorical sense, but Walter Slovotsky didn't mind that, not at all. He had been on a real battlefield or two in his time, and a real killing ground wasn't filled with the smells of roasting meat and garlic, the tinkle of fast-picked strings of a Holtish lute, and acres of firm cleavage to go along with miles of smooth leg, and at least yards of full lips. Walter Slovotsky had never had a breast fixation—he always tried to enjoy all the parts of a woman's body.

Bren Adahan was quickly at his side.

"Good evening, Proctor," he said.

"And good evening to you, Baron Minister," Slovotsky answered, with equal formality.

As usual, the baron was impeccably dressed, from head to toe. He had chosen a leather motif for the evening, from tunic to trousers to boots. His tunic was of a snowy white calfskin, split almost to the navel—probably as much to show off his well-muscled chest as to give him access to a hidden knife strapped to that chest, although Slovotsky had to admit that the baron was getting better at hiding his weapons, because Slovotsky couldn't see where it was.

A short sword hung from the left side of his waist; the pommel was made of age-darkened bone inlaid with gold and jewels, but the hilt itself was of rough-textured, leather, bound tightly with brass wires. That was Bren Adahan for you: always willing—hell, eager—to show off his perquisites of rank, but not at the risk of leaving himself less well armed for the sake of fashion, style, or elegance.

"The women wait for us at table," the baron said. "But Tyrnael said that he wanted to have a word with you, and perhaps share a glass of wine before dinner. He's out on the veranda."

Well, it would be too much to hope for that Tyrnael would freeze to death out on the veranda, given the balmy weather. And for that matter, Tyrnael was hardly the most difficult and annoying of the Biemish barons—Niphael was much worse, albeit less slick.

Walter Slovotsky liked the Holtish barons better, by and large—something about being under military occupation tended to make them quite reasonable, most of the time.

"Join me?" Slovotsky asked.

"I wasn't invited," Adahan said, his expression flat and unrevealing.

Slovotsky returned the expression, or rather the lack of it. "Nor were you asked if you were invited. You were asked, 'Will you join me?' "

Two could play at this game, even if only one of them could enjoy it, and that one would be Walter Slovotsky. Slovotsky prided himself on his ability to enjoy just about anything that didn't involve pain and suffering—particularly his own.

Adahan's too-handsome face split in a smile. "I guess I wasn't, at that. And, yes, I think I will join you. It might be interesting."

They made their way through the fringes of the crowd, past where young Lordling Arondael, the heir apparent to that barony, held court in front of the massive fireplace, alternately using the fireplace poker to rearrange the burning faggots and to illustrate some fine point of swordplay—or at least what he thought of as a fine point of swordplay, as he was far too young, and far too unscarred, to have earned his opinions the hard way; past where some old dowager's chins shook and wobbled as she whispered in the ear of a young woman who was manifestly her daughter—add around three decades, fifty pounds, five childbirths, a hundred thousand frowns to the daughter and she would become the mother; past where a thick, barrel-chested decurion of the Home Guard passed out appetizers from a silver tray, spoiling any possibility of his servitor's tunic fooling anybody by scratching at himself with his free hand; past a long table, piled high with gifts—the usual run of knives, bone sculpture, rolled tapestries, and dark bottles of wine for Thomen, as one did not come to visit the emperor empty-handed; past where the Holtish barons and their entourages clustered and plotted and schemed, something they would not be able to do during dinner, as the seating plan alternated Holtish and Biemish delegations with a careful, or at least carefully thought out, overlap.

He nodded to himself. That was best. After a couple of centuries of brush wars and one major one, you couldn't expect all the children to play nice right away, not even with Daddy—in the person of the emperor and his troops—watching carefully.

Adahan nodded. "Give it a few generations, Walter Slovotsky."

Slovotsky raised an eyebrow. "I wasn't aware that I was thinking out loud."

"You weren't." Adahan's smile was halfway between contagious and insulting. "But you looked carefully down the rows, then sighed and nodded to yourself."

"I'd better watch myself more carefully," he said.

"I knew you'd take my point."

Half a dozen men and as many women, including Vika Tyrnael, tried to catch his eye while pretending not to try to catch his eye—apparently, Slovotsky being named imperial proctor made him just ooze irresistible sexuality—and he returned the former's glances with a smile-and-nod and the latter's with a smile and a slightly elevated eyebrow.

Maybe it was his present, barely interrupted run of monogamy that was increasing his prowess to legendary—translation: bullshit—proportions.

Or maybe both.

It would have been enough to give a lesser man a case of performance-anxiety impotence.

"What are you grinning about?"

"Just some private thoughts, Baron Minister," he said. "Nothing of any concern."

The night was clear and cool, with only a film of clouds that more frosted than obscured the stars and the slowly pulsating Faerie lights off in the distance.

Torches crackled and sputtered on the inner ramparts, where doubled patrols of the House Guard kept a more than usually close watch on what was going on inside the keep, as well as looking for trouble from outside. Baronial troops were always in the capital, and less often seconded to the Home Guard, but, except when there was outlying nobility in residence, so much as a single baronial soldier within the walls of the keep was a rarity.

"Good evening, Baron," Walter Slovotsky said.

Tyrnael—Walter Slovotsky always thought of him by his family name, by the barony's name, rather than by his given name—was alone as he waited for them on the veranda, the baronial butt elegantly perched on the stone railing, showing off the long, lean lines that a combination of heredity and exercise had enabled him to keep well into his fifties. His close-cropped hair was full, despite the high widow's peak, and dusted with silver at the temples only.

Eyes that blinked a fraction too little watched closely. A mouth that smiled a touch too often was framed by a close-cropped strip of beard that accentuated already sharp jaw and cheekbones. The effect was always somehow reptilian, although for the life of him Walter Slovotsky couldn't figure out how the baron's appearance added up to that.

"Good evening to you, Proctor," Tyrnael said, his thin lips barely moving, as though it would be too much trouble. "And a good evening to you, too, Baron Adahan," he added, as though in afterthought.

"If we are going to be so formal, Baron Tyrnael, that should be 'Baron Minister Adahan,' " Bren Adahan said.

Walter Slovotsky frowned at him, and Adahan shrugged an apology, which Slovotsky accepted with a gracious nod. Which was the proper thing to do, after all, particularly considering that Slovotsky had been just about to correct Tyrnael himself.

"Please accept my sincere apologies," the Baron said, only the slightest of frostiness at the edges of his voice giving the lie to his words.

"I don't think you asked me out here to talk about forms of address, Baron," Walter Slovotsky said.

Tyrnael nodded. "There's some truth there, indeed. No, I want to know what you mean to do about the Keranahan succession."

"I?" Slovotsky raised an eyebrow. "I'm not going to do anything about it at all. That's a matter for the emperor to decide, not for a lowly proctor."

"Or even for a baron minister," Bren Adahan put in. "Though I think I'm probably rather more familiar with the precedents and relative claims on the barony. There was a Keranahan baron failing of an heir five, six generations ago, if I remember correctly." From his slight smile, Walter could tell that not only did he remember correctly, but he knew exactly how many generations ago it was, and what the circumstances were. "I wouldn't suppose that you are inclined to support the Euar'den claim on the baronial throne?"

Tyrnael's lips pursed. "On which baronial throne, Baron Minister? Yours? Or shall we go back to the Nifne Dynasty and dispute the settlement of baronial estates in Bieme? Looked at from the right perspective, we don't stand on solid ground at all, but on floating flows of rearranged territory, drifting and rearranging themselves down the river of time." He stamped a baronial boot against the flat stone of the terrace. "As to me, I prefer something more substantial, something to be relied upon, to be stood upon, not merely to be hoped might possibly persist for a few more years."

Slovotsky nodded, conceding the point. "Yes, there is a value to consistency. But it's not the only value."

"And that is as it should be," Tyrnael nodded. "I do have a suggestion, though, which maintains that value, perhaps as well as others."

Here it comes.

"Were the emperor to declare that Forinel, Nerahan's oldest son, is still the presumptive heir, it would maintain that stability, as well as giving the Council reason to believe that the emperor will not be quick to take Keranahan as his own. If, on the other hand, he marries the lovely Leria, he'd have a proper claim on the barony as father of the presumptive heir, and—"

"I've heard nothing about any such intention," Walter Slovotsky said. "And I don't expect to, for that matter."

"About marrying Leria? Or about claiming the barony?"

"I've heard nothing about either."

Which was a bold-faced lie about Leria, although true of the barony.

Walter Slovotsky never minded a little falsehood. Thomen was apparently rather taken with Leria—and who could blame him? She was, after all, attractive, well-mannered, and relatively politically uncomplicated, both in intellect and in connection. Beralyn, of course, favored the idea—cementing the Furnael line to a direct descendent of the old Euar'den princes would appeal to her, and Leria had cultivated that malicious, crooked, evil old bag with uncharacteristic skill and style.

Bren Adahan cocked his head to one side. "Forgive me if I'm mistaken, but isn't Forinel supposed to be dead?"

"Yes," Tyrnael said, "that's precisely the case: most do suppose that he is dead. But there's been no body produced, no witnesses. Some years ago he rode off—some say to the Katharhd, some say to join the Home raiders—and he has never been heard from since."

Which is why Elanee's son, Miron, had been the presumptive baronial heir. Which was also why it was, in retrospect, strange that Elanee had been only weakly politicking for a declaration that Forinel was dead. Slovotsky had always assumed that was because she wasn't ready to share power with her son, becoming dowager baroness.

She had, in fact, had other plans.

Walter Slovotsky didn't hold a grudge, even though those plans had included his death and had come too fucking close to causing that death. Elanee had made her play for power, and it had cost her her life. No point in staying mad.

Bitch.

Bren Adahan nodded. "I can't speak for the emperor either—"

"Save when you're warming his throne for him."

Slovotsky kept his nod to himself. That was, of course, the source of Tyrnael's jealousy and irritation. As, at least arguably, the senior line of Biemish barons, Tyrnael had had a better claim on the throne than the Furnaels, and certainly better than the Cullinane usurpers. If Thomen were to die without naming an heir, both precedent and politics would likely cause the other Biemish barons to turn to Tyrnael.

Which was, as far as Walter Slovotsky concerned, a good argument for keeping Tyrnael either in Biemestren, under close watch, or out of the capital entirely.

It was not a good argument for having him act as chief of staff when the emperor was out riding or hunting or taking some other break from affairs of state, as important as that recreation was to keeping Thomen from going bugfuck crazy.

"—but," Bren Adahan went on, as though he hadn't been interrupted, "I think you've a sound point, and I'll recommend it to the emperor." His lips twitched. "Of course, he could leave the matter to Parliament."

Tyrnael nodded sagely. "Yes, I suppose he could." Walter Slovotsky had never heard sarcasm played with such a light touch. Tyrnael turned to Slovotsky. "And you, Proctor?

"Me?"

"Will you support keeping the succession open, at least for now?"

It would have been nice to know what Tyrnael's real motivation was. Oh, it probably included his desire for stability. Did he have Forinel stashed somewhere? Or some connection with Treseen, the Keranahan governor?

Slovotsky nodded. "Your position sounds reasonable to me . . ."

"Ah." Tyrnael's lips barely turned up at the edges. "You've turned into a cautious noble in your old age, Walter Slovotsky."

I'm not that damn old, Walter Slovotsky thought, *as your second-oldest daughter found out a few days ago. Twice in the same night.* Vika had been very sweet, and while Walter Slovotsky was glad that Aiea had been born without a jealous cell in her body, he hadn't thought to mention their encounter to her, and had no intention of bringing it up here and now.

"Perhaps it's just age," Walter said. "But I like to think that when I commit myself, I'm sure as to what I'm committing myself to, and why."

"Why?" Tyrnael's face was studiously uncommunicative. "I've certainly given you good reason why."

"You have, at that," Slovotsky said. "I'll think about it. I don't see any need to rush into anything. It's usually been my experience that it's much easier to rush into trouble than to rush out."

"Ah." Tyrnael said. "Another of your famous aphorisms. How nice." He brightened. "Well, shall we join the others? I would not want to keep the Emperor waiting . . ."

Walter Slovotsky and Bren Adahan had joined their ladies at table when the decurion pretending to be a servant quieted the chatter in the Great Hall by pounding the butt of his staff on the floor, three times.

Thoom. Thoom. Thoom.

"Gentles and Barons, Barons and Lords, Lords and Ladies, Ladies and Gentles," the decurion called out, his blaring voice more suited to a parade ground than the Great Hall, "the Dowager Empress Beralyn and the Emperor Thomen."

Beralyn and Thomen entered through the private door to the emperor's study, the dowager empress on Thomen's arm. They moved slowly, probably more out of necessity than for dignity and dramatic effect; Beralyn looked older, day by day. And, still, her eyes moved across the crowd until they met Slovotsky's, and burned in.

Amazing how fresh and unyielding her hate could be. Yes, Walter Slovotsky had been in the room when her husband was killed— but it hadn't been his fault, and Slovotsky had killed Zherr Furnael's murderer seconds later.

Her holding a grudge was, well, inconvenient at best, dangerous at worst.

It would be convenient if she simply keeled over and died, but the dowager empress was unlikely to do anything at all for Walter Slovotsky's convenience, not even so small a favor as dropping dead.

Aiea bent her head close to his and whispered, her lips barely brushing his ear. "I'm beginning to wonder if she's ever going to let it go," she said, her breath warm and surprisingly erotic in his ear.

Slovotsky could more feel than see Kirah, out of the corner of his eye, glaring at him. Wonderful. His ex-wife resented his and Aiea's relationship, even though—as far as she knew, although there was much Kirah didn't know—it hadn't amounted to anything before their marriage was over, and their marriage had long been over when Walter had stumbled upon Kirah and Bren Adahan fucking— in his own damn bed.

He turned to Kirah and gave her a genial smile that he hoped would either reassure or irritate her.

Damned if he knew which he really wanted.

The tables had been arranged, as much as possible, to alternate Holtish barons with Biemish, attempting to keep traditional enemies—Nerahan and Arondael; Selahan and Benteen; Nerahan and Niphael; Nerahan and Adahan (Nerahan didn't seem to get along with anybody; particularly understandable, considering the legendary brutality of his soldiers during the war)—as far away from each other as possible. It reminded Walter Slovotsky of Doria Perlstein's stories about her Bat Mitzvah and other gatherings of the remarkably dysfunctional Perlstein/Silverstein/Rosenberg clan, where the combinations of who-couldn't-be-next-to-whom often seemed to approach the mathematical limits, and the organizer would always, at some point, have to throw up her hands (and it always was a her) at the sheer frustration of trying to get some semblance of civility for even a short celebration.

Here, it had been the job of the baron minister and the imperial proctor, and Walter and Adahan had done the best that they could.

Robald Nerahan's table had been put next to the emperor's in the hope that that would keep him away from most everybody else—and, perhaps, give Beralyn somebody else to glare at besides Walter. Nerahan, a short, bristle-mustached man, reminded Walter of a weasel not just in his appearance, but in the way he was busy attacking the pile of herb-encrusted squabs on the trencher in front of him, as if he had been turned loose in a henhouse, or at least in a squab house, if there was such a thing, rather than a pigeon coop. His party included half a dozen lords—or at least, putative lords, from his barony; Walter suspected that the biggest, most broad-shouldered of the lot was an imposter, brought along as an extra bodyguard who could be brought into the castle while Nerahan's soldiers were relegated to the barracks in town—and a half dozen ladies of the barony, all of whom seemed to run to large breasts, hair the light brown of molasses honey, high cheekbones, large lovely eyes . . . and buck teeth and piercing, nasal laughs that ruined the whole effect.

Tyrnael seemed almost alone at his table, accompanied only by two minor lords and their ladies. All were dressed in appropriate formal wear—well-tailored linen tunics and leggings for the men and long, floor-sweeping gowns for the ladies—but despite the variety of colors, each garment was hemmed in Tyrnaelian red and black, as though in none-too-subtle reminder of where their allegiance lay. But Tyrnael seemed unembarrassed by the empty expanse of wood, and chatted quietly but animatedly with his party, listening with at least feigned absorption as one of his lords, a big, unabashedly fat man who reminded Walter of Sidney Greenstreet, gestured with an eating prong to emphasize some point he was making.

Selahan, accompanied by his military governor as all the Holtish barons—save for Bren Adahan, of course—were, watched the goings-on at Tyrnael's table with barely concealed envy. Big-boned, sunburned, and lantern-jawed, he kept spilling sauces on his formerly white tunic as he tried his best, no doubt, to convey food to his mouth while the conversation at his own table eddied around him, splashing up against the rock of General Dereneer, the real power in Barony Selahan.

It was hard to tell Barons Hol'sten, Benteen, and Derahan apart, except by the baronial colors of the filigreed decorations on their sleeves. Probably not more than a couple years separated them in age: all the men were in their early fifties, with sagging jowls that were barely concealed by their short-cropped beards, and receding hairlines that were more emphasized than concealed by careful attempts at comb-overs. Walter had to remind himself that Hol'sten was yellow and green; Benteen was brown and gold; Derahan, crimson and cerulean.

The Keranahan table was one of the two empty ones—General

Treseen, not having a baron to accompany, had elected to quarter himself with his officers. Walter wasn't sure whether or not he approved—that was the intelligent, competent thing to do, and if Treseen wasn't an incompetent boob, then he had likely been involved in Elanee's treason, and that was worse.

Niphael and Verahan were next, for no particular reason except that they reminded Walter of Jack Spratt and his wife—Niphael, thin enough to look sickly, his complexion made to look only worse by his choice of the baronial orange and green as colors for his striped tunic, rather than merely decorations; Verahan, who apparently had never met a pig part he didn't like, managed to munch on a huge joint he held in his hand without so much as dropping an ounce of fat on the vast acres of linen that covered his heroically massive belly. Which was just as well—pig fat probably wouldn't go with black and orange piping, and definitely wouldn't go with the snowy white of his tunic.

There would have been an argument for Walter and Aiea to be at the emperor's table, but nobody had suggested that—at least, not in Walter's presence—and if the alternative was sitting with Bren Adahan and Kirah, while there was some discomfort involved with that, it had to be better than sitting with Beralyn, watching her every move and wondering if she was going to sprinkle some poison in his soup.

Then there was the other empty table: Cullinane. Every once in a while, somebody would glance over at it, as though to make the point that Jason Cullinane wasn't here, and how that showed at best marginal respect for the emperor.

Shit. Walter Slovotsky wished that Ellegon were here. It would be nice to slip out and take a quick dragonback ride over to the barony and find out what the hell was going on. Pulling Cullinane heads out of Cullinane asses was something that Slovotsky had been doing for twenty years, and it was a habit he apparently wouldn't be able to give up, not yet.

Still . . .

Parliament hadn't opened yet, so the boy wasn't—at least technically—late.

But where the hell *was* Jason Cullinane?

Soon enough, he thought. *The boy will be here soon enough. He'd damned well better.*

7

✠ The Road

Morning broke all sunny and blue-skied and clear, the threat of storm and rain that had hovered over their campground all night having melted in the light of the early morning sun, along with the thin pre-dawn fog, as well as Pirojil's nightly nightmares.

It was good to lie still in his blankets, warm and cozy until he moved, while somebody else started the fire and got things moving. Off in the distance, the quiet whicker of Pirojil's big bay gelding announced that somebody—probably Kethol—was tending to the horses.

The baron was, as usual, quick to rise, and—likely over the objections of Kethol, who had had the last watch—he had started the morning cookfire, and had a billy of water already boiling by the time that Pirojil rolled out of his blankets and got to his feet, the rough ground hard and cold beneath his callused feet.

His boots stood, waiting, at the foot of his ground bed—Pirojil had been a soldier long enough to know that while wearing your boots at night gave you a few extra moments in case of an emergency, it was better as a matter of policy to let your boots air out and the scabs on your feet air-dry at night whenever possible.

Jason Cullinane's smile was, as usual, natural and easy as he eyed Pirojil over the rim of his cup. "Tea's had enough time to steep this morning," he said, "and it's pretty good." He raised an eyebrow. "Can I pour you a cup?"

Pirojil grunted, not sure whether he meant yes or no. He didn't like waking up in the morning.

Oh, in an emergency, he could go from deep sleep to instant, violent wakefulness in just a few heartbeats, but that wasn't his natural tendency. He was no noble, used to dallying in bed while the servants cooked and served him breakfast and brought him a warmed chamberpot, but it would be nice to try that once again—to try that, for once.

The baron misread his grunt. "Yes, yes, yes, I know: the baron doesn't cook the food and serve the soldiers." His smile broadened. When he smiled, he looked about twelve years old, instead of almost twice that. There was nothing of artifice in that smile, nothing of calculation. "You'd think, by now, that people would be used to the idea that we Cullinanes do things our own way."

"I noticed that right away, myself." Toryn smiled. Pirojil didn't like that expression on him; it seemed too condescending. And, for that matter, Pirojil didn't like the way that the tall, slim man seemed fully rested and refreshed as he dawdled over his mug of tea, every hair on his head and pointed black beard combed neatly into place. Pirojil didn't like much about the slaver—no, the ex-slaver; it was important to remember that—but, as usual, the world didn't much care what Pirojil did or didn't like.

Toryn took another sip. "You've served the Cullinane family for some years; one would think you would have accustomed yourself to their ways." His tone was just this side of an overt insult.

Yes, Pirojil didn't say, I'm used to it. I was long used to it when doing things his own way got his father, the Old Emperor, blown to bloody little bits on a Melawei beach. And, if I have to, I'll get used to Jason Cullinane's doing things his own way killing him every bit as dead.

But, Pirojil didn't say, it would be nice if I didn't have to.

"I . . . it's good tea, true enough," he said, then took a sip, his first sip.

Toryn chuckled.

And it was good tea, strongly flavored with cinnomeile, with a vague but biting touch of pepper to it, smoothed out by sweet honey.

Ahira, the dwarf, walked out from behind the remnants of an old stone wall, buckling his thick belt around his even thicker waist.

"Good morning, all," he said, his voice a gravelly basso rumble, curiously smooth and melodic around the edges. "We'd best be up and on our way; there's been a fire burning down the road since before dawn." He rubbed a thick hand against his face, smearing blood from jaw to cheekbone. Ahira had, for some reason or other, taken to shaving lately, and the effect was to leave his huge, massive, improbably wide jaw even more prominent and as ugly, perhaps, as Pirojil's own.

You got used to having the dwarf around after a while, but then, every now and then, the differences were somehow more shocking for your not having noticed them: the improbably wide body, massive shoulders and torso over stumpy legs; the craggy, ageless face that could have been thirty years old or three hundred; the knobby knuckles, like walnuts under the skin. You could forget easily, too easily, that Ahira wasn't really human, but another, older kind entirely, but only for so long. Then it would hit you like a slap in the face.

The dwarf sang a quiet little song as he packed up his gear, thick fingers moving with a dexterity that was no less surprising for its familiarity. Pirojil couldn't make out the words—it wasn't in Erendra, and Pirojil knew only a little Dwarvish—but it was a cheerful sort of thing, with a recurring refrain something like, "he ho," or something similarly cheery.

Pirojil grunted. Again. If there was anything more irritating in the morning than a cheerful baron and a condescending former slaver, it would have to be a cheerful dwarf.

It was best to keep such opinions to himself.

He walked over to the cookfire, and warmed his fingers. There were times when his opinion would be listened to, and times when it wouldn't.

Splitting the party in two was one of the times it hadn't been. The idea was that, if there was a problem at one campsite, there was a rescue party close by. Pirojil would rather—much rather—have had the entire group under protection. Yes, in theory, it wouldn't be his and Kethol's fault if something happened to the Cullinane women, if somehow, somebody got past their five guards.

But when you went soldiering, you didn't sign up for avoiding blame—you signed up to obey orders, to protect those to whom you owed fealty, to stand between sharp metal and soft flesh . . .

Shit. Well, it wasn't his choice. If what he wanted was a world full of choices, he could take his share of the money the three of them had cached, and go out and make all his own choices.

Instead, he squatted in front of the fire and warmed his fingers.

He could tell that it was Erenor who had started the fire; while Erenor wasn't much of a wizard, except, of course, for his illusions, he was a good hand with a fire. Come to think of it, that probably came with the territory—Andrea Cullinane, whom Pirojil still thought of as the empress, even if, technically, she was one of two dowager empresses, had always been quick with a fire.

And he wasn't too terribly slow himself, not since he had discovered, quite by accident, that a little bit of gunpowder—a quarter charge was ample—combined with a spark from flint on steel or steel on flint, would let an ordinary soldier such as himself start a fire as readily as even a wizard.

"Sleep well?" Erenor asked, as though it was something that he cared about, which seemed unlikely on the face of it. Pirojil could swear quite easily and honestly that he hadn't been so solicitous when he had wakened Erenor for his turn on watch. Pirojil had simply toed the wizard awake, waited until Erenor had grunted and gotten to his feet, then staggered over to his own blankets, kicked off his boots, and was asleep before his head actually hit the ground.

Pirojil just grunted.

"One would think," Erenor said, "that you think that I don't care if you passed a pleasant night."

Pirojil didn't think, he didn't say, that he didn't see why Erenor would have any reason to care if he had passed a kidney stone.

The wizard raised an eyebrow. "But of course I do," he said, as though he had read Pirojil's thoughts with the same ease that he could read the blurry glyphs on the vellum pages of his spell books. "And not merely because you are far more grouchy when you have not gotten your rest." The long, almost aristocratic fingers of his left hand made a complicated and pretentious gesture.

"And what would that reason be?" Jason Cullinane asked. "I'm curious."

"Lord Baron, may not even a simple soldier have a secret or six?"

Toryn laughed. "It's much easier to keep a secret, Erenor," he said, "if you don't announce that you're doing so."

Erenor started to say something, but stopped himself and turned back to the baron.

"Well . . ." Jason Cullinane's mouth twitched. "Well, I don't see why not."

Pirojil didn't like the way Ahira looked long and hard at Erenor.

Yes, yes, he and Kethol were loyal to the Cullinanes, but they weren't mere appendages. They were soldiers, and their loyalty was that of soldiers, not tenant serfs. Erenor's status as a wizard was as much their own property as their swords and their cache of gold, and while circumstances had forced them to share the secret with Walter Slovotsky, circumstances had not forced them to share it with the young baron.

The young fool, was more like it. Jason Cullinane had been the heir to the silver crown of the Prince of Bieme, and Emperor of Holtun-Bieme, and he had given it over to Thomen Furnael on little more than a whim.

That had always bothered Pirojil. It was wrong to give up a position without a fight.

He hadn't, after all. He had lost the fight before it began, of course, the moment that the elf—

No. He had other things to think about, he thought, his fist clenching, the inward-turned stone on his ring pressed hard against his hand.

Kethol, his own hands protected by thick leather gloves, slid down the rope from his perch high in the old oak tree. "There is some movement on the road to our south; the others are on their way. When we get moving, we will not be the first to do so this day." He gave the end of the rope a hefty shake: the end tied around the high branch loosened, as if by magic, and the rope fell to the ground all in a neat heap.

Kethol grinned at him; Pirojil had never quite gotten the hang of that trick, and it gave Kethol innocent pleasure to be able to best Pirojil at something where the only thing at stake was convenience.

Kethol looked pointedly at where the horses were hobbled, still unsaddled, and then at Erenor, whose job it was to saddle and unsaddle the horses.

Jason Cullinane chuckled. "Go a bit easy on our friend," he said, handing another steaming mug to Erenor, unself-consciously, as though it was the most natural thing in the world for a baron to wait upon his soldiers, as though they were the nobility and he was the servant. "He reminds me a little of Walter; the Slovotsky family tends to wake up slowly." He smiled smugly over the rim of his mug, as though over a private joke.

The top limb of the sun was above the far hills by the time camp was broken and they were on their way.

Too long. Pirojil didn't like it. If it had been up to Pirojil, they wouldn't have been traveling in the daytime in the first place, or heading back toward the capital at all.

Yes, the night was in some senses a better time for an ambush, but with the dwarf with them, ideally riding point, that danger would have been minimized. Pirojil wasn't sure exactly what Ahira could see in the dark—he couldn't read, for example—but his night vision was a lot better than even Kethol's night vision.

And if it had been up to Pirojil, they wouldn't have been traveling along the Prince's Road at all. The direct route was fine for most travel, and necessary for trade—but escort duty was a different matter.

Not that anybody had asked his opinion. Or Kethol's. Or Erenor's. Working for the Cullinane family was better than working for any other nobility that Pirojil had been involved with, but it wasn't all that different.

"Let's get moving; we're wasting daylight," Jason Cullinane finally said.

About time.

An old tune his father used to whistle ran through Kethol's head as he rode, although he didn't let it come to his lips. That was the thing about riding point. Even though you were out of the immediate hearing of the others—you would have to yell, or at least raise your voice, in order to be heard—part of the job was to keep your ears clear, as well as your eyes open. There wasn't any particular reason to be expecting trouble—except that was a big part of what their job was: to expect trouble, and then to handle it.

Kethol missed Durine's reassuring bulk, but he could more feel than sense Pirojil's presence half a kalikan behind, riding just behind the baron, and Erenor was riding drag—the perfect spot for him, as Erenor seemed to have been born to be looking and listening over his shoulder, waiting for some trouble he had no doubt earned to catch up with him.

Kethol liked taking the lead—yes, there was a bit more risk to it, supposedly. But any bones player wasn't averse to risk, and any soldier who was, was either crazy or a fool, and Kethol was neither.

Yes, he went along with Pirojil's idea of stashing some money for the three of them to buy a farm, or tavern, or brothel, or something else to support them in their old age, but now there were only two of them, unless they decided to cut Erenor in—which wasn't impossible, but wasn't particularly likely—and in some way that he couldn't quite explain, not even to himself, Durine's death had taken all the pleasure from thinking of it. He had pictured the three of them sitting on a porch somewhere, drinking wine—out of glasses, perhaps, and not just mugs—being waited on by women in low-cut, short shifts, who had to be careful when they bent over, lest their breasts come tumbling out . . .

. . . and that used to be a fine daydream.

Shit.

It probably wouldn't be a problem, anyway. It wasn't like they were likely to reach old age, after all. It could happen, particularly if by some magic the peace persisted, but there was trouble on the Kiarian border, and increasing orc problems in the north, and Kethol had no particular faith that the emperor's plan to return control of the Holtish baronies to the Holts wouldn't end up triggering a war of secession, or rebellion of the Biemish barons, for that matter.

He smiled to himself. Maybe he *was* crazy or a fool, or both: he found that reassuring. Perhaps he wouldn't have if Leria had been back in Keranahan, but she wasn't. She was safe, in Biemestren, and well-guarded, and even if streams of war were to overflow the banks and run red all across the land, it was unlikely that they would so much as touch the hem of her dress.

He was so caught up in his own thoughts that he suddenly realized that it was too quiet. Yes, he could hear—and count, if he had a mind to—the clopping of the hooves of the horses behind him, and the rattle and whisper of the breeze through the brush and the leaves of the trees, but . . . where were the birds? Where was the high-pitched chittering of the brown squirrels and the lower tones—almost grunts—of the black?

Kethol had been raised in the woods—not, granted, these woods, but an older, darker forest—and he knew the smells, the sights, and the sounds. Particularly the sounds.

He cursed himself for an idiot and a fool, but cut off the thought with a savageness that was just this side of physical. There would be time enough for blaming himself later on.

He pulled his horse to a stop, then dismounted, pretending to check its left rear hoof. Pirojil kicked his dull brown gelding into a quick canter and was quickly at his side.

"Your horse wasn't limping," he said, dropping heavily to the dirt of the road.

"Listen," Kethol said. Sometimes Pirojil could be as thick-witted as Kethol himself.

Pirojil cocked his head to one side, thick lips pursed together in thought. "I don't hear anything."

"Me, neither. Nothing. The birds aren't singing, or chirping, or anything." Kethol drew his belt dagger and pretended to pry at a stone lodged in the hoof. "Which means," he said, "that either the animals and birds around here aren't used to men and horse traveling along the Prince's Road—"

"Which I beg to doubt."

"—or something else has them frightened into silence."

Pirojil's mouth twitched. "An orc, or two?"

"Maybe." But this far south? Granted, they had recently run to ground an orc farther north in Barony Cullinane—vicious creature, almost as vicious as the three of them were, although not quite— and it was certainly a possibility.

Maybe Kethol was wrong, but he felt sure that he could smell an orc far off, and with the way the wind was blowing, it should have brought that acrid scent to him. After a few years in either the woods or the kind of soldiering that the three of them had been doing, you developed a sense of when you were and weren't being watched.

The only trouble with that sense was that it was unreliable.

"For what it's worth . . ." Pirojil shrugged.

"Me, neither."

Either Erenor hadn't been doing his job or the baron had over-ruled him: instead of staying in place like they should have, Jason Cullinane rode up, Toryn lagging only a little behind on the huge white mare that made the slim man look almost doll-like, while the dwarf brought up the rear on his sad-looking brown gelding, leading the three pack horses. Ahira always seemed to pick a small, sad-looking horse, one that could, seemingly, barely bear up under the considerable weight of an armed, armored dwarf, but he was always considerate enough to mount his heavy gear on one of the pack animals.

"Some problem?" he asked.

Well, if they were under observation, it would probably be best to keep moving. They could make better time on the road than almost anything could make through the woods, even an orc.

"I'm not sure," Pirojil said, swinging his leg back over the sad-dle. "I think Kethol needs to walk his horse for awhile; I'll take point and we can let him catch up later."

The baron nodded. "I could—"

"No." The dwarf was already out of the saddle. For someone so strong, he always seemed to have a hard time mounting up, but wasted neither time nor motion in dismounting. "Kethol is best in the woods; Pirojil and I can back him up if need be." The dwarf's smile said that he was looking forward to that sort of event, which made him either a liar or a fool. Or both, perhaps; a fool could lie as well.

"I'm not totally useless in such situations," Toryn said.

Ahira grunted. "Are you volunteering?" He raised a hand to forestall an answer. "Never mind—if three isn't enough, four won't be. You stay with Erenor and the baron, and send up a signal rocket if it all breaks loose."

Kethol approved. Toryn was a good hand with a sword, but he

was no woodsman, and Kethol didn't trust him the way he did Pirojil, or even Erenor—for a wizard; Erenor was awfully good at moving stealthily. Probably came from having to sneak out of town all the time.

And Ahira? If the dwarf thought he could be useful, Kethol would trust him.

Crashing through the woods was a good way to get yourself killed, if there was anybody around who had the ability and desire. Moving silently through the woods was impossible off a beaten path, and difficult on one. So, his longbow strung, an arrow nocked—he could drop it to one side and draw his knife, if need be—Kethol walked down the road, Ahira and Pirojil trailing well behind him, until he found a game path, separated from the woods by just a fringe of windbreak. Deer might well like to take a nibble—or more than several nibbles—from a cornfield, but they would avoid the open throughout the day, and perhaps the night as well. The strip of forest alongside the road was, legally speaking, a baronial hunting and foresting preserve, where only squirrel, rabbit, and fox—nuisance animals—could be taken, and where cedar, oak, maple, and willow were also protected from harvest without a warrant.

But the emperor, back when he was a baron, before Jason Cullinane had abdicated the throne in his favor, had indefinitely extended the wartime blanket permission to hunt deer on farmland, and the deer had become increasingly wary. Which, of course, made them more insistent on sticking to cover, staying out of the open, and, ironically enough, made the hunt even easier for somebody patient enough to find a stand along a game trail, and wait.

And which, at the same time, made travel along the same game paths more likely for everybody.

Kethol shivered for a moment as he left the sun-warmed road for the forest.

Whether it was ancient road builders or equally ancient wizards that had prevented the Prince's Road from being overgrown, neither had worked their craft beyond the roadbed itself; leafy giants twisted their limbs overhead, swallowing Kethol up into green coolness before he went half a hundred paces in.

Dozens of years and thousands of hooves and feet had beaten the dirt of the path solid, only pierced here and there by a projecting tree root. Little light trickled through, but there was enough for Kethol to see where an occasional misplaced hoof had planted itself off the path and in the rotting humus that covered the forest floor.

He followed the trail inward, past where little balls of droppings told of an owl's nest, high above, hidden from view, past where two small, beady eyes peeked out of a shadow beneath an upthrust root, disappearing into that shadow before Kethol could decide whether it was a ground squirrel or a gopher, past where flattened grasses told of a place where a deer had rested, and recently . . .

. . . until the trail suddenly broke on a clearing ahead: a meadow.

Kethol signaled for a halt, and knelt down, listening.

No, it was still too quiet. No farther. There was something out there, certainly; something watching them, clearly; something waiting for them, perhaps.

But dashing out from the cover of the forest and into an open clearing, exposing himself—and worse: the others, following him— to attack by whatever it was . . .

Yes, he would do it under orders. There was a lot you did when you were ordered to do it, and more that you would do if you had to. He would probably do it if there was something, someone across the clearing who needed rescuing. Kethol had been roundly cursed by both Durine and Pirojil for what they called his stupid heroics.

But not just to see what it was.

Pirojil knelt beside him, breathing heavily. He wiped the sweat from his forehead with his sleeve. Yes, he had stamina, that one, both of body and of mind, but he didn't have the woodsman's knack of keeping up a fast pace without tiring. Maybe you had to be born with it.

He turned to Pirojil, who frowned. *I don't like it, either,* Pirojil mouthed. *Something ahead?*

I think so. Kethol wasn't sure. The meadow was crisscrossed with paths of trampled grasses. Deer? Orc? Man? Some of each?

Ahira stood beside where they knelt, his chest level with Kethol's eyes for once, instead of the other way around.

"I smell something," he whispered. "Something rank."

That wasn't much help. Was it an unbathed man, or an orc? A harsh smell in the forest was the sign of an animal that didn't have a need to hide its scent—try to catch a whiff of rabbit some time!— but it could be a skunk or a boar or a bear as easily as an orc or a man.

A skunk would be annoying, and a bear would likely flee at the sound of their approach, but boars were mean, and stupid enough to be unafraid. Hunting a boar was not something Kethol would want to do right here and now. Yes, bow and arrow would be fine, if there was a low-branched tree within reach. Even if your first arrow killed it—and that would require a side shot, as even the fastest-driven arrow wouldn't penetrate the bone and gristle and muscle that covered the pig's chest—a boar was too stupid to know that it was dead, and would gladly charge you and rend you with its tusks before it finally keeled over.

No. They hadn't been trailing a boar. Kethol would have spotted its spoor, and it wouldn't have moved quietly, except by accident.

He had worked that out, but in doing so he felt disappointed in himself. Surely, somebody with his experience in the woods could do better than figure out that whatever it was, it wasn't a boar.

"Let's let it go," Pirojil said, his lips close to the dwarf's.

That was the prudent thing to do, the wise thing to do. And if Kethol didn't know that Pirojil would have imprudently followed him, he would have dashed out into the clearing, trying to draw the attention of whatever-it-was, hoping that his speed and reflexes would save him.

"No." Ahira shook his head. "Let's finish things here," he whispered, and straightened himself.

There was something strange about the dwarf's very ordinary-looking roughspun cotton tunic, as he stood, his ax held lightly in one gnarled hand. It took a moment for Kethol to realize what it was: the dwarf wasn't wearing his chainmail armor. That made sense, but it was somehow surprising that Ahira would instantly see the problem with rattling and clanking through the forest, and would leave it behind without a moment's hesitation, as he must have—particularly considering his short legs—to have kept up with Kethol's pace.

I can move faster than you'd think, Ahira mouthed. *Let me handle it.*

Pirojil frowned. He had little patience with stupidity. That Ahira could run faster than Pirojil would have guessed was probably true, and all to the good. But could he move faster than an orc, a boar, an arrow, or a bullet?

Asking silly questions was unlikely to improve matters. And there was a real question in Kethol's mind as to whether Ahira would let the two of them overrule him.

Even if he did—even if Ahira backed down at their insistence—the baron was all too likely to put himself in harm's way, and there would be no arguing with him. Compared to the baron, or the dowager empress, Ahira was as expendable as Erenor.

The good thing about working with somebody for years is that you don't have to say everything out loud. Pirojil would no more look forward to explaining a dead Ahira to the baron than Kethol would.

Kethol was a good enough bones player that he could have made something of a living at it, assuming that he could find enough competition, and survive the after-game fight when the competition realized how badly they had been had. It wasn't enough to have a steady hand, and a keen eye, necessary as those were. Sometimes the bones fell against you; sometimes you were two or three moves away from having no play at all. You had to learn how to bluff, to persuade the other guy that he was in the position you were really in, trick him into making a bad play, and watch the bones tumble to the table, looking surprised at the *rickitatickitatickita* sound.

So he shook his head and loosened his arrow from the bow-string. "No," he said, his voice more than a whisper, though little more. "Not a good bet," he said, not looking to Pirojil for support—that would have been too obvious, and the wrong way to play this board. "It's too open, we're too far away from help, and there's only three of us."

For a moment, he honestly didn't know how it would all fall, but then Ahira's wide face split in a grin, and he broke for daylight, his short legs pumping hard, faster than Kethol would have thought possible. The dwarf was right about that, at least; Kethol wouldn't have thought that he could have run so fast.

"Shut up," Pirojil said.

Kethol realized that he had been muttering curses and oaths under his breath, so he stopped.

Ahira dashed across the meadow, not taking more than two or three or four steps straight in any one direction before angling off. If there was somebody trying to line up a rifle or a bow on him, that would make it more difficult. If that somebody was an inexperienced shot, it might well make it impossible.

"I think he's going to make it," Pirojil said, the unvoiced next question: and, if he does, do we follow him?

It would be silly to follow—there could be somebody behind the treeline, just waiting for the next fool to dash out into the open. It's what Kethol would have done, if it had been him on stand, waiting. Let the first one go, at least for the moment, and then collect two nice, juicy kills when the others followed. On a good day, Kethol could have the second arrow in the air before the first one struck home.

The dwarf was barely a manheight from the concealment of the treeline when a feathered bolt seemed to sprout from his thigh in midstride. It didn't slow him for a moment, not until his leg came down. It crumpled beneath him, and he let out a shout as he fell, hard, his ax falling from his hands as he tumbled to the tall grasses.

Kethol was already in motion, his bow tossed to one side, his quiver of arrows falling from his right shoulder as he shrugged out of the strap to draw his sword with his right hand, while his left reached for the nearest of the brace of pistols on his belt. There had been a motion out of the corner of his eye—he knew where the crossbowman was.

Pirojil's boots thumped behind him, and a pair of shots rang out as he ran. From behind him—was Pirojil . . . ?

No. Pirojil would no more shoot at Kethol than he would at himself. He was just firing to keep the enemy crossbowman occupied, to give him something to think about besides the two men charging at his hiding place—Kethol had just bet both of their lives that they *were* charging his hiding place, but the path of the bolt glowed in his mind, sharp and bright like the edge of a knife. It was a race: if they could reach the hunter's stand before he had a chance to recock his crossbow, if the sound of the shots and the image of the two of them charging, running, deep-throated growls coming, unbidden, unsummoned, to their lips, if . . .

Kethol fired off his pistol, just as something whisked past his right ear, his neck suddenly wet.

The pain came a moment later, a fiery stroke that burned him to the bone. But he couldn't stop for pain, he couldn't stop for fear, he couldn't stop for knowing that his gamble had failed, that the crossbowman could not have had half enough time to reload, and that Kethol had not only bitten off more than he himself could chew—*Leria, remember me*—but had dragged the closest thing to a friend he had ever had along with him.

He crashed through the brush, brambles clawing at his throat and face, and into a cleared space, no wider than a manheight, where a bowman knelt, trembling fingers pulling back at the string of his crossbow.

Somehow, somewhere, he had learned to size up an adversary at a glance. The bowman was a tall man, half a head taller than Kethol himself, his blond hair and beardless, flat face suggesting some Salke in his ancestry, or perhaps Kiarian. He wore the dark green tunic and deerskin leggings and buskins of a woodsman, be it a woodsman of Holtun or Bieme or Osgrad or Salket. You could move invisibly through the forest in such clothes, limited only by your silence. You could—and Kethol had—stand motionless in the crotch of an old oak, invisible against green leaves and rough brown bark, the fringes of your leggings helping to break your outline.

Kethol felt a strange kinship with the taller man as he lunged forward, in full extension, the edge of his sword not pausing for even a heartbeat as it cut through the bowstring, then rose to bury the point deep within the chest, and then, after a quick twist and pull, slash open the other's throat as he charged past. You couldn't stop and congratulate yourself over a quick kill, not in the middle of a fight, not when he didn't know where the other bowman was, not with Ahira down and Pirojil right behind him. He had to keep moving, to find the other—

Something tangled up his feet and he fell, hard, headlong. He tried to turn it into a roll-and-recovery, just as he would have on the practice ground, but he had been too long a soldier, and too little a woodsman, and what his mind should have remembered without effort, his blood and bones and muscle had forgotten: that the floor of the forest was not a flat and level surface, not a straw-covered parade ground, and he slammed, chest-first, into an up-thrust root that knocked the wind out of him.

He tried to force himself to his knees—first to all fours, then to your feet, and then back to the fight, that was the way of it—but his traitor body refused to cooperate. It was all he could do to try to breathe, to try to suck a puff of air into his lungs, to wave his arms and legs, to try to get them into motion, because in a fight, if you were pinned to the ground by anything, you were no use to yourself or to anybody else. It would be trivially easy for some blade to reach out of the black borders of his narrowing vision, and pin him to the ground, ending any usefulness he might ever have.

No. It took every bit of strength, every bit of effort, he could muster, but he managed to get his knees and elbows beneath him, and then, distant, disobedient fingers clawing at the rough bark of the tree, to pull himself to his feet.

He found he could breathe, just a little, as long as he kept the breaths shallow, and didn't try to fill his lungs.

Not that it mattered much. It was all over. Pirojil wouldn't have been standing over the body of the enemy bowman if it wasn't.

The big blond man was dead—the shit stink broadcast that into the air, for all to smell—but Pirojil was still Pirojil: he had kicked the dead man's knife to one side, and one of his heavy boots rested firmly on the dead man's wrist.

A sound from the brush sent Kethol stooping to retrieve his sword, but Ahira's voice made the move less urgent.

"Ta havath," the dwarf shouted, "it's just me. Give me a hand here, eh?"

Pirojil gave a final, tentative kick to the corpse's head—it left the neck cocked at an impossible angle—and picked up the dead man's sword, using it like a machete to hack a path through to daylight. In a moment, he came back, stooping awkwardly, one of Ahira's thick arms around his waist.

The bolt had been snapped off—not cut cleanly; Ahira clearly had been rushed—almost flush with the skin, and the wound was still leaking blood, although only slowly. The dwarf followed Kethol's glance at it, then looked down and furrowed his brow for a moment, the thick, ropy muscles in his neck and leg tensed, and the flow of blood stopped.

The dwarf grinned, but the unusual pastiness of his complexion made the grin a brave lie. "Try that sometime, eh?" He released his grip on Pirojil to lean against the bole of a tree. Blunt fingers probed at the stub of wood protruding from his leg, then fastened, tightly, and pulled. The stub of bolt, complete with razor-sharp head, slowly eased out of his flesh, darkly wet. He gave it a casual flick, and it stuck in the bark of the tree over Kethol's head. "Better save it. Might want to scratch his partner with it, and see if he thinks it's poisoned, maybe?"

Pirojil shook his head. "No partner. This one had two cross-bows," he said, gesturing with the point of his sword to where first one, then the other lay. "Kethol tripped over the second."

Kethol's mind was still a bit foggy, and he winced as he brought his hand up to his cheek, and it came away wet with his own blood. No partner. He and Pirojil had killed the assassin, which was better than getting killed by the assassin, no matter how he looked at it, but . . .

Ahira knelt down next to the body. "Anybody care to bet we don't find anything to identify him," he said, quickly stripping the tunic and leggings from the corpse. "Be nice to find an identifying ceremonial scar, say, or a tattoo, or a list of prices and targets in a familiar hand . . ."

Kethol bit his lip until it hurt more than his torn ear did. He had messed it up; it was his fault.

He could just hear Pirojil: if only Kethol had just waited for the assassin to come out and try to finish Ahira off, he could have disabled the man with an arrow to the leg, say, just as the assassin had done to Ahira. Ahira had been willing to be their bait, and if only Kethol hadn't gone off again, playing the hero. Yes, the assassin was dead and they were all alive, but the dead man was just a tool— and with him dead, there was no way to know whose hand had wielded the tool.

Unless, of course, there was some evidence on the body.

Which there wouldn't be.

Pirojil clapped a hard hand to his shoulder, and Kethol nodded in thanks.

That was the thing about Pirojil: he knew that Kethol was in the wrong, but more than that, he knew which side he was on. That was important. There was more than enough right to go around, but trust was always in short supply.

Ahira looked up at Kethol. "You just going to stand there bleeding, or are you going to give me a hand with this?"

Part Three:

Parliament

8

Bren Adahan

The best time to get in a little private sparring, it occurred to Bren Adahan, probably for the thousandth time, was the early morning, just at dawn. The keep was quiet then, save for a few early-rising servants and some late-posted guards, and the heat of the day had yet to bake the horse urine–soaked parade ground outside the inner barracks, releasing the scent of ancient horse piss. With a little luck, a stiff wind at the ramparts level would translate into a light breeze at the ground, perhaps bringing a distant smell of sun-warming wheat, but certainly carrying away sweat before it had the chance to bead on your bare chest.

These days, of course, what with everything else he had to do, getting up early probably meant meeting with some noble or notable so that he would be able to talk intelligently to Thomen, about whatever was bothering or interesting the emperor, over their usual breakfast together.

So an early morning bout had gone the way of his old early morning ride, and he missed it almost as much.

Almost as good as an early morning bit of sparring was a late night bout. With the night wind whispering vague threats and vaguer promises, bodies moving under the light of flickering torches with the tips of the practice swords disappearing into the darkness, reappearing moments later, you could concentrate—you simply *must* concentrate—on nothing more than the bout itself. It felt too real, the threat too imminent, when your sight couldn't always reassure you that your opponent's sword was blunt and button-capped, like your own.

Of course, what with Parliament in session, and with the danger of the other barons, particularly the Biemish barons, thinking him aloof, and therefore dangerous, or isolated, and therefore vulnerable, his evenings were filled with endless dinners and interminable drinking bouts with the rest of the visiting nobility. He would be lucky to stumble back to his rooms, not sure whether he was more tired than drunk or more drunk than tired, where Kirah—warm, soft, patient Kirah; what a fool Walter Slovotsky had been to let her slip away—waited with warm cloths, warm hands, and a warmer mouth. Sleep was a dark but friendly pit that he could fall headlong into.

The worst time was now: noon on a busy day, when what he really ought to be doing was going over tax figures and expenditure reports with the engineers and accountants, so that he would have facts not merely at his fingertips, but at his lips, when arguments arose during a session of Parliament. But sword practice was like riding, and hunting, and sex: even when it was bad it was pretty good, and when it was good it was terrific.

It was also better than the alternative way of earning some respect from the fighting men of the Home Guard, for this reason: it was possible.

If you were going to command fighting men, his father had long ago taught him, you had to command the respect of fighting men, and the simplest and best way to do that was to lead them in battle. Not the safest, mind, but the best.

You couldn't always be right there when steel met steel and flesh, not in person. But if you demonstrated, from time to time, that you were willing to put your own steel—and your own flesh—out in front, you could earn that respect. You could make the men believe that the only reason you weren't here, right here and now, was that you were busy somewhere else, and the least they could do was to shoulder their share of the burden. Much of the time, they would. You could earn that respect by winning a few scars in battle, early on, and let your legend grow in the telling, the way the Old Emperor had.

That wasn't a possibility that was open to Bren Adahan.

Forget, for the moment, all the silly talk about a unified empire. That was just talk, and talk was always the cheapest of coin. He was a Holt, and Holtun had been conquered by Bieme, and commanding fighting men in Bieme was something that was not going to happen, no matter his title.

But he could earn their respect, even the half-sneering sort of respect that might be the best that an outlander noble would be able to earn.

The way of the sword is the way of timing and balance and speed, and very little of sheer force, but while strength wasn't the key to it, strength mattered. You needed power not just in your wrist and arm, but in your legs and torso, and with some effort, you could make your opponent spend his strength fighting phantom menaces while, slowly, bit by bit, his legs tired, and his arm drooped, until you could beat his sword—practice, as now, or a real sword—to one side as you moved in, leaving him open from nose to ankles.

Bren Adahan did just that, yet again, and lightly tapped Captain Garett on his left nipple, then stepped back. The objective was not just to beat the captain, but to do so in a way that would not cause the other to lose stature and credibility among his men. There was no need for that. Stature, like wealth, was not a fixed commodity; it could be created as well as destroyed, and to destroy it without need was not just cruel, it was wasteful. Bren Adahan was willing to be cruel—you simply couldn't wield power if you weren't willing to be cruel when necessary—but he wasn't willing to be wasteful. Too much of both Holtun and Bieme had been wasted during the war.

"Very nicely done, sir," the captain said. The set of his jaw showed that the admission was at war with his pride, but the words showed that his pride, in a deeper sense, was still the winner. There was some shame in admitting that you had been bested, but much more in denying it.

Bren Adahan nodded to himself. This one would do. It was hard to keep track of the idiotic Biemish system of ranks that, in the Biemish victory, had become the imperial system of ranks, but Garett was now a captain of patrol—by one way of looking at it, the second-lowest ranking officer class.

Well, what with deaths and promotions, the Home Guard was in need of two captains of companies, and three of troops. Garett could fit in either way, and while it was usually General Garavar's call as to promotions, the general probably was ready for retirement, and it wouldn't do to have too much of his hand in shaping the new Home Guard on his way out to pasture.

At Adahan's nod, Garett gave a quick salute, dropped back a full step—Adahan had already caught him when he had ignored his proper spacing—and re-engaged.

This was almost too much fun. It would be wonderful to spend the rest of the day sparring, to exercise nothing more than wrist and thigh muscles, to keep his mind blank—thinking too much was a bad habit that the loss of a few points could correct quickly—but it was time to get back to work.

He deliberately let Garett win the point—something that probably would never have occurred to most people, he thought smugly—and then let his point drop, as though tired.

"Well done, Captain," he said.

"Do you fancy another point, Baron Minister?" The captain's stony face betrayed his self-satisfaction only in the twinkling of his eyes.

"I think not," he said. "At least, not now."

It was tempting, though. There was much to be said for having a reputation for knowing everything that was going on, and since it was impossible to actually know everything that was going on, the only way to gain that reputation was to be able to produce information with seeming effortlessness, and being ready for effortlessness took a lot of work.

This wasn't work.

Truth to tell, it was fun. Necessary fun, but fun.

I am, he thought, *not quite entirely alone and generally hated, in a foreign land. But at least I'm having a good time.*

Adahan—the town, as well as the family—had been destroyed in the war, and if it hadn't been for the Old Emperor . . .

And what was not to like? His bed was warmed every night by a warm, willing, and remarkably pleasant woman, one who, unlike his former intended, had better things to do with every moment of the day than compare him—unfavorably—with her adopted father and her "Uncle Walter." And with the Spider's assurance that Kirah was still fertile, he had every reason to hope for an heir.

And if not, well, the world was filled with warm, willing, pleasant women, wasn't it?

"Nicely done," sounded from the walls high above, in a familiar voice.

Tyrnael leaned over the balustrade, his fingers widely spread on the rail. "You wouldn't mind giving a quick lesson to a lesser baron, would you, Baron Minister?" he asked, then headed for the nearest staircase, taking the answer for granted.

He hadn't seemed to hurry, but his pace must have been brisk; it was only a few moments later that Tyrnael exited from the darkness of the tower staircase, his hair still damp from his morning ablutions. The older baron was dressed casually for the morning, in little more than a blousy spidersilk white shirt over linen trousers, his thick-soled boots the only note of utility, save for the plain-hilted sword at his left hip.

"You're up and around early, Baron," Bren Adahan said. That was the way things were when Parliament was in session—drinking and talking until all hours of the night, with most of the visitors sleeping until the afternoon heat drew them from their beds.

Tyrnael smiled. "Oh, I'm meeting the lovely Lady Leria

shortly," he said, casting a quick glance where the short shadow on the sundial was nearing the fifth hour. "I'm hoping that I can persuade her and her entourage to visit us, out in the country. She's developing quite a reputation as a horsewoman, and I think she might like some of what my middle son has been breeding in our stables."

Bren Adahan kept his face studiously blank. Tyrnael's eldest living son, Lord Lefernen, was very much not in evidence; probably back in Tyrnael, keeping everybody there in line, while acting as a reminder that the mass of baronial troops were under local, not imperial, command. It was one thing to make the barons put their own necks under the emperor's sword—and while it was rarely spoken of, it was understood by all that that was a major reason for Parliament gathering—but their bringing along their whole families as hostages, implicit or otherwise?

That was too bad, in many ways. Lefernen had quite a reputation as a troop captain, won honestly in riding the Kiaran border after his elder brother had been killed doing just the same thing. Bren Adahan would have liked to have met him here, to have taken the measure of the man. But Thomen was reluctant to order other than the barons themselves to the capital, just as the Old Emperor had been.

And—baron minister or not—Bren Adahan didn't have the authority to give such an order himself. Vertum, Bren Adahan's father, had taught him that you should never give an order that you knew would be rebelled against, or ignored. Better to relieve the commander or warden instead. It was even worse with subordinate nobility—you couldn't just relieve them, not if they had their own fealty-held troops.

Barking out orders could be a bloody thing. Think twice and cut once, his father used to say, was a good maxim to apply whether you're measuring wood for a spear or judging a man for a grave.

"But that wasn't why I asked your clerk for a few moments of your time," Tyrnael said. "I do have a small request."

"My clerk?" Bren Adahan raised an eyebrow. He hadn't spoken with Deretty since before breakfast. "I'm sorry; you have the advantage of me. What did you ask my clerk for?"

"It's nothing major," Tyrnael said, "but there's a small party from the barony—my barony—arriving today, and I would much appreciate a pass for its captain. He should have brought a few trinkets that I didn't quite have time to gather together before leaving." His smile was sure innocence. "Just a few gifts and surprises I've been having some of our local craftsmen work on to give out at this Parliament."

Bren Adahan nodded. "Of course," he said. *And,* he added silently, *Walter Slovotsky and I are going to each have a* very *close look at these trinkets of yours, and at the captain bringing them.*

Tyrnael's smile broadened. *I wouldn't have any other way,* it seemed to say.

9

☩ Kelleren's Farm

Some things and some people heal slowly, and maybe some never heal at all, Pirojil thought. There are, after all, wounds to the body, and to the mind, and to the spirit.

He rubbed at his face with the back of his hand, the smoothness of his ring comforting in its familiarity, the signet warm against the palm of his hand.

Prince's Road still hadn't recovered from the ravages of the war, although there had been more than enough time. In the old days, there had been, by princely edict, inns with suitable accommodations for travelers, no more than a day's ride apart, as the road snaked its way through the Biemish landscape.

And then the Holts, aided by the Pandathaway Slavers Guild and their own version of gunpowder, had torn through Bieme, playing out ancient enmities with sword and torch, burning the harvests and harvesting the people to be marched off north and east as slaves. That had been understandable. Not, of course, at all pleasant to be on the receiving end of, but understandable. There would be something satisfying about turning an ancient enemy into jingling coins.

What most people would not have understood is why the Holts had so often burned everything behind them as they ravaged their way through the baronies.

There was no profit in that.

No, most people would not have understood, but Pirojil understood. War was not just about profit and money and pride; it was about destruction and killing. You could ride into a village and kill all who opposed you, and march the rest out in a line, destined to become slaves in other lands, but could you leave behind their homes, untouched? Wouldn't you have to build up your anger and hatred, and wouldn't it be all too easy to touch a torch to a thatched roof? If there were any left inside, you could close your ears to their screams.

Pirojil had closed his ears, his mind, and his heart to a scream or two in his time.

"I don't like this." Andrea Cullinane swung a leg over the pommel of her saddle—and why did the Cullinane women always seem to choose the biggest horse available?—and vaulted more than dropped to the ground. "I don't like this at all," she said. She sniffed the air. "Something smells wrong, and I don't know if it's in the air or in my mind."

She was dressed for the road—women wore trousers for riding, for obvious reasons—but in a discordant note, a short sword was strapped to the left side of her hips, balanced by a flap holster on the right. It was unusual to see a single pistol—when Kethol intended to rely on gunpowder and lead rather than tempered steel, he never carried less than a brace—but the dowager empress (and to Kethol and Pirojil, Andrea Cullinane would always be the real dowager empress, and Beralyn Furnael but a shriveled, shrunken, mean-spirited usurper) undoubtedly had her own reasons for arming herself as she did, and it wasn't the place of the likes of Kethol to question her judgment on that or anything else.

If she wanted his advice—or his belly sliced open so that she could warm her toes in his guts—all she had to do was ask.

Pirojil would have found her strikingly attractive, if he had let himself. Her forty years had left only the start of wrinkles at the corners of her eyes and particularly her large and generous mouth, but if there was any sag to her breasts, the tightness of her leather vest concealed that. The blouse beneath the vest had started the day white and clean, but road dust had turned it a dingy gray already.

Her skin was smoother than it should have been at her age, and there were no visible scars, not to her body, but, from time to time, when her eyes forgot to lie, there was a wildness and an ancient pain there.

Well, that was understandable. One moment she had been the wife of the emperor, mother of the heir, and a powerful wizard in her own right. The next, she was a widow, her husband blown to bloody little bits on a Melawei beach. Now, she was just a dowager empress, and that only a courtesy title, as her son had abdicated the crown and throne to Thomen Furnael.

"I don't know, either," Jason Cullinane said. His eyes kept sweeping their surroundings, never quite resting on anybody or anything. He was too inexperienced to make it less than obvious that he half-expected things to go crazy on them at any moment.

Ta havath, Pirojil thought. Stand easy.

The rest of the guards—Pirojil could have remembered their names if he'd bothered, but he didn't like to get too close to the regulars—were still on their horses, the animals snorting and shuffling in impatience.

The young baron was no unblooded, effete noble, but he was, after all, still young. Yes, it made sense to stay alert, but if an attack was going to happen here and now it probably would already have happened. You had to learn to husband your energies, to get what little rest you could from the situation, or when it all went to shit around you, you would not have any reserves left.

Pirojil was just a simple soldier, of course, but it made sense for even the simplest of soldiers to look at his own personal reserves from a lofty perspective. And it was a lot easier than remembering how scared he had been when he had charged out into the meadow behind Kethol. It was amazing, if you thought about it: Pirojil had been doing this for more years than he cared to count, but he still hadn't outgrown the fear. Maybe that was something you were born with, and that stayed with you when your baby teeth, your easy youthful erection, and your belief that you could depend on people abandoned you.

Andrea Cullinane turned to Kethol. Which figured; women found Kethol to be brighter than he was. Probably just because his features were even and regular, nice-looking in a rugged sort of way.

"What do you think?" she asked.

Thinking wasn't Kethol's best skill. He took a moment, glancing over to Pirojil for support or help, but Pirojil just shrugged. It was one thing to follow Kethol into a bloody piece of work, but Pirojil felt no obligation to make him look bright in front of the dowager empress. That would be, somehow, disloyal. It wasn't Kethol's—or Pirojil's or Erenor's—sterling intellect that the Cullinane family had hired; it was their swords, and the arms and will behind those swords.

"I think we should go back," Kethol said.

What? For a moment, Pirojil wasn't sure that he had heard correctly. Kethol, the one who was always first, always eager to dash into some dangerous situation, urging caution? Kethol, who had just this morning charged a bowman, hoping that he could outrun a crossbow bolt? Kethol, who had gotten Pirojil and Durine into more trouble than anyone could reasonably expect to survive?

No, it made sense. Kethol was doing his job, after all. "There's a troop quartered in Manderel's Green—and that's just a quick day's ride. We would be only a couple of days late for Parliament, and it would be a lot safer."

Ahira frowned. "I know we found only one assassin, but I'm not sure I believe in just one assassin."

The Old Emperor used to say something about the test of a man's intelligence being how often he agreed with you, and Ahira was sounding awfully intelligent to Pirojil. If he had been setting it up, there would have been at least three or four men involved: a scout, to keep track of the baron's party; a lookout, to give the final signal for the bowman to move into position, and at least two bow-men.

But just one? One who gave up and ran back to a previously prepared position, ready to snipe at any pursuit, or just give up and try another day if nobody pursued?

It was possible; but it wasn't likely.

Toryn nodded. "It does sound too . . . convenient. Or inconvenient, depending upon how you look at it."

Convenient for whom? Betrayal by Toryn didn't seem likely—he had been kicked out of the Pandathaway Slavers Guild for his failure to kill Jason Cullinane, and it was unlikely that even if he did finally complete the job, they'd take him back, and certain that the baron's friends and family would hunt him down.

"I know we would have heard about a troop of foreigners moving through the barony, but a couple, maybe half a dozen, could be traveling along the Prince's Road." The young baron nodded, agreeing with himself.

So did Pirojil. Traders of various sorts were often coming through, now that the war had ended, bringing buttons or spices or bolts of cloth from near and distant lands, trading for the imperial marks that were the only coin that could buy New Pittsburgh steel. And that was a good thing; trade, in some way that Pirojil never really did understand, did seem to make fixed wealth grow. It didn't make sense, not really, but if you kept swapping things around, everybody seemed to end up better off.

But the increase in trade did mean an increase in travel, and that meant more strangers wandering through the baronies.

Erenor shook his head. "I don't like it."

Pirojil cocked his head to one side. He could not have cared less whether or not Erenor liked it at all.

Ahira held up a hand. "Hear him out," he said, his fingers spread wide.

"Whenever . . ." Erenor licked his lips. "Whenever something gets complicated, you've got to wonder why. One man, left alone?"

He shook his head. "If somebody wants the baron dead, and is able and willing to pay well for having it done, why can't he afford to hire three or half a dozen men?" He pointed with his chin toward where the deer path led into the woods. "And leaving one alone, all by himself?" He waved his fingers back and forth. "Go forward, and we may well be into an ambush; move back, and we are even more likely to be riding into trouble."

"I don't see why," Jason Cullinane said. "It should be safe to go forward—if this is some sort of elaborate trap, then the purpose of putting the assassin here was to get us to go back, which we wouldn't have done otherwise . . ."

His mother smiled. "That's too neat by half," she said. "Maybe it's not as elaborate as Erenor is thinking—Erenor, you seem to be the sort who likes things complicated, but not everybody is that way. Maybe somebody sent just one assassin. Maybe that's all that Beralyn could locate."

Well, the other dowager empress was the obvious candidate.

"Or," she went on, "perhaps she's hired several, and this one was just the first put in our path."

Ahira nodded, smiling. If Pirojil didn't know any better—and, come to think of it, Pirojil didn't know any better—he would have thought that the dwarf was enjoying all this. "So, heads they're in front of us, tails behind." He removed a silver quartermark from his pouch and flipped it.

Erenor snatched it out of the air. "When you've got a six-to-six bet, the wise man doesn't play," he said, holding up the coin and considering it in the bright light of midday. "Half the time, you lose. Or more than half—perhaps there is a party of assassins in front of us *and* another in back."

Can't go forward, can't go back. Pirojil didn't much like that, but there always was an alternative. "Everybody," he said, his voice pitched to carry, but not very far, "on my signal, everyone is to mount up, and follow Kethol straight across the cornfield to the farmhouse across the ridge."

"Pirojil." Jason Cullinane shook his head.

"No." Ahira laid a thick hand on the young baron's arm. "It's his job to get you safely to Biemestren. Fire him there, if you're of a mind to, but for the time being . . ."

Jason Cullinane nodded.

"Very well." Pirojil let his hand rest on his horse's neck. "Kethol first, Toryn and you two," he said, indicating two of the mounted soldiers with a quick jerk of his thumb, "the empress and the baron next, and the rest of us after that. Ahira and I will bring up the rear."

Pirojil was not surprised to see that the others were looking to Jason Cullinane. There was no particular reason they should be obeying a simple soldier, particularly an ugly and misshapen one. But it was a good thing—they were looking to the baron, and not to the dwarf or the dowager empress: he was no longer just the heir, or just the baron-to-be.

Pirojil wasn't the only one to notice. Kethol gave him an encouraging grin, while Erenor's was amused, the way that the wizard was always amused by the vagaries of lesser—which was to say: all—humans.

The baron drew himself up straight. "Make it so, all."

Kethol, his hand just happening to rest on the butt of his flintlock pistol, rode between the two stacked-stone pillars at the main gate.

The farmstead had been restored, and looked prosperous enough. Perhaps two dozen chickens ran loose and wild inside the low stone wall, and beyond it, and a half-dozen large plowhorses stood lazily chewing on bales of hay over in the corral in front of the barn. Smoke puffed into the air from the chimney of the main house and from two of the workers' cottages, as well.

He had to look for it, but the scars of war still showed: the cluster of barns and crofters' shacks along the main road were too new, and the main house was roofed in slate, rather than thatch.

Probably not the right choice, if you were looking at it reasonably. Slate was expensive, leaked when it rained, sucked the heat from the house in cold weather, and retained it in hot weather; thatch warmed you when it was cold, let in air to cool you when it was warm, and shed water like a duck's back. But slate didn't burn, and thatch did.

Somebody who had been burned out once would understandably not want to look up at his roof and see it, in his mind's eye, once again in flames.

A dog—at least, he guessed it was a dog: it was definitely a small, noisy, floppy-eared animal of no particular breed—came running up, clearing the stone fence with a quick bound, yapping all the while. Kethol kicked it away from his stirrup, resisting the urge to do something more violent and more effective. That was the trouble with peacetime. You had to put up with indignities like a small, bite-sized dog yapping at your heels, while in wartime you could easily end that with one quick stroke of the sword.

Well, there were disadvantages to wartime, as well . . .

A young girl, no more than eight or nine, perhaps, ran out of the main house, a bulky woman after her in hot pursuit. Both were dressed in the cheap blousy tunics and pants common in the country, although belted with leather, rather than the usual piece of rope, and the woman was in boots, not sandals.

"Efanee," the woman shrilled, not meeting Kethol's gaze, "stop right there."

She snatched the girl up as the girl—Efanee, was it?—was reaching for the still-barking dog. "Your pardon, noble sir," the woman said, more to Kethol's feet than to Kethol. "She means no harm, and the dog—"

"—is no problem, either," Kethol said, trying to sound reassuring. "I've been bitten by a dog before, and it didn't kill me then." He had, of course, killed the dog, but that didn't seem like a reassuring thing to mention, not at the moment. He waved the problem away. "I'm Kethol, with the baron's party."

"The baron?"

"Yes, Baron Cullinane. *The* baron. Unless you have another in mind?" He waved a thumb at the party following him down the dirt road.

She didn't know quite how to take that, so she just stood there, mute. Probably the right decision.

"I'll need to see the landowner," he said. "The baron will need quarters for his party, and someone to see to the horses."

"He's . . . he's out working in the fields—it's a workday, after all." She bent and whispered in the girl's ear, then sent her on her way with an affectionate pat, and turned back to Kethol, the set of her jaw belying the loose tone of her words. "Efanee will bring him back quickly, along with some . . . people to help you with your horses and gear."

Pirojil brought his horse to a prancing halt beside Kethol's. "Is there anyone in the house?" he asked.

"No." She shook her head. "The rest of the children are at work in the fields—Efanee is helping me and two of the crofter women with the housework."

"So there are two people in the house."

"Well, yes, but I didn't mean that—"

"Don't worry about what you mean," Pirojil said quietly, his voice pitched low. "Worry about answering carefully."

"I don't understand—"

"That's correct," he said. "What you don't understand is that the baron's company has killed an assassin, one who was sent to murder the baron," Pirojil said, sounding more sure of that than Kethol was, "and the assassin was hiding out in the woods, just across from your cornfield." He held up his left hand, fingers spread wide, and the clopping of hooves on the road behind stopped.

Kethol almost smiled. When Pirojil forgot that he was just an ordinary soldier, he had an air of command about him. That probably had something to do with that signet ring of his, the one that he always wore, with the stone turned inward. Did he really think that even somebody as slow-witted as Kethol hadn't noticed that? Kethol was hardly the brightest of men, but you couldn't stay alive in Cullinane service as long as he had, doing the things that he had been doing, if you went through life with blinders on all the time.

"I think," Toryn's voice sounded from the darkness of the main house's doorway, "that what we have here is just a case of people being cautious—too cautious, for my taste, but my taste in caution of others is limited—preferring, as I do, to keep caution conserved for myself." He herded three men and two women out onto the porch, his sword held at a jaunty angle. "Then again," he said, "it's possible that these are the fellows of the assassin we encountered earlier this morning." He made an ornate flourish of a gesture back toward the house. "They were waiting with cocked crossbows, inside."

"They—we . . ." she cut herself off before anybody else could. She was a typical peasant—although, apparently, a landowner's wife, and not just a crofter or plot owner—face weathered by sun and wind, arms thickened and hands callused from too much work, muscles too hard, skin too saggy, teeth gapped from too-infrequent visits from the Spider, face white in fear, knowing that whatever the armed men looking down on her wanted to happen was going to happen.

Pirojil looked down at the woman. "We wear the green-and-gold of Barony Cullinane," he said, running a blunt finger down the embroidery along the seam of his tunic, "and you greet us with lies and hidden bowmen?" Pirojil's voice was calm and even enough, but Kethol felt the undertone. He was deciding whether or not to ride her down, probably slashing at her neck in passing.

Kethol disapproved, but it wasn't his decision, and nobody was asking his opinion, after all. If things were going to go to shit here, better it was here and now than later and by surprise, and if killing a peasant woman who was setting them up to be assassinated was what Pirojil wanted to use to trigger all the excitement, well, then Kethol could just back him up, and criticize him for it later, in private.

If there was a later.

"Stand easy, Pirojil," Jason Cullinane said, trotting his big red mare up, putting himself between Pirojil and the peasant woman. "No apologies necessary, freelady," he said, using the honorific more commonly used for middle-class merchants and tradespeople of the cities, rather than a peasant woman, even a relatively glorified one, "if there's any fault to be found, it's likely mine, not yours." He removed his feet from his stirrups, and in a move that Kethol had never seen anyone do before, popped his feet up onto the saddle and stood on the back of his horse, balanced easily, while the big mare stood, rock-steady, beneath his boots. "In case none of you know who I am, let me introduce myself: I'm Jason Cullinane, your baron. I've been, so I'm told, spending far too much time away, instead of making a tour of the barony, as I've been told repeatedly."

Ahira chuckled thinly. "Where have I heard that before?" he asked.

"Shush, dear," the dowager empress said. "It's not nice to say, 'I told you so.' "

"Allow an old man some idle pleasures."

Pirojil turned and gestured at the soldiers. "Melden, Arvin—check the house," he said.

One of the men on the porch looked to Toryn for permission, and at his slight nod stepped forward.

"My name is Kelleren; I'm the landowner," he said. "We were . . . unsure." He and his wife could have been brother and sister—entirely possible, at some points in Biemish history; he was flabby where she was flabby, wrinkled where she was wrinkled, and his upper arms and thighs were treetrunk thick, like hers.

"Unsure as to what?" Toryn asked. "Whether green and gold are green and gold? Whether Cullinane troops wear Cullinane livery?" His thin lips tightened further. "I don't know, Baron, but I think we have traitors here, and I know what to do to traitors, being a traitor to the Slavers Guild, and all."

At that, there was a trickling sound, and a dark, spreading stain at the crotch of one of the prisoner's trousers. One of the Cullinane soldiers snickered, but shut up at a quick growl from Ahira.

Pirojil grunted in irritation—not at the prisoner, but at the soldier. Kethol agreed. If shit and piss were gold, nearly every soldier would get rich in damn near every battle.

Jason Cullinane dropped easily to the ground, letting his knees soak up the shock of his landing. The courage of youth—that was an easy way to sprain your ankle, if you landed wrong. But the young baron was spoiled nobility—with a healer or a flask of healing draughts almost always at hand, you could take risks as a matter of course that an ordinary soldier couldn't and wouldn't, not a sane one.

"Well, Kelleren," he said, "I think it's time you make your choice—are you a loyal imperial subject, or not?" He softened the question with a smile, but only a little.

Pirojil let the talk flow over and around him as he sat back on his sleeping blankets, his back pressed up against the front wall of the house, his eyes closed. He probably looked like he was sleeping, and perhaps he was drifting in and out. It was restful, is what it was. There was something about the solid wall of a house—no, of a home that people lived in—a home, not just a house, had a solidity that was more, well, solid and reassuring than could be explained by the materials alone. It was as though the stone and mortar and wood had taken on a personality of their own, a tender and motherly one, that whispered quietly, so quietly that only your soul could hear it, *I'll take care of you. Don't worry. Lean on me.*

He folded his arms across his chest and let his head loll back against the rough surface. He was comfortable enough. The farmhouse contained a total of six chairs, and those were for the noble guests—if you included Ahira and Toryn as well as the baron and the dowager empress—and, at the baron's insistence, Kelleran and Bekana.

He grinned. Not that Bekana was using her chair much; she bustled about, making sure that every glass was kept constantly full of the sour beer that came, pitcher by pitcher, from the cellar.

Pirojil didn't mind the lack of a chair. He had long since learned to take his ease when he could, and with guards posted on the lookout platforms on the roof of the house and barn, there was little or nothing to worry about, at least in daytime.

Which meant that he could eat and let the beer go to his head, and perhaps even nap. Once those in charge figured out what they wanted to do, there would be little enough time to rest for a while.

He could see it coming, after all. You didn't have to be a sword-maker to know a sharp edge when you saw it.

"I don't keep track of your troops, Baron," Kelleren said, his tone getting less scared and more irritated as the day went by. "We can go tendays here without seeing a patrol. But, as far as I know, the nearest group, company—"

"Troop," Toryn put in. "They are called a troop."

"—the nearest *troop*, then, is at Dernal's Ford. Or possibly Belneten's Spring is closer, if you take the shortcut through the forest."

Whether out of fear, hospitality, or a desire to ingratiate them-selves with the ruling family, Kelleran and his wife had laid out a midday luncheon spread that would have done U'len proud: ram-ekins of potted meat and preserved fruit, along with fist-sized loaves of bread, still warm from the big stone oven that filled the baking-house behind the main house, although some of the loaves were burned on the bottom, Bekana having left them in the oven too long, what with the excitement of earlier in the morning.

"Then that's where we get help," Ahira said.

"Help?" Toryn's voice dripped sarcasm. "If you're going to scour the woods for some unknown number of assassins, you're going to need more than a troop of soldiers. How about, oh, the entire Home Guard, and maybe a baronial army or three? Just for a start?"

"We don't have to go looking for them." Ahira's voice was endlessly patient, entirely dwarvish.

"You think they'll come looking for us?"

"That," Jason Cullinane said, "would be very nice. I'd like to find out who sent them."

That was all well and good—yes, it would be nice to know— but it wasn't all that important. The world was filled with people who wanted the Cullinanes dead, for reasons good and bad, and finding out who had sent this particular bunch of assassins was, in the long run, probably as unimportant as figuring out what farrier had shod the assassins' horses.

"No," Ahira said, "they're minor players. It's who sent them that's important, and we don't have the need to track them down, or the resources to track them down."

And even if they had, Pirojil thought, it might not matter. If the killers had been hired in Enkiar or Pandathaway, it was entirely possible that they'd been put under a geas that would prevent them from speaking the name of the one who hired them, even under torture.

It could even be simpler. There were enough former soldiers around, tired of working as day laborers in the cities or on the farm, feeling that they deserved something better than a croft, a bag of seed, and a scythe as a final bonus, men who had gotten used to the taste and smell of blood during the war. All it would take would be one of them, and he could probably raise others.

They wouldn't be local here. But they could easily be imperials, Holt or Biemish.

But the dwarf was right. They weren't important, except as an obstacle to Jason Cullinane getting to Biemestren on time.

Loyalty to the Cullinane family didn't make Pirojil feel one whit guilty for thinking that the boy had been an utter idiot to wait until the last minute to leave for the capital. He understood it—when you were trying to make a place your home, you needed to spend time there, to walk the halls in your own bare feet, to ride the paths and hunt the woods—but it was still a mistake.

He shook his head. But it wasn't his problem. Pirojil was—what was it that Ahira had called the assassin? Ah, yes: a minor player; a nice term, that—a minor player, merely an ordinary soldier, and grand strategy and imperial politics were not his responsibility.

"Some other time," Andrea Cullinane said. "It's politically important that you get to Parliament—Thomen didn't just *ask* all his barons to show up. You—all of you—appear by imperial command."

She had a point, a good one. Jason Cullinane had abdicated the throne in favor of Thomen Furnael. There were those around the new emperor—his mother, in particular—who were sure that Jason was waiting for an opportunity to take it back. Showing too much independence was sure to get tongues wagging and minds working.

"Let's not make more of that than it is." Jason Cullinane snorted. "Thomen isn't going to do anything if I'm late a few days, or even if I miss Parliament altogether."

"That," she said, with some heat, "isn't the point. The point is that if he puts up with it from you, he has to put up with it from the other Biemish barons, and probably most of the Holtish ones, too, and Parliament isn't just about spreading responsibility—it's about joint responsibility, about making the barons responsible and responsive to each other, as well as . . . are you listening to me?"

"Of course I am, Mother. It's just that, well, I thought I'd gotten out of politics when I gave up the crown."

She snickered. "You should have thought of that before you took on the barony."

It had been a glorious gesture, Pirojil thought, the boy giving up the silver crown to Thomen Furnael, and truth to tell, Thomen Furnael was probably a better emperor than Jason Cullinane ever could have been, if only because the Cullinanes seemed to have the knack of making glorious gestures born into their very bones.

But that was the trouble with a glorious gesture, whether it was a noble one of abandoning the throne to a more worthy ruler or of, oh, barring the doors and windows of the man who had denied that he was your father and cast you out for your ugliness, and then touching fire to the wonderfully thatched roof.

Just as an example.

Pirojil forced the image from his mind. He was just an ordinary soldier, and the work of an ordinary soldier was to see what was in front of him, not to strike a pose, gazing off heroically into the distant future or longingly, regretfully, into the long-dead past.

And for here and now, it was entirely possible that—

"—It could be," Ahira said, "that making him late for Parliament is the whole purpose of this. Or, at least, the second choice, assuming that the killer doesn't get him."

"And who, would you think, would want to drive a wedge between my son and Thomen?" Andrea Cullinane's voice was even; she had self-control, that one. That was one of the things that Pirojil liked about her. Women were usually impulsive and notional.

"Oh," Ahira said, "perhaps all the barons, both Holtish and Biemish, plus Beralyn, and the Kiarians, and maybe Nyphien, too, for that matter."

"Your point is well-taken," the dowager empress said. "You are quite right."

It didn't bother Pirojil at all that the other dowager empress, Beralyn, was every bit as self-controlled as Andrea Cullinane. Beralyn was an enemy, not somebody on their side—in her, self-control was a flaw, not a virtue, just as her increasing physical weakness over the years was a virtue, rather than a flaw.

The difference between virtue and flaw, between strength and weakness, between good and bad, well, it all depended, as usual, on which side you were on.

Pirojil didn't have much use for political maneuvering—an ordinary soldier could only lose in the games that nobles played—but he did know which side he was on. That kept things simple.

And, for now, things were, indeed, simple enough.

The question was how to get the baron out of here with reasonable safety, assuming that there were a few more assassins waiting on the road. Eight soldiers acting as guards would have been enough, under ordinary conditions—but not now, not with somebody that close.

Pirojil would have pointed all that out, but nobody had asked his opinion.

Dernal's Ford, eh? He had been through there, some years ago, with the Old Emperor, he thought, but he couldn't remember anything about it. Just another town on a river, the smell of horse piss filling the air after a quick rain. You didn't have a lot of time to take in the sights when you were keeping your eyes on every window, every doorway, every alley.

He heard Erenor's footsteps, and waited deliberately for a long moment before opening his eyes when Erenor squatted down next to him. "I have a question for you," Erenor said, quietly. "Although I'm sure you know what it is."

Not only didn't Pirojil know, it would have taken a serious effort to care less.

Admitting that, well, that was another matter. "Well," he said, "of course I do. You may be able to put something over on me, Erenor. But . . ." he shrugged. "Some day, perhaps. But not today."

"Well? What do you think?"

"That should be obvious. Even to you." Pirojil was in too deep now. He would have to either keep bluffing or admit that he had been. "Say it right out and be done with it."

"I . . . well, I don't see the point, but you're in charge, after all."

"Don't you forget it. Not for a moment." Unspoken: not if you want to see your spell books, which I have very carefully hidden. And: in the field, not if you want to keep your tender skin unpierced. "So say it. Now."

"I'm . . . fairly good at seemings, you know. It wouldn't take much to disguise him as just an ordinary soldier, and put one of the troops on his horse, looking like him." He seemed to consider the matter for a moment. "Although to do a good job on it, I would need at least one of my books back. Erendel's dominatives aren't easy to reconstruct, and—"

He should have known it would come to that, and quickly. Pirojil rolled his eyes. "You'll get the spell books back when I think you should, and not before.

"As to this, do you think a Cullinane would agree to that?"

Silly question. The Cullinanes were, if anything, far too stupidly courageous. Was it contagious? Or were they born with it? The whole family was as bad as Kethol at taking chances, most of the time, and substituting somebody else as target for him was not something that Karl Cullinane's son would agree to.

Besides, it wasn't necessary.

Pirojil shook his head. "As to that, if we just put him and his mother in green-and-gold cloaks, it would be close enough." Somebody might be persuaded to risk his life on a shot that would kill the real target, but a single bowman, or two or three, would hardly fire into a whole troop of cavalry just for the chance to kill a couple or three mounted soldiers; the rest of the troop would quickly be on them like a bunch of angry, deadly bees.

Bees with lead and steel stings.

Taking him in under a large enough guard would be a reasonably safe risk. The trick would be to convince the young baron that he would never be at peace, that he would always have to travel fully guarded, that regular movements—an afternoon ride, a regular tour of the barony, an autumn hunt—would always require precautions. It would probably be sensible to see if Ellegon could fit taking the baron to and from Parliament into his schedule—although there was some danger in letting anyone know where the dragon was going to be at any particular time. It wouldn't be difficult for an assassin—armed, say, with a half-dozen dragonbaned arrows—to rendezvous with him. Forget, for a moment, that Ellegon was, among other things, a symbol and source of imperial power—

although he was that, and that was important—Ellegon had been Jason's friend and a constant one as long as he could remember. Longer really; Ellegon always said that he had first mindspoken with Jason when Jason was still in the womb.

Pirojil sighed. Just when things looked like they were settling down for a while, at least, they weren't.

So, the question was how to get the troops here, and with the nearest telegraph across the baronial border in Pirondael, that meant sending somebody out after them, and soon.

It wasn't much of a mystery to Pirojil who would be sent. He and Kethol and Durine had had a well-deserved reputation for being just this side of unkillable, a reputation that had been only slightly marred by Durine's getting himself killed in Keranahan.

And Erenor, for any number of reasons, was seen as a worthy replacement for Durine.

Dernal's Ford, eh? If they left just after sunset dark, they could probably be there before morning.

10

A Matter of Succession

It had been longer than she could remember since Beralyn Furnael had been without pain, but there were worse companions, just as there were better ones, equally faithful.

Hate, for example.

Her joints burned with a constant fire as she stalked the halls of the keep like an arthritic ghost, pure will forcing each foot to follow the other. If she stopped—if she permitted her traitor body to overrule her—she might never be able to start again. Her nightly walk around the parapet had, bit by bit, become insufficient to quiet the pain in her hips, and particularly in her left knee. Sleep—or a thin, restless, sweaty thing that was the closest she could come to the long-gone dark warmth that sleep had been, long, long ago—would not come easily, and was hardly worth the trouble.

She paused for a moment at a hallway balcony, and stepped out into the night.

The courtyard was filled with brightly colored canopies, lit by flickering torches set into the walls of the donjon, the residence tower, and the inner curtain wall. The guards seemed to spend most of their time walking from torch to torch, replacing the burned-out ones with freshly lit ones.

She sniffed in disapproval. That was probably that accursed Walter Slovotsky's doing, once more. She had seen him pacing off the distance between the tents, as though reassuring himself that they were far enough apart, and it had been he who had supervised the laying-down of gravel paths between them, as though the noise of footsteps on gravel could dissuade a Biemish from taking revenge on a Holt sleeping in the nearby pavilion.

Had it been up to her, all the visitors' entourages would have been housed, along with their guard detachments, down in the city in the barracks, but there was a point, she had to admit, to keeping them all within the walls of the castle, although at times that felt too much like clasping a poisonous snake to one's bosom.

There were already enough of those.

She ignored the rhythmic stomping of boots on the hard stone of the third-floor hallway behind her. Just a pair of guards, making the rounds.

She nodded. There was no harm in conceding that not everything that Walter Slovotsky did was necessarily wrong, or stupid. Adding an internal watch to the castle, and keeping soldiers moving through the halls night and day, would tend to prevent any private arguments from becoming violent, and make it clear that the emperor would not tolerate his hospitality being used as an opportunity to settle old grudges.

She smiled. And not necessarily just the Holtish-Biemish grudges, either. Old Ferden Arondael had been looking daggers at Tyrnael all through dinner. Was that over that minor border dispute? Or was it that Arondael was angry that Tyrnael had chosen to marry off his middle daughter to a minor lord from Barony Adahan? It wasn't like Arondael wanted the girl for one of his own sons; Stevan, his heir, had been married off last year, to a remarkably bovine young woman from a family with links to an old Tynearean dynasty.

She set her hands on the cold stone railing, and let it support her weight. There was a slim possibility that the railing could break loose, tumbling her two stories to the hard flagstones of the courtyard below, and that would be the end of pain, and of responsibility, and if Thomen chose to blame, say, Walter Slovotsky for that, let that be his problem.

She heard quiet footsteps behind her. "Please, my Empress," sounded from behind her, "if you need something to lean on, may I proffer my arm?"

She jerked upright, sending rivulets of pain through her back and her left shoulder. She had half been expecting it to be Derinald—he clearly had the servants alerting him to her movements—but the voice wasn't his.

It was Willen Tyrnael, instead. He was dressed for sleep, at least mainly—he wore a light robe, belted tightly at his waist, over his trousers and boots, as though he had awakened suddenly and had decided to go out and use the garderobe at the end of the hall rather than the thundermug in his rooms.

But that was just an illusion. His hair and beard were well-combed, and his face freshly washed, and if there was any trace of sleep in his eyes, her vision was too dim to see it, and she didn't believe that for a moment.

No, it was no accident that he was here. He wanted to talk to her about something, although what he could possibly want with a useless and ignored old woman who wanted nothing more than the safety of her family and the death of its enemies wasn't at all clear.

"Good evening, Willen," she said. "I hope my midnight pacings didn't wake you."

He had the White Suite, down the hall, a triplet of rooms floored in white marble, their walls whitewashed rather than covered with tapestries. She found the rooms too spare and drafty, but the number of available rooms in the residence tower was limited, and some of the baronial parties were quartered in what had been—and what served as, most of the time, when Parliament was not in session—the barracks, as well as the tented pavilions. But as, at least arguably, the senior of the Biemish barons—in lineage, although not by any means in age—Tyrnael had to be given a suite in the donjon.

"Not at all," he said. "I find it difficult to sleep in a strange bed. At home, I rarely tour the barony anymore." He sighed. "Which,

I'm sure is said but has not reached my ears, is probably attributed to the orc problem." His mouth twitched. "Which means, I would guess, that I should make it a point to go along orc-hunting more often."

"Oh?" she asked. "How often have you gone orc-hunting of late?" She was as little interested in it as he probably was, but let him come to his point, whatever that might be.

"Well, never. I know that the hunt is a noble activity, building of character and connecting us with all the generations that have gone hunting before, but I've found it usually boring and sometimes dangerous, and never have much cared for it." He smiled shyly, and a chill went through her. He reminded her of Zherr when he smiled. She must be careful not to make him smile more often. Zherr Furnael could always get her to agree to anything when he smiled, even the time that he had apprenticed their older son, Rahff, off to Karl Cullinane, something that had so quickly gotten Rahff killed.

It was probably no coincidence that he exactly mirrored her own feelings about hunting.

She let the silence build for a moment, watching him.

"May I?" He gestured a request for permission to join her on the balcony, at the rail; she nodded.

"A pretty night," he said. Off in the distance, a trio of Faerie lights seemed to play a children's game of touched-you-last just at the lowest level of dark, looming clouds. The light pulsed quickly through a series of blues and reds, with an occasional flash of orange and green, as they whirled about each other, sometimes momentarily ducking into a cloudbank, and then emerging. "A light, cool breeze; the sky is clear to the west. Nature seems to smile on Parliament, wouldn't you say?"

She grunted. "It's not Parliament, not yet. My son has not called it into session, and there's one baron missing."

Tyrnael seemed to stiffen, slightly, as he stood beside her. "Two, really. Keranahan, as well as Cullinane."

"Cullinane," she said.

He laughed lightly. "You make that sound like a curse, my Empress."

"It's been a curse on my house," she said. No, that wasn't entirely fair. The Cullinanes had tried to do well by her family, and that was part of the problem—doing well by them had meant Karl Cullinane taking on Rahff as an apprentice, and getting him killed; doing well had meant Walter Slovotsky taking Zherr to Biemestren to put him on the throne, and getting him killed; and doing well had meant Jason Cullinane trading Thomen's barony for the throne.

That that had not—yet—gotten Thomen killed was her fortune.

"Times have been difficult," he said, "and may yet be difficult again. But a Furnael graces the throne, and rumor has it that there is a wedding—and heirs, perhaps?—in the offing, and instead of Bieme and Holtun poised on the knife-edge of war, there is the Empire of Holtun-Bieme." He gestured at the canopies below, their fringes making quiet snapping sounds in the light breeze. "And below, Holtish and Biemish lie sleeping, side by side, in peace."

She looked pointedly at the guards walking the ramparts, and he laughed. His laugh really was ingratiating.

"Yes," he said, "peace at the point of a sword, but that's peace nonetheless. Peace and stability, with the promise of wealth and peace and stability to come. The Adahan iron mines and steel plants turn out more and better steel every year, and with Engineer Ranella building—"

She raised a hand. "Yes, yes, yes, I know. But . . ."

"But it all," he said, "rests on, well, on the expectation of stability. That's what worries me about the succession."

She nodded. "I'd see my son married, and with an heir. Or several."

"Yes," he said, "but that wasn't the only thing I was thinking about. With Barony Keranahan under the leadership of Governor Treseen, rather than—"

"You'd have Elanee back?"

He shook his head. "No. She plotted treason, and it overtook her. But legitimacy is important."

Beralyn didn't see his point. "Forinel is years gone, and Miron fled when his mother fell," she said. "The direct line ends there, and, as to indirect claims . . . I'm tempted to think that the Euar'den claim is the best, although there are other Tynearean families that might disagree."

"One is as good as another," Tyrnael said. "Perhaps."

"Or perhaps not?" Was that what he was about? Did he have some preference between the houses of Lord Moarin and Virael? Virael was more closely related to the Holtish baronial houses, but old—Moarin was years younger, and could more reliably be counted on to rule the barony longer. Both had possible heirs a'plenty.

"Oh," he said. "I see little difference between the two, look-ing—as I do, I must confess—from the point of view of a Biemish baron, rather than an imperial. What's important, I think, is the legitimacy. Whether one likes one candidate or another, the im-portant thing is that he be legitimate, that he be seen as the one and proper heir to the barony. Don't you think so?"

She frowned. She had played the game as well as she could, but he had somehow brought the conversation to a place where she could only agree, and not know what he was getting at.

"Of course," she said. Yes, stability was important. Would any-body whose son sat on the throne of an emperor ever doubt that?

"I thank you," he said. "And I'm pleased that you agree with me." There was a light rustle of cloth and the rubbing of metal links on each other, and he held a thin silver chain in his hand. "The stone," he said, "is, I'm embarrassed to say, simply a garnet, al-though a well-polished and utterly flawless one. But it's been in my family for more than six generations, passed down through the gen-erations, never from father to son."

He placed it in the palm of her hand. "Oh, there's a little magic on it, just the mildest of glamours; it tends to make sweet things taste a little sweeter, cool water a tad more refreshing, and pain hurt just a trifle less—but that's not the point. I hope you'll accept it as a memento of this conversation," he said.

Well, she could—and would—have it checked by Henrad, but since he knew that she could and would, there was little chance that it was other than what he said it was.

Her fingers closed around the coolness of the stone. "Of course, Baron Tyrnael," she said. "I'm not sure, my dear Baron, what is it that you think you've manipulated me into agreeing to, but perhaps you'll enlighten me some time, if not now."

"I wouldn't think of trying to manipulate you, my Dowager Empress," he said, carefully.

"Of course not," she said. He wouldn't think of it any more than he would think of breathing, or of pissing; he would do it naturally, without having to think.

But just because he was trying to manipulate her, that didn't mean she was unwilling to go along.

If what he wanted was stability, then he and she were on the same side. For now.

11

Night Moves I: Erenor and Pirojil

Erenor's feet hurt. Pirojil could tell that, because every few moments, he'd grunt and groan in pain, then heroically stifle the grunts and groans, and force himself to keep going, waiting for somebody to applaud. It was the sort of thing that made Pirojil more than idly fantasize about pounding Erenor's face with his fist until it resembled raw meat.

But, to be fair—and Pirojil tried to be fair, when possible—Erenor wasn't, in fact, making any more noise than Pirojil himself was, and less than Ahira.

They moved quietly, single file, along the edge of the road. Kethol, probably, and Ahira, certainly, could have made their way through the dark down the twisting forest paths, but neither Erenor nor Pirojil could have.

Ahira, of course, had the darksight that enabled dwarves to tunnel through stone in what was utter blackness to any human eyes—it was said that a dwarf could see, although not far, simply by putting a hand up in front of him, and make out forms, even in complete darkness, by seeing the reflected heat from his palm. Following a road under the twinkling of the overhead stars and the pulsating Faerie lights didn't even cause the dwarf to squint a little.

And Kethol, having exchanged his soldier's boots for a woodsman's buskins, could have kept up a careful and virtually silent run, if he had been alone, for hours on end. It was all Pirojil could do to keep up without sounding like a cow stomping down the road.

Well, at least Pirojil wasn't as much of a drag on the party as Erenor was. It would be terribly embarrassing to be the limitation.

He wished that they could have taken the horses, but the idea was to sneak out, to make it to town without anybody who might be watching the farm knowing, without putting hunters on their own backtrail. The sound of a horse clopping down the Prince's Road at night would travel far and wide, and Pirojil knew from personal experience that a thin leather rope or steel wire strung across a road at rider-height would be invisible in the dark, and could knock a man off his horse and leave him turtled on the ground . . . if it didn't snap his neck, first.

So they walked. You made your own luck in this world, most of the time, and Pirojil would do his best to make his luck good. All the precautions might be unnecessary—if there weren't other assassins, or if the ones left were busy breaking themselves against the rock of the defenses at the farmhouse, they might be able to make their way to Dernal's Ford without any interference, no matter what they did.

If they didn't run into an orc, say, or a wolf, or a boar.

Well, a boar was unlikely, at that. After all, they tended to sleep the night away, the way decent people did, the way Pirojil wished, with every step, that he was doing. And, as to wolves, it was a rare wolf that would attack a human, or—so he hoped and thought—a dwarf, either.

And an orc? They were, he thought, too far south for orcs, at least for now. Like all vermin, though—mice, insects, rats, slavers—they tended to spread themselves far and wide. Did they hunt at night? Pirojil certainly didn't know, and didn't know anybody who knew.

The night, though, was alive with sounds. That boded well. It took quite a woodsman to keep himself quiet enough to not disturbed the fidgetbugs, with their *clicketyclicketyclick*ing, and—at least, according to Kethol, who ought to know—the distant *taroooo* of a hairy owl was a sure indication that the bird thought it was safe to announce to potential mates and possible rivals that he had seized enough mice to fill his belly, and that he was ready for less immediate needs.

A quiet trilling that Pirojil couldn't have distinguished from a robin's song was Kethol calling a halt, and Pirojil dropped to a squat, while Erenor staggered on a few steps first. Each pebble along the road that he kicked sounded louder in Pirojil's than a drumbeat, but, realistically, it probably couldn't have been heard very far over the whispering of the wind through the trees.

The wind appeared to be picking up, in fact. Pirojil looked up.

The sky to the west was dark now, the twinkling of stars obscured by clouds.

Kethol, moving like smoke—his silent movement was, even after all these years, still a matter of some amazement to Pirojil—worked his way back to where Pirojil and Erenor were, Ahira with him.

"I smell rain coming," he whispered. "It's not far off."

Erenor sighed. "Then we should find some shelter and hole up until it passes, yes?" The note of fatality and depression in his voice said that he already knew what the answer was going to be.

"No," Pirojil said. "We can make faster progress in the rain." With raindrops pounding down on the forest, it would be somewhere between difficult and impossible for even a careful listener to hear footsteps over it.

It would, of course, be miserable. But it would also be a spot of good luck to be able to move quickly down the center of the road—its long-dead builders had made it convex, probably to increase the number of centuries it would take to wear it down—without having to worry out being heard.

The farther they got away from the farm, the better off they were. A half dozen—at most—men could only be spread so far. And as soon as Pirojil and the rest came to the first fork in the road—a crossroads, actually, where the road from Dernal's Ford to Belneten's Spring crossed the Prince's Road—there would be three more ways for them to go, and therefore one-third the chance that they'd meet up with anybody lying in wait.

At least, that was the idea.

"How soon?" Ahira asked. "I can smell it coming, too, but I don't have a feel for it."

Kethol shrugged. "I don't know. But soon." He turned to Pirojil, although Pirojil could not make out his expression in the darkness. "There's another possibility," he said. "Kelleren talked about a trail off the Road, one that's a shortcut to Dernal's Ford."

"But Erenor and I couldn't make any speed along it in the dark." Forget, for a moment, the branches dangling down, waiting to tear at your face and eyes; ignore the difficulty in staying on an ever-twisting path that followed the lines of the land, not the will of a builder; they'd be stumbling and falling over every root, rock, and divot along the trail.

"No," Kethol said, "you couldn't. You'd be lucky to be able to keep up a slow walk. But Ahira and I can," he said. "If you two stick to the road, you should be able to reach the crossroads, and get to Belneten's Spring at about the same time that we make Dernal's Ford. You can move a lot faster once it starts raining."

And if one party didn't make it, the other one was more likely to.

It was hard to tell from Kethol's tone what he thought of the idea, which probably meant that he had only brought it up because he felt he ought to. That was the thing about Kethol, he would do what he thought he had to, and let others fall around him, or not, as they pleased.

It was one of the things that had always kept Durine and Pirojil reminded that Kethol was as much in charge as they were.

Splitting your forces was, whether you were part of an army or just a pair of comrades, always something to be approached with caution. At least Kethol would have Ahira to watch his back. Pirojil would have Erenor, and while Erenor wasn't entirely useless in everything, his swordsmanship was pitiful, striving toward weak, and not striving very hard. He was a perfectly fine hand with a flintlock pistol, of course—as long as he had the muzzle of the weapon pressed tightly against the target.

And not that the pistols would be of much use in the rain. The pan practically sucked water out of the air. Well, there were advantages—slaver rifles were even more useless in the rain.

Erenor touched him lightly on the arm. "We might be able to make a quick time, by ourselves," he said. "Perhaps even with a source of light—"

"How you'd expect to keep a torch going in a hard rain escapes me," Kethol said. "And if you've packed a lantern in your rucksacks, I'd want to know why."

Pirojil didn't answer. No, they didn't have a torch, but . . . "Very well," he said. "Let's separate."

It was just as well that he knew that Kethol was not a schemer by nature, it probably wouldn't occur to him until much later, if ever, that he had ended up saddling Pirojil with that dead weight of an Erenor.

Pirojil shook his head. Well, if somebody was loyal, wise, and forward-thinking, he'd probably have found another means to make his way through life than soldiering.

"Let's go," he said.

The rainstorm didn't start so much as it shattered. One moment, Pirojil and Erenor were walking down the road in a darkness that was, at best, shades of darkest gray on lightest black, and the next moment, with a flash of lightning followed almost immediately by a crash of thunder that left his ears ringing, cold rain smashed down on the Prince's Road, clawing at it and at them with icy fingers.

Erenor tried to run for the shelter of the trees, but Pirojil grabbed at his arm.

He shouted, *No, you idiot, lightning likes to strike at trees,* but the ringing in his ears drowned out his voice, even in his own head, and his vision was wiped out in another white flash that he more felt than heard.

He grabbed at Erenor's sleeve and ran, the wet stones of the road slick beneath his boots. Only a heroic fool would be looking out for somebody traveling now, and the nearest heroic fool that Pirojil knew was on his way to Dernal's Ford with Ahira. Erenor's boots pounded on the hard road, and after a few staggering steps he began to match Pirojil's long strides. Pirojil had spent most of his time soldiering as a horseman, but the trouble with the damn horses is that they tended to die on you at the most inconvenient times—times when you had to be somewhere else, and fast, because if you didn't, you weren't going to be able to do what you had to do, and when soldiers didn't do what they had to do, the people they were protecting died.

And sometimes they died anyway.

Ill-used skills came back slowly. The trick was to pace yourself, to keep up a jog that ate the road in bites you could stand, but didn't leave you gasping for breath. That was easy to do on a cool day, the straps of your rucksack bound together with a length of rope to keep it tight against your back instead of bouncing with every step, some officer calling out a cadence to keep the pace even and constant, or at least it was easier than it was now, with some cursed thing in his rucksack poking at the same spot on his back every time it slapped against him, which it did with every step, and with every step making him colder and wetter than he had been the moment before.

The rain eased from a horrid downpour to a steady pace, and that only seemed to make him colder. That was infuriating—the rain easing up should have made him at least a little less miserable.

What was even more infuriating was that Erenor was keeping up with him, his steps matching Pirojil's, one for one. Sometimes it was too easy to forget that Erenor, despite his failings, was at

least ten years younger and in good shape, and had probably made
it a point to keep his wind good, out of the necessity of taking to
his heels out of town more often than not.

But where the flesh was weaker, an iron will could be stronger;
Pirojil kept running. If he lowered his head and only watched the
ground in front of him, he could forget, or at least pretend to fool
himself into forgetting, how much farther he had to go. If he
stopped, even for a moment, he would feel how cold and miserable
he was, how his clothes had soaked up probably half his weight in
water, how his boots were waterlogged, as well, how the fire in his
lungs burned hotter and hotter with every step, how . . .

His feet shot out from underneath him, and he landed, hard,
on his right hip, his sword somehow coming loose from its scabbard
and rattling off in the darkness, his pistols tumbling to the wet road.

"Pirojil!" Erenor was at his side, helpful hands shaming Pirojil
as Erenor guided him to his feet. "How badly are you hurt?" he
asked.

"I can manage," Pirojil said, ignoring the way his hip pulsated
in bright red agony with every heartbeat. He thought about reaching into his pouch for the flask of healing draughts, but put the
thought aside. Those were expensive, and hard to get, and they
weren't for his comfort, but to make it possible for him to do his
job, and—pain or no pain—he would not be stopped.

Erenor scooped up Pirojil's pistols, and tucked them in his own
belt.

"I'll need those back," Pirojil said, holding out a hand.

Instead of complying, Erenor stooped to retrieve Pirojil's
sword, and handed it to him, properly hilt-first. "You can have them
back anytime you want, Pirojil," Erenor said, tossing his head to
clear the rain from his sodden hair. "Anytime, that is, that it's dry
enough for these to do anything useful." He drew one of the pistols,
cocked the hammer, and pointed it toward the sky.

"No, don't." Pirojil took a half-step toward the wizard, stopping
when the pain in his right hip brought a gasp to his lips.

"But these are wet . . ." Erenor pulled the trigger, which fell with a loud *snap*.

Wham. Flame shot skyward, and the stink of sulfur filled the air.

Pirojil slapped the pistol from Erenor's hand, although what the point was of that escaped him. It was empty—now—and besides, it was Pirojil's pistol.

"You can't count on them to work in the rain," he said. "Unless, of course, some feeble-minded wizard posing as a soldier pulls on the trigger to show how useless wet powder is, which—since my luck is bad enough that I'm saddled with you as a companion—is guaranteed to be the one time that water hasn't quite reached the pan, and that the greased cloth wrapping the bullet has kept any water from getting into the barrel."

Well, at least Erenor hadn't demonstrated how useless the pistol would be by pointing it at Pirojil's head. Too bad he hadn't used his own head as a target to show how safe it was.

Pirojil used a relatively clean spot on the front of his own tunic to wipe the mud off his sword, then sheathed the sword—in its sheath, not in Erenor's guts, tempting though the idea was. "We've wasted more than enough time," he said, as the rain again intensified. "Let's get moving."

He set out at a slow walk, each step with his right leg a stab to his right hip. But it was just pain. In the long run, pain could sap your energy probably almost as quickly as a hard, cold rain. The thing to do was to keep yourself warm, and the metal flask of corn whiskey in his rucksack would have done just that.

But that would have meant stopping to rest for a moment, and although he feared only distantly that he could not start up again once he had stopped, he would have cut off any finger except his trigger finger before showing such weakness in front of Erenor.

Erenor, a part of Pirojil's mind noted with savage glee, was starting to fall behind. Maybe he was younger, and surely he was less damaged, but there was still an advantage to being resolute and determined. It was a matter of strength of character, and even an ordinary soldier—a good ordinary soldier, at least—had to have more character, more will, more determination than some illusionist and swindler. It certainly took intelligence and cunning to separate people from their coin, having them exchange entirely real copper and silver for amulets, scrolls, and potions of at best dubious puissance, but it did not take iron will, a resolution to ignore that which could be ignored and proceed anyway over the screaming of bruised flesh and battered bones when it could not be ignored.

He heard Erenor mumbling something behind him, but he couldn't make out the words without dropping back, and there was nothing that Erenor could say that would have made him want to drop back. Let the bastard fall behind, let him collapse on the wet road, let him seek shelter under a tall tree and have it shattered by lightning, let him . . .

It was strange. Maybe Pirojil was better off than he thought he was, or perhaps he was so far gone in pain and effort that it just didn't hurt anymore. No, that was an overstatement, but it was true that the pain in his hip and back and the pounding headache were receding, moment by moment, settling down to a state that was not by any means comfortable, but was merely uncomfortable, not agonizing.

Whatever it was had apparently affected Erenor, as well; he caught up with Pirojil, and kept pace with him.

The rain eased even further, but the lightning—now so far away that it was often several steps between the flash and the crash of thunder—was coming faster and faster, lighting up the road every few moments.

And ahead—praise be to whatever power was listening!— around the next curve, a crossroads waited, one sign that Pirojil could make out in the lightning flashes holding the glyph for spring, a stylized fountain spewing forth water, and while he was sure that the other held a glyph of a ford, he didn't need to see it to know that that was the way that he and Erenor were to go. The village would not be far down the road, and having somehow or other found a reserve of strength and will in his body and mind, it would only be a matter of time until—

There was the quietest of splashes behind him, and he was never sure if it was instinct, judgment, or accident that caused him to duck to one side just as the big man with the sword lunged by, the tip barely grazing his side in passing.

The cool wetness of the metal told him that it had pierced his side, just below the ribcage, but there was, strangely, only the slightest of pain. Of course, he thought, as he slammed his body into the other, tackling him to the ground, that was probably only a momentary respite, particularly if there were other attackers.

Rough fingers clawed at face and throat, and a knee smashed into his outer thigh. Pirojil fought back, breaking the hold of the fingers on his throat with a quick grab that snapped finger bones in the attacker's hand.

He missed Durine and Kethol like he would have missed an arm and a leg. If he didn't finish this one off quickly, rolling on the ground, in the dirt and water and mud like this, he could be speared through the back or side like a fish on a plate.

It never occurred to him that his opponent could take him. Clumsy fool—if he was any good, Pirojil would already be dead, and—

Light flared, bright and yellow, dazzling his eyes momentarily.

But only momentarily—his vision cleared almost immediately, and he rolled away from where his attacker knelt on the road, hands clawing at his own face, while another man, mostly concealed in a thick cloak, staggered blindly toward where Erenor stood, proud and upright, his arms raised, fingers spread widely.

They were all surrounded by a bright, golden glow that seemed to radiate from the stones of the road itself, a glow so bright that it washed out all colors, and should have blinded Pirojil as much as it did the others.

But it didn't. And when Pirojil drew his own sword and hacked down at the swordsman's arm, the other let out a grunt as the blade fell from his fingers, and he turned toward Pirojil, away from Erenor.

Pirojil stopped him with a low lunge that changed target and took him neatly in the throat, followed by a kick to the side of the knee as his attacker staggered past, emitting wet, horrid burbling sounds.

It was then that the exhaustion and pain hit him, all at once.

He had long had the belief—in retrospect, the conceit—that he could soldier on through any pain, that physical discomfort, even agony, could not stop him from doing whatever it was that he needed to do, and on more than one occasion, he had been able to force himself to function, no matter the pain . . .

But red agony washed up his injured side, leaving his right arm useless, his sword falling from fingers that no longer would obey him.

And there was one man left. He staggered toward Pirojil, his mouth wide in a soundless scream, his dazzled eyes blind and unblinking. This one was a big man, easily a head taller than Pirojil, the saber in his right hand and short, stabbing sword in his left hand trying to weave some sort of pattern in the air, for defense or attack.

Pirojil pulled his remaining pistol from his belt with his left hand, thumb-cocked it, leveled it carefully at the big man's chest, then pulled the trigger.

Click.

It would have been too much to hope, too much to ask, for the other flintlock pistol to have kept its pan dry through the storm and the fighting and the rolling around on the ground. The only way

Pirojil could have made sure it would work would have been to point it at his own crotch.

He hobbled to one side, but an involuntary grunt of pain escaped his gritted teeth, and his attacker turned, lunging wildly toward him.

It should have been an easy thing for Pirojil to take on a blinded man, but it was all he could do to shuffle to one side, out of the way.

And then Erenor, his belt knife held clumsily in his hand, was on the big man's back, his arm rising and falling, over and over again.

Pirojil wouldn't have thought that such a big man would have such a high-pitched scream.

He crouched over the body in the pre-dawn light, barely able to keep his eyes open. He must have bled more than he had thought, more than the shallow slash along his side should have.

There was nothing about either of the dead men that gave any indication as to who they were, or where they were from. Not that he would have believed that, say, tunics in the red and gray of Barony Adahan would have meant that Bren Adahan had sent these killers.

Well, not killers. Would-be killers. Pirojil was more than a little worse for wear, but he and Erenor were still breathing.

He took his belt knife and sliced through the tunic, leaving the strangely motionless, hairy chest bare to the cold morning air. The dead man wouldn't mind.

No, there was nothing useful hidden under his clothes.

"There's gold in his pouch," Erenor said, jingling coins in his hand.

"I'm surprised," Pirojil said, forcing the words to come out calmly and evenly, not as grunts of pain. "I would have thought that you would have found only a couple of coppers, and made any gold vanish into your pouch."

Erenor's lips thinned momentarily. "Yes," he said, "after all the many times I've stolen from you, taken the very food from your lips, the coin from your purse, the stiffness from your organ, and the sense from your speech, surely, surely you should suspect me now."

He smiled as he spoke, his usual easy—too easy—smile firmly in place, as though he was speaking for somebody's amusement, if only his own.

His long fingers delicately probed at Pirojil's side, pulling away torn cloth so that he could get at the wound. "I'm not a healer— I've no channel to Hand, Great Spider, nor Eareven Powers—and my own skills are of illusion, not reality, but I don't really think you want to keep bleeding to death. Of course, I could be wrong, and I could be right and you could choose to contradict me, as usual, just for the sake of making me out to be wrong, but maybe we should just pour in a vial of healing draughts, perhaps, possibly, don't you think?"

Those were for emergencies, not for comfort. They weren't just expensive—but hard to get. "Sew it up."

"I'm sure I did not hear you correctly. I'm no apothecary—I'm just a wizard, technically an apprentice wizard, at that, with some skills of illusion." He smiled, smugly. "And not entirely useless skills, either, as these two would be happy to say if somebody were to reanimate them long enough."

"There's a sewing kit in my rucksack," Pirojil said. "Just sew the edges of the wound together, and then let's get going." It would take some time for infection to set in—the spirits of gangrene and wound rot were lazy. There should be a healer in the village, or one nearby, and that would be enough for that.

"And as to the pain?"

"Just *do* it." Pain was a private matter, as long as you could

keep it to yourself. Pirojil could clench his jaws as tightly as anybody. And never mind that he was chilled to the bone, that it was
all he could do to keep his teeth from chattering like a coward's,
that every breath came with its own stab of fiery agony, that cut
through his side over and over again.

"As you will." Erenor slipped his forearm under Pirojil's left
armpit and levered him to his feet. "I'd like to sit you down on a
firm bench in front of a roaring fire, but, given the present situation," he said, as he guided Pirojil to the side of the road, "I'm
afraid this cold rock is going to have to do."

Pirojil seated, Erenor retrieved his rucksack and rummaged
through it with annoying familiarity. "Oh, here it is." Erenor shook
his head as he produced the leather pouch and loosened the draw-
strings. "You do always have to make things difficult for yourself,
don't you?"

He crouched next to Pirojil, and brought up his hand, fingers
cupped, as though gripping an invisible ball right next to Pirojil's
side.

His voice low, barely audible, Erenor murmured strange words
that Pirojil tried to remember, but couldn't. He listened as carefully
as he could, and could make out each syllable distinctly, but as
Erenor completed each word, it vanished from Pirojil's mind, as
though it had never been there, like a snowflake disappearing as it
struck a hot skillet.

He didn't know what Erenor was up to, but the time to argue
with a wizard, as anybody but a fool knew, was before or after the
wizard was casting a spell, not during. There were powers and
forces involved that Pirojil was not capable of understanding, but it
wasn't necessary to understand magic—it wasn't necessary even to
be able to see more than a blur on the page on which spell runes
were written—in order to fear it. Or, at the very least, to have a
healthy caution.

For a moment, the pain in his wound became a cold tingling,

as though instead of cutting him open, somebody had simply applied the cold flat of a blade to his side, and then there was no sensation at all.

None.

Erenor looked up and smiled. "Actually," he said, "it still hurts you every bit as much as it did before, but I've put a minor seeming on it, to fool you." He took up the needle, and threaded it with a small length of sinew, then quickly began to sew up Pirojil's wound, the thumb and forefinger of his left hand pressing the ragged lips of the cut together.

It was a strange sensation: it was as though Pirojil was watching somebody else's wound be treated.

Wait. And it had been like somebody else having been tired before, when Pirojil had found himself not nearly as tired as he thought he should be.

"Is *that* how we got through the rain?"

"Well . . . since you asked, I don't think you have any real question about the answer."

Pirojil's lips tightened. "You mean, you fooled me into believing that I wasn't as dog-tired as I was."

Erenor had finished sewing up the wound, and he tied a clumsy knot in the end of the sinew, then trimmed off the remainder with his belt knife. The spare sinew and the bloody needle went back into the pouch.

"Fooled is such an . . . *unfriendly* word," he said. "Let's just say that I used my talents to help you along, for which I can, no doubt, expect the usual gratitude, expressed with a curse and a cuff of the hand, that has so endeared the both of you to me." His brow furrowed for a moment, and then he reached into Pirojil's rucksack and produced a metal flask, which he opened. "You know, the usual objection to killing wound spirits with whiskey doesn't apply right now, and even if it did, well, I guess that would be your problem, now, wouldn't it, Master Pirojil?"

He brought the flask to his lips and took a small swallow, and then a larger mouthful, which, without any warning, he spat into the wound.

Pirojil clenched his jaws tightly together to keep from screaming. Raw whiskey on a wound should have, at the least, hurt terribly.

He felt silly. It didn't hurt. It didn't even feel cold. Just wet.

"Drink. You look like you could use it."

Pirojil accepted the flask and tilted it back, letting the fiery whiskey burn his throat, warming him to the core. Walter Slovotsky had once said something about how a drink actually chilled you rather than warmed you, but that just went to show that Walter Slovotsky didn't know nearly as much as he thought he did.

Pirojil forced himself to his feet. It was harder to stand than it should have been, but he managed to remain standing, and took first one step, and then another.

"We still need to get to the village," he said.

Erenor shouldered both rucksacks. "Why don't you take the swords—you're probably of more use with them, even in your present condition, than I am." He turned and began to walk away down the road. "Not," he said, not bothering to sound anything but smug and self-satisfied, "that I am as entirely useless, as some people have all too often suggested that I am." He started to whistle some silly tune, but stopped when Pirojil told him to shut up.

They weren't more than a couple of hundred paces down the road when the flapping of leathery wings filled the air.

12

Night Moves II: Kethol, Ahira, and Another

It never bothered him that other people were good at other things—that was, after all, the way of the world—but Kethol had always hated it when somebody was better at something he, himself, thought he was particularly good at. At bones—rare as it was to find a bones player who was better than he was, although it was, thankfully, common to find more than one who thought he was better than a none too sober looking soldier—it would mean losing money; with a bow, it would mean losing a bet, or, under the wrong circumstances, it could mean losing his life; with a sword, it would mean that he would have had to rely on Pirojil and Durine, rather than have them rely on him.

He hated that. Kethol liked being somebody that others could rely on. He knew he wasn't the most quick-witted of men, but he liked to think he was reliable, and good at, well, what he was good at.

And moving through a forest quietly was something that he was good at, day or night.

At night, though, Ahira was better at it than Kethol was, and he should have resented that.

But there was something about Ahira that simply didn't let that bother him, didn't make him resent the dwarf taking the lead through the forest. It was, maybe, as simple as the fact that the dwarf wasn't human, and that Kethol could not compete with Ahira in a test of night vision any more than Ahira could compete with him in a longbow competition. He almost smiled at the idea of the dwarf trying to manipulate a bow whose length was half again his height. Yes, the dwarf was actually quite a good shot with his short horn bow, and even Durine hadn't been strong enough to string it.

But there was something about a good longbow—be it of yew or horn or both—that made its clothyard shafts fly farther and truer in the hands of an expert bowman than could be accounted for by anything short of magic.

Working their way down a trail at night, though, it simply made sense for Ahira to take the lead, as he could see the path better than Kethol could.

You had to proceed mostly by feel at night; the wan, thin light of the overhead stars gave little illumination, but that little was enough.

Or, at least, it was enough until the clouds above slipped silently over the forest, leaving only an idle quartet of dancing Faerie lights, high above the forest, to provide illumination.

And then it started to rain. Not gently, not even at first; within moments the drumming of fat raindrops against the canopy of leaves above drowned out the forest noises, but it also frightened the Faerie lights away, leaving Kethol in the blackest of darkness, wet and miserable as the storm broke.

He could have panicked, but that wouldn't have done any good. Yes, he was in the woods in the rain and the dark, but he had been in the woods in the rain and the dark before, and he would manage now as he had managed then. He had a working map in his head of the twists and turns of the path for a dozen paces ahead, and that was all that he and Ahira needed. There was no point in trying to push their way through a nighttime rainstorm, after all. Even Ahira's darksight wouldn't work well enough in the rain.

The only thing that made sense would be to take the oiled groundcloth out of his rucksack, find a small tree—not a large tree; they attracted lightning like an open sore attracted flies—and huddle under it until the storm passed.

"Ahira," he called out to the dwarf, not afraid to raise his voice, knowing that it couldn't carry far over the manic drumbeat of raindrops against the overhead leaves.

No answer.

"Ahira."

Ahead on the path, light flared, bright enough to hurt his eyes. It seemed to be originating from Ahira's hand, and that impression was proven true when the dwarf hid the light in his massive fist, then let a beam shoot out from between two spread fingers, the effect the same as that of a hooded lantern, except much brighter.

His face was split in a broad smile, despite the way that rain ran down his water-stringy hair. "What do you think," he said, smiling, "the chances are that anybody is dedicated enough or stupid enough to be watching a trail during a thunderstorm?"

The rain had already chilled Kethol thoroughly, but he smiled, too.

Comfort was a good thing, but safety was better, and the dwarf had a good point. He nodded.

"Then let's get going." The dwarf set off at a trot.

The forest protected them from the direct impact of the driving rain, but forests always leaked: Kethol was thoroughly chilled and utterly soaked by the time the rain stopped, shortly before the path broke on a narrow dirt—mud, now—road, that led downhill to Dernal's Ford.

Downhill, off in the distance, wisps of smoke from stone chimneys beckoned, with promises of warmth and dryness, and while the wind was blowing the wrong way, Kethol could have almost sworn that he caught an occasional whiff of stew cooking over some fireplace.

Stew. Just the thought made his mouth water. There was something about a peasant stew that always sat simmering in the hearth, the stewpot never emptied but constantly refreshed with new vegetables, water, and meat, that warmed more than the belly it filled.

He must have been more tired than he thought, or perhaps he was paying more attention to the stirrings of people in the village below, but he only heard the whickering of a horse a few moments before two men rode out of the darkness of the forest, their horses' hooves making deep sucking sounds in the mud of the road. They both had lances, pointed only generally toward Ahira and Kethol, and one held a hooded lantern high on a pole, the butt end of the pole resting in the socket on his saddle.

The lantern hood slid back as the horseman manipulated the control wire, and Kethol and Ahira were bathed in its light.

Everything is relative. The lantern light would have seemed puny and impotent compared to the elven glow that Ahira had concealed in his fist, but in the dark of night, relieved only by the vaguest glow of starlight and Faerie lights above the thin layer of clouds, it was almost painful to Kethol's eyes.

"And what do we have here?" one asked. "A drowned dwarf and his soggy companion? Stand easy, the two of you, and identify yourselves."

Ahira laid a restraining hand on Kethol's arm, not that Kethol was going to do anything at all, much less something stupid and violent. The muddy road sucked at his buskins with every step, and while Kethol was normally fairly fast on his feet, the horsemen could run him down without any difficulty at all, and wouldn't hesitate to do so.

It would be a shame to be killed by Cullinane soldiers, after all.

Besides . . . "My name is Kethol," he said. "Soldier, fealty-bound to Baron Cullinane."

A skeptical snort from one of the horsemen was echoed by the other's horse. "And who is your short friend?" he asked. "Ahira Bandylegs, no doubt?"

"My friends call me Ahira," the dwarf said, his voice calmer even than usual. "Particularly the baron, whose swaddling clothes I used to change, some years ago, and whose errand I'm on."

"Our captain knows Ahira Bandylegs very well, and he's not likely to take kindly to somebody pretending to be him." The tip of the lance didn't waver for a moment. "He, like the village warden, is a humorless fellow; both are very likely to be wondering what you two are doing wandering around his domain at night."

Kethol was wondering why a small village would have a pair of soldiers on watch on a rainy night—and it would, of course, be more than a pair. There were two roads in and out of the village, and that would mean at least four guard posts, at a minimum, eight men on duty at a time, and at least two watches overnight.

Yes, it wasn't uncommon to station a troop in or near a village—for one thing, it gave troop captains more contact with the people of the barony, and that helped with recruitment—but putting a guard out meant something was going on.

One of the horsemen brought something to his lips, and blew a quick tune on his fingerwhistle that was echoed back from the village, below. Kethol recognized it instantly as a call for three horsemen, with the four-note theme, repeated twice, that made it not an all-hands-turnout request.

"A Cullinane man should recognize that," the horseman said. It was a question.

"You should think about finding a better test," Ahira snickered. "Anyone with more wisdom than a snail should be able to figure out that you've signaled for relief, and never mind that Karl Cullinane and I put those signals together back during the raiding years, and I know that you've asked for exactly three horsemen—although why you chose three rather than two or four or just letting your captain, down in the village, decide for himself, well, that is something you can explain to him, as I don't much care."

"You really are Ahira Bandylegs?"

The dwarf unclenched his fist, so that the light source in his palm bathed his face in its painfully actinic, white light. "Yes. Now blow that little quickstep-march that tells them to hurry. We've got some matters that need attention, and the sooner the better."

A hot mug of cloyingly sweet tea warming his hands, his belly, and his soul, Kethol sat close enough to the fireplace that an occasional spark was flicked out of the fire to hiss itself to death on his still-damp tunic.

Ahira was in the chair opposite, his legs folded underneath him, tailor-fashion, a joint of mutton in one hand and a preposterously large tankard of beer in his other.

"So, Captain Sterlen," Ahira said, around yet another bite of meat, "how many good men can you have, armed, rested and ready to ride at dawn?"

The captain seemed young for his position; his mustache was thin and his face unlined, unmarked save for a ragged scar that ran from the corner of his mouth to the point of his jaw. Kethol hadn't asked how he had earned it, although it was a story that the captain likely thought worth telling, given that a beard would have easily covered it.

"I've one troop's horses saddled," the captain said, "and my men are ready to ride right now, or whenever you command, Master Ahira. I'd sooner take the second troop, but—"

"Second troop?"

That didn't make much sense to Kethol, either. He didn't think a small village like this one would need to house as much as a single troop, normally, not unless there was some sort of orc nest about, and he surely would have heard about that.

Sterlen looked at Kethol and then back to Ahira. "It's just temporary. We're expecting a delivery at . . . shortly, that is. I brought in an extra troop from Emdeen—better to be on the safe side than not—"

"Ellegon?"

Sterlen kept his face impassive. "Excuse me?"

Dwarves were known as the Moderate People, but that didn't prevent the excitement and relief in Ahira's voice. "You're expecting *Ellegon*. He's bringing in something valuable—" Ahira's brow wrinkled"—oh, say, a generator from Home, to take advantage of the grainmill when it's not grinding, and after the way things went in Keranahan, not only is the dragon nervous about getting shot at, but Doria is nervous about it, too. When is he due?"

"I don't know—"

"Think about it, Captain. We've got to get the baron out of the barony safely, and to the capital for Parliament. And with the dragon due here, that's the best news I've had all day. So when and where?"

Sterlen dragged up a chair and looked from Kethol to Ahira, and back again. "I have my orders, from the regent herself—"

"—who does not outrank the baron, himself, who is the one who sent me—"

"—to keep matters quiet until Ellegon has come and gone. Word is, there was an attempt to kill the dragon out in Keranahan not too long ago, and there are those of us who think he's more important to the realm than just as something to put on the reverse of a coin."

He fingered an old copper halfmark—Kethol could tell by the unmilled edges. The face of it would hold the image of the Old Emperor, just as more modern coins would have the Emperor Thomen's face on it, but the reverse of both was a dragon, perched on a castle wall, breathing flame.

The Holtun-Bieme war had been won by soldiers on the ground, not a dragon in the air, finally—but it would have been lost, just as finally, if the Old Emperor and the dragon, Ellegon, hadn't involved themselves.

And what would have happened if the Baroness Elanee had managed to have Ellegon killed, leaving her magic-tamed dragon the only one in the Middle Lands? Would the emperor have had to come to terms with her? And if he didn't, would the empire itself have dissolved into baronial wars between—and among?—the Holtish and Biemish baronies?

That was the nice thing about having the dragon around, even only occasionally. It might not really be immortal and its appearance might not actually be inevitable, but it felt that way, and that discouraged revolt.

"You don't have to tell me anything," Ahira said. "Just give me a troop to escort the baron to Biemestren, and when the dragon shows up, tell him. Ellegon can work out what the right thing to do is."

Sterlen didn't answer.

Kethol didn't understand why. They had proved who they were, and—

"Of course." Ahira's smile threatened to split his face in two. "That's why all the guards—he's due *now*, tonight. He's dropping off whatever he's dropping off here on his way to Parliament, planning on circling a few times above the assembled heads, flame flashing through the sky."

The dwarf was on his feet, Kethol only a beat behind him. "Take us to the rendezvous, now."

"I—"

"That will be now, Captain Sterlen," Ahira said, in a voice that brooked no disagreement.

The captain didn't answer right away.

"Very well," he finally said.

Kethol spotted the dragon first.

He had been scanning the sky to the east, looking near the horizon. He had seen the dragon fly in perhaps only half a dozen times—ordinary soldiers, even those who were often assigned to protect nobility, had little to do with Ellegon, which was fine with Kethol, all in all—and the only time he had seen it coming, it was skimming quickly, low to the ground, following the contour of the land, flying as low as possible, not high.

But, finally, a dot that he thought was just a speck in his eye grew larger and larger, and circled in from high overhead, until—

Kethol. And Ahira, sounded in his head. *And Captain Sterlen.*

The dot grew larger, and became a bat-like shape, a slim, tubular body suspended between two huge wings. The dragon, wings flapping not at all, circled in and down toward the hilltop.

"Look alert, all of you," Sterlen shouted to the horsemen arrayed along the road to the hilltop. "There's nobody who should be anywhere near here."

A smoldering fire told of where a thick raspberry bramble had cupped the side of the hill. There was probably no reason to waste the wild raspberries—and the few remaining ones were terribly sweet, even though they had dried on the vine—but it was, at least in the captain's mind, at least theoretically possible that somebody could have been hiding in the brambles, and Sterlen had been ordered to keep the hilltop secure within a long bowshot.

All it would take would be one arrow, its tip coated with dragonbane extract, to pierce Ellegon's otherwise almost impenetrable hide, and send the dragon to his death.

That would be a horrid waste. Humans lived only a few years, but dragons lived forever, if they weren't killed. And while Kethol had never had much contact with any other dragons, he found that he liked Ellegon—at least as much as he could like a creature that was easily capable of burning him to death with an idle breath, or biting him in two with teeth the size of a short sword.

Have I ever burned you to death or bitten you in two? the mental voice asked.

Ahira turned to Kethol and smiled. "The dragon makes you nervous, doesn't he?"

Kethol didn't answer. There was nothing wrong with being scared, as long as you didn't let your fear stop you from doing your job, but it wasn't something that he was particularly eager to discuss.

*I seem to recall that *you* were not overly calm around me the first time we met, my young friend,* the dragon said.

Young? With the lines in his face and the gray in his hair, Ahira had to be at least a hundred, a hundred fifty years old.

Well, no, he doesn't have to be, and in fact he isn't, the dragon said.

Was there no way to keep it out of his mind? That was the thing that Kethol always disliked about being around Ellegon: he had no privacy, not even between his ears.

Yes, I can shut out your mind, if I'd like, and no, I don't enjoy poking around humans' minds. I spent a couple of centuries chained in a sewer, being forced to flame it to ashes or live with the smell, and the recesses of most human minds smell worse than a sewer does.

The dragon landed in the tall grass with a thump that shook the hill, forcing Kethol to reach for Ahira to steady himself.

The great beast folded its huge wings underneath it—

Him, if you please. I am a him, not an it, thank you very much.

—and settled to the ground, its—*his* long neck stretching out first so that he could scan the surroundings from side to side, and then so that he could lay his immense, triangular head on the ground.

The outer lids sagged shut. *Don't be surprised. Even a dragon gets tired sometimes.*

Sterlen's soldiers were already swarming over the dragon as it— as he lay on the grass. He was a huge beast, gray-green in color, his scales ranging in size from that of a serving platter on his wall- like sides and belly to tiny ones, barely the size of a palm, around the edges of his eyes.

The eyes opened again. They bothered Kethol, as they always did. They seemed to see too much.

It isn't the eyes, it's the mind.

Thick leather straps circled his chest, just aft of the forelegs and forward of the hind legs, supporting a woven rope rigging, to which half a dozen canvas bags and one large box had been carefully lashed. The box was put on belay by a team of six men on one side of the dragon, while another tried at first to untie the knots, then at Sterlen's command used his belt knife and cut through.

The soldiers slowly lowered the box to the ground. *One low-flow electrical generator, as promised,* the dragon's mental voice said, although it didn't bother to explain what that was.

It doesn't involve killing anything; you probably wouldn't understand. Or care.

"That's unfair," Ahira said. "And—"

—and life is unfair, and if it was fair I could lie around here for awhile, maybe snatch a sheep or two from some field, and not get back in the air to ferry you over to Kelleren's farm, and then the lot of you to Biemestren.

The dragon craned his neck until his head, easily the size of a carriage, was almost an arm's-reach way from Kethol.

The massive jaw sagged open, wisps of steam escaping from the corners of the ropy lips.

Well? What are you waiting for? Life isn't fair, and we'd best be going.

13

Parliament, and a Can of Worms, Opens

Walter Slovotsky took his place at the head table, next to where Thomen would sit—the place of service, on the left, not the place of honor, at the right—when he came down from his rooms and officially opened Parliament.

It would have been nice to be able to sit in the back of the room, able to slip out if—when—the session became boring. Which was inevitable. Yes, Parliament would handle matters of life and death.

But just because something was important didn't mean it wasn't godawful boring.

Walter Slovotsky sipped at his morning cup of tea while others gathered and took their seats. Servants bustled in and out from the side door, bearing platters laden with mugs, and plates and pots . . . and notes: with few exceptions, Slovotsky being one of them, people other than nobility and imperial governors were excluded from the Great Hall while Parliament was in session.

The tables had been arranged in a broken circle, leaving plenty of room for servants to pass between them, keeping mugs refreshed and passing messages.

Of which there were plenty. Baron Nerahan, a short weasel of a man, seemed to be constantly answering telegrams—reading a note brought by a runner, and then dashing off a quick response. He had been the first of the barons in the Great Hall, according to the majordomo.

Slovotsky smiled quietly to himself. He had had a word with the engineer on duty in the telegraph shack on the southwestern tower; there would be a detailed log of all telegrams received, as well as sent. Nerahan was probably just showing off—the telegraph lines were almost complete in Holtun, although not in Bieme, and while the purpose of that had, originally, been for the benefit of the military governors, the Holtish barons were perfectly capable of making it look like a luxury that the Crown provided to them, and hadn't quite got around to providing to all the Biemish barons.

Tyrnael, of course, had been the first Biemish baron to have a telegraph station in his baronial seat, and not just or even mainly because he was the senior Biemish baron—by lineage, although not by age.

But Arondael—who was showing every one of his sixty-plus years in the lines of his face—glared at Nerahan with undisguised hatred as he entered the room and took his seat. He sat back in his chair and murmured to General Forsteen, the Arondael military governor, who had arrived with him, practically arm-in-arm. If it had been up to Walter Slovotsky, Forsteen would have been given another barony to govern years before. He was far too cozy with Arondael, and, for that matter, what with them graying and balding at the same rate, and sharing some of each other's gestures, the two of them were starting to look alike, like an old gay couple.

But it wasn't up to Walter Slovotsky, and with Thomen eager to return the Holtish baronies, one by one, to the rule of the Holtish barons, Forsteen was likely to stay right where he was, particularly considering that he had married one of Arondael's daughters, a widow half his age.

Not that I have any business objecting to that sort of thing, Slovotsky thought. Aiea, after all, was just about half his age. He could protest all he wanted that it was different with him and her—

and, well, it was—but that sort of protestation would get him laughed at by Aiea. And Andrea Cullinane. And Jason Cullinane. And particularly Ahira and Doria.

And then there was Treseen. Treseen, the governor of Keranahan, was the next to arrive. General Treseen. Treseen the asshole.

He was ten, fifteen years older than Walter Slovotsky, but he wore his age well, his black hair curled about his scalp in well-oiled scallops, his beard only touched with gray, and his jaw wide and solid.

Walter Slovotsky was careful not to stare at Treseen, the only governor there not accompanied by a baron—or vice versa, depending on how you looked at it. But Walter Slovotsky could see quite a lot out of the corner of his eye; he pretended to look, once again, at the mural decorating the far wall as he considered the governor.

Treseen's tunic was of thick linen, edged with silver thread and laced tightly across the chest and belly, probably to hide the sag of one into the other, but the effect worked. Slovotsky didn't know quite what to make of the short, informal cape mostly over his left shoulder, fastened in place with a silver chain. It was an affectation, perhaps.

And perhaps Treseen was a trifle too richly dressed for a baronial governor. It was probably better and safer for a governor to overdress than underdress—too much of a protestation of poverty would probably draw more attention than a bit of ostentation.

That was the problem with the Occupation—tax money, by necessity, flowed from the village and district wardens to and through the governor, and it was certain that in some—many? most? all?—cases, some coin would stick to any but the most honest or clever governor's hands, and you probably didn't get to be an imperial governor by an excess of honesty.

How much coin, of course, was the real issue. A little embez-
zlement here and there was no problem, as long as it was only a
little.

And if it was too much? A governor could be hanged for em-
bezzlement just as legally as a peasant could be hanged for poach-
ing. The trick was to hang him only if necessary, only if a governor
made a pig of himself, to encourage prudence in the others. You
didn't want the other governors spending more time fiddling with
their books than watching for signs of brewing rebellion.

Still, since neither Thomen nor Karl had had a governor
executed—Karl had relieved a couple; Thomen hadn't—the Crown
could probably get away with doing in one, *pour encouragez les
autres.*

That might not be a bad idea in this case. Slovotsky didn't like
Treseen, and he kept coming up with reasons why, although the
obvious would serve just fine: Treseen hadn't been able to keep
Baroness Elanee from secreting an injured dragon out in the hills
of Keranahan, raising it to kill and replace Ellegon, intending not
only to put her son on the baronial throne of Keranahan—which
had been, in the absence of Forinel, the older son, likely enough,
but . . .

. . . but there was no way of knowing what she had really intended, not now, not with her dead and Miron, who had conspired
with her, fled the empire.

But . . . Ellegon. Treseen had best not have had anything to do
with the assassination attempt on Ellegon.

It wasn't just that Walter Slovotsky liked the dragon—although
he did; the dragon was one of the very few people who knew Walter
Slovotsky as he was, with all his flaws and limitations, and loved
him just the same—but the dragon helped keep the peace, just by
existing, just by being around every now and then.

The fear of Ellegon dropping out of the night sky, flame roaring from his cavernous mouth or—perhaps better, and certainly
safer, what with the proliferation of the cultivation of dragonbane

ever since the exodus of magical creatures from Faerie while the rift at Ehevnor had been, temporarily, open—a bag of rocks dropped from a great height, a sort of nonexploding cluster bomb . . .

. . . well, just the idea was enough to at least give a possibly rebellious baron pause.

"So, Walter Slovotsky," Niphael said, as he stalked into the room, and stood in front of his own chair across the room from Walter. He leaned forward, his palms firmly on the table, "How are you this fine, fine morning?"

Vertum Niphael was a fat man, his cheeks permanently reddened with burst veins near the skin. It was tempting to think of him as a drunk from the way he slurred his words, but his injuries had come in battle, during the war, in a blow to the head that would have scrambled the brains of a less hard-headed man, and while it had left him with a withered left arm and a way of slurring his speech, it didn't seem to have affected his mind.

"I am well, Baron," Slovotsky said. "And thank you for asking." Honesty was not a particularly useful tool of statecraft; Niphael would get around to his point sooner or later, and it was simplest to let him.

"Your new wife treats you well?"

"Yes, and—"

"Soldiers and other servants of the empire respond promptly and obediently to your commands?"

Smirks passed across the faces of several of the barons. What was Niphael up to?

"So, all is well with you, now, is it?"

"Yes, but—"

"Then where," the baron said, all false joviality gone from his manner, "have you hidden that Jason Cullinane of yours, and why haven't you made sure that he's here with the rest of us?"

There wasn't an easy answer for that. He could say, of course, that Jason Cullinane didn't answer to him, not anymore—the boy was not a boy, and hadn't been for a while. He could say, truthfully, that he didn't know where the hell Jason and his party were, and that he had dispatched Pirojil and his two companions to that barony in part to make sure that Jason made it in time for Parliament, although mainly it was to get Erenor out of town before Henrad twigged to his identity as a wizard.

But, as he kept reassuring himself, honesty was not a fundamental tool of statecraft.

Still . . . "To be honest, Baron," he said, dialing for an expression of honest concern, "I don't know what's kept Baron Cullinane, and I'm increasingly worried."

"Hmph." That didn't satisfy Arondael. "It seems to me," he said, his voice low and reedy, "that on an occasion or two when other barons have been tardy in responding to an imperial summons, they've been met at their gateposts with a detachment of the Home Guard, and perhaps the dragon, Ellegon, circling overhead, and on at least one occasion the emperor himself, threatening to pry the baron loose from his castle like a mussel from its shell, if the castle didn't quickly disgorge itself of said baron."

"Are you suggesting we sit in trial of Baron Cullinane?" Bren Adahan's voice came to Walter Slovotsky's rescue, which both relieved and irritated him. "How . . . interesting an idea. Why not bring it up to the emperor himself?"

Bren Adahan stopped in the doorway, but Ranella didn't break stride. She was another one of the exceptions; as a master engineer, she had been given the military governorship of Barony Adahan, and even after Adahan had been released from direct imperial rule, she had stayed on to manage the development of the mills in New Pittsburgh.

Short, fortyish, and thick at waist and neck, affecting a mannish tunic and leggings rather than a dress or shift, she didn't look particularly attractive—well, she wasn't particularly attractive—or particularly bright, but looks could be misleading.

She wore no knife that Slovotsky could see—and he suspected

that she probably had none—but there was a brace of pistols on her belt, gold and bone inlays on their curved grips proclaiming that these were to be paid attention to, bragging of her permission to come not only armed, but armed with a gunpowder weapon, into the imperial presence.

She took her seat quietly, and without making a fuss of it placed both of her pistols on the table in front of her. "I think," she said, quietly, "that Baron Arondael means nothing of the sort, and that he's just as concerned as the rest of us are at Baron Cullinane's absence." She raised a palm toward where Bren Adahan still stood, framed in the arch of the doorway. "I'm sure, Baron Minister, the proctor has tried to find out what he can—aren't you?"

From the cynical expressions decorating the faces at the tables, this little charade wasn't fooling anybody. If Bren Adahan and Walter Slovotsky were to have a disagreement—not an unusual event, granted—it would not be in public at all, much less in front of all of the barons.

Oh, well. Most of what we do is wasted effort, after all, he thought. The only trouble is, you could never tell which part was wasted, so you had to do it all.

A page—Walter was tempted to claim that he wasn't even a paragraph, but the double meaning wouldn't have worked in Erendra—stepped in through the side door.

"Barons of the Parliament," he said, the drama of the moment ruined when his voice momentarily cracked into a pubescent screech, "Thomen Furnael, Prince of Bieme and Emperor of Holtun-Bieme."

Two pikemen marched in cadence through the side door, and took up positions next to it. They wore the black-and-silver imperial livery, from their helms to the enameled armor that covered them down to their toes, and their pikestaffs had been enameled black, the blades silvered, although Walter Slovotsky had no doubt that good steel lay beneath.

Not that they would have used the pikes indoors. It was a silly weapon here, more ceremonial than threatening, given the difficulty in wielding any sort of polearm indoors. If either had to use a weapon to defend the emperor—and they were ready to do just that—they would use the very businesslike and plain swords at their waists, or the flintlock pistols in holsters that had been welded, two on each side, to the sides of their chest-pieces.

That was little more than a distraction. Walter Slovotsky had had a word with General Garavar about security for Parliament, and trusted marksmen from the Home Guard, each with a half-dozen flintlock carbines at the full-cock, hid in niches in the tapestries to the right and left of where the emperor would sit, the walls of the niches protecting the emperor from a stray shot more surely than even loyalty could.

Trust was a nice enough thing, but it was better to make sure.

Thomen entered, his mother waddling along just a few steps behind him.

There was a lot wrong with inherited position—not necessarily the worst system in the world, but not the best, either—but one of the good things about it was that the nobles learned young at least part of how to behave.

The barons and governors were quickly on their feet as Thomen walked in, moving neither quickly nor slowly, a certain dignity to his mien that Walter Slovotsky frankly envied.

Even after twenty-odd years on This Side, he still had the built-in American disdain for inherited titles. Virtue could, perhaps, be something you were born with, and it could, certainly, be something that you learned, but it was not carried by sperm as it wiggled its way toward a waiting egg.

Still, whether it was, as Slovotsky believed, training and education, or was something he had been born with, Thomen Furnael carried himself well. The silver crown of Bieme—now of Holtun-Bieme—sat easily atop his head, the bright metal burnished to a high shine, each jewel glistening as though from an inner light.

He nodded to his right and left, and then took his seat on the throne, to Slovotsky's right, and let the assemblage stand for a few long seconds before folding his hands in his lap.

"The Parliament is called to sit," he said, formally, his voice low and conversational.

Walter Slovotsky plopped down in his seat, and looked over at Thomen. He suppressed a frown. If the emperor had a weapon—other than that entirely decorative knife at his belt—it was well-hidden, and while, as a matter of firm policy, Walter Slovotsky always assumed that he had missed a concealed weapon or three, that was purely policy, and he didn't believe for a moment that Thomen had concealed as much as a hunting knife on him.

Yes, this was Parliament and astronomically unlikely to turn into some sort of fight—physical fight, that is—but stranger things had happened, and rulers who wished to become old rulers were well-advised to take pains with their own safety. Yes, that's what the soldiers in the alcoves were for, but there were damned few people whom you could count on to do their jobs right. Particularly when the shit hit the fan. As it always did, sooner or later, one way or another.

Chairs squeaked on stone as the assemblage took their seats.

Nerahan muttered something to Forsteen, his lips close enough to the governor's ear that Walter Slovotsky couldn't see them move enough to guess at what he was saying.

Is this something you can share with the whole class? he didn't quite ask.

Arondael leaned forward. "I didn't quite hear that, Baron. Something about special privileges for some?"

The old man must have had better hearing than Walter Slovotsky would have given him credit for; Nerahan reddened. "It was nothing."

Thomen Furnael steepled his long fingers in front of his face. "I can't speak for the barons," he said, his voice quiet but penetrating in the still air of the room, "but I'd be interested in hearing what it is that you had to say."

"I—it was nothing, Emperor," Nerahan said. "Just a quiet comment to Governor Forsteen about how we have two seats empty."

Actually, there were several unoccupied chairs at the tables; the Biemish barons had elected to come alone. But the chair with the green-and-silver filigree work along the edge of its upholstery, and its black-and-orange mate next to where Treseen sat, showed that there were two barons missing.

"And you see some equivalence, Baron?" Bren Adahan asked. "There is no baron in Keranahan at the moment—are you suggesting the same thing for Barony Cullinane?"

Tyrnael grunted. "He doesn't need to suggest anything, Lord Minister." He sat back, and in either deliberate or unconscious imitation, steepled his fingers the way Thomen had. "What's clear, and what needs no suggestion, but merely simple observation, is that Baron Cullinane is absent, and unless he's not received the same summons that the rest of us have, I don't see how he can—"

"Be permitted to keep his barony?"

Bren, shut up.

Even if that was what Tyrnael was suggesting, it was clumsy for Bren Adahan to bring it out in the open. Bren Adahan was usually too slick for something like that, but something about Tyrnael had him irritated, and while Walter Slovotsky shared the irritation and suspicion, it was one thing to feel it and another entirely to act upon it.

"—flout the emperor's command." Tyrnael's expression grew grave. "Unless, of course, some tragedy has befallen his party." He shook his head. "It's sad, but it's true: we live in unsettled times."

Verahan, the youngest of the Holtish barons, leaned forward.

"I think we live in very settled times, my Lord Baron Tyrnael," he said. He gestured toward the emperor. "The emperor is on the throne, the Crown is on the emperor, and we are at peace, are we not?" He didn't wait for an answer before continuing. "With the Holtish baronies being returned to the rule of the Holtish barons, we can look forward to even more settled times."

It hadn't escaped Slovotsky's notice that the governor of Verahan sat at Verahan's right, the position of honor, but also, by local custom, the position of a subordinate when only two men sat together. Claressen was probably the oldest of the governors, although he had never been more than a troop captain—but he had, so Bren Adahan, who knew him better, thought, a better feel for details than for combat.

Claressen leaned back in his chair, folded his thick fingers over his massive belly, and laughed. "That's the thing I like about the young," he said, patting the baron on the arm in a way that was clearly affectionate, and not condescending. "Always looking at the bright side of all such matters." His smile dropped away. "As for us older folks—or, at least this older folk—I'm concerned that Governor Treseen has been left to run his barony without a baron to help shoulder the load, as young Arta has been doing for me." His mouth twitched. "I'm an old man, and I'm looking to step down—emperor willing—as soon as my young baron, here, can take over."

Tyrnael looked over at Niphael, and gave a slight twitch of his fingers. Nothing much; if Walter Slovotsky had blinked, he would have missed it.

So that's how it is. It was a good thing to know that Niphael would take a hand signal from Tyrnael.

"Do I take it that you vouch for this . . . young baron?" Niphael asked.

"Yes," Claressen nodded. "I do. I vouch for his intelligence, and his industriousness, and I shall even vouch for his loyalty to the Crown, should anyone be so impolite as to suggest otherwise." His smile had no trace of warmth in it. "But I'm neither so young or so foolish—and aren't those so often the same thing?—that I'd vouch that a boy of twenty, even one like young Arta, with a wife and two sons, would be ready to rule a barony without some help, and even direction." He shrugged. "I'm just not at all sure that direction, that help, needs to come from a military governor." He drummed his fingers on the table in front of him. He turned toward Thomen and addressed him directly. "I had thought there were matters more pressing, but if Baron Tyrnael—I mean Baron Niphael, of course—wishes to discuss whether Verahan should be the second barony to be released from direct imperial rule, I'm not unwilling. But it seems to me that the succession in Keranahan is more pressing."

Well, at least it hadn't gone over everybody else's head that that challenge had come from Tyrnael.

Would you do me the favor, Lord Baron, Walter Slovotsky thought, *of falling down the stairs and breaking your neck immediately upon your arrival home?* It wouldn't do to arrange an accident for him here, as even a real accident under the emperor's roof would be perceived by the other barons as a successful assassination—but if it were to happen back at the barony, that couldn't be held against the emperor. Or the imperial proctor.

Tyrnael nodded, conceding either the point or that his manipulation of Niphael had been noted. "As, indeed, it should be. As, indeed, the absence of Baron Cullinane is."

The emperor shook his head. "Jason Cullinane has been summoned; he will be here. I've no doubt that he simply has run into some difficulty, and were Ellegon here, I'd ask the dragon to go investigate." His crooked smile reminded everybody in the room that while the dragon belonged to himself, Ellegon could reliably be counted on to run an errand for the emperor, and wouldn't much mind if that errand involved stomping on somebody.

Unspoken was the question of whether Ellegon would be more loyal to the Cullinane family than he was to the throne, but there was little political profit in trying to exploit that, even if—as Walter Slovotsky certainly hoped—it was indeed the case.

Bren Adahan leaned forward. "I hardly think that simply because a baron is late for Parliament any sensible person would wish to take away his barony."

Slovotsky wasn't sure why, but that was the wrong thing to say: Tyrnael sat back, trying just a little too hard not to look smug.

14

✠ The Road to Nowhere

Pirojil frowned, while ahead of him, his tunic flapping manically in the wind, Jason Cullinane stood on the dragon's back, nothing between him and the ground but leagues of clear air and a too thin safety line.

And, worse, when he turned to look behind him for a moment, the young baron had a grin on his face. It was bad enough that he was doing something so risky and stupid; it made it worse that he enjoyed it.

Pirojil would have to keep him as far away from Kethol as possible; Kethol's mindless bravery was apparently contagious. No, that was unfair, and Pirojil wanted to be fair. The Cullinanes seemed to pass along that sort of pointless courage with their blood.

Pirojil hated the whole idea. Not that it mattered. There were good things and bad things about being an ordinary soldier, but having your opinions count wasn't on the table as either.

But that didn't matter. Pirojil was used to doing his job, and his job was to obey orders, and the orders right now were to keep the baron alive without interfering with this silly idea of his.

Looking for the assassins made sense—although just barely; getting any profit out of it was a slim possibility at best—but having the baron along while they were doing that made none at all, except maybe to the baron.

Pirojil swore under his breath. It was bad enough having to

watch his own back, and Kethol's, and Erenor's—watching out for the baron and his mother would make it worse.

It wasn't that he objected to protecting them. Pirojil would have waded through fields of soldiers' guts to protect the dowager empress's little finger from a slight scratch, or hacked his way through walls of innocent peasants to make his way to the baron's side, and if that made him a bloodthirsty murderer, well, then that's what he was, and the best he could do would be to not think about it any more than he had to.

What bothered Pirojil was that he couldn't do two things at once, and this was going to call for about four, maybe five. There was no way he could properly watch out for both of them at the same time, much less do that and simultaneously protect not only Erenor and Kethol but himself.

And adding in trying to search for some assassins? That was lunacy.

Up here, high in the sky, it didn't all matter.

Karl used to call it 'the morality of altitude.'

Eh?

I'm not sure what he meant, not exactly, the dragon thought, as he banked into another turn. *But there is something about being high above it all that gives you a sense of detachment.*

Right. And you could conceal a gold coin at midnight by tossing it high up in the air—for a short while.

But it would come down, and so would the dragon. You couldn't stay up here forever, as tempting as it was. Still, maybe the dragon had a point, as—

Thank you so very much for admitting the possibility. I'm touched, I am.

—as the ground was far away, and anybody or anything that could reach this high was something that Pirojil simply didn't have to worry about because it could kill the baron and the dowager empress as easily as Pirojil could a swat a fly or stab a man.

So, it was best not to worry about that, but to relax and rest for a moment. Which didn't explain why Pirojil's eyes kept scanning the sky as well as the ground.

Silly thing to do. He closed his eyes and leaned back in the straps.

You couldn't do everything at once, and to try to was to guarantee that you couldn't do any one thing really well.

Changing the baron's mind wasn't one of those things that he could do. Making sure that the baron and the dowager empress had been strapped in properly before Ellegon had taken to the air was something he could do; keeping the baron properly strapped in wasn't one of those things.

Divide the world into two piles, and keep the piles separate.

What mattered was making sure that Kethol was strapped into the rearmost position on the dragon's back, well back of where Jason Cullinane stood—not sat, despite Pirojil's request, but stood— just ahead of the dragon's shoulders, the rush of wind whipping his hair as he braced himself by clinging to the long rope that ran down the center of Ellegon's back, his feet jammed in between two scales.

There was nothing to keep Jason Cullinane from falling except his grip, and a single safety rope tied around his waist, the other end made fast in a hole in one of the dragon's impossibly tough scales.

There is also the fact that I've known and loved the boy since before he was born, the mental voice said. *I'd no more let him fall to his death than I would have his father. Surely, Pirojil, you should know something of loyalty.*

It would have been nice if there was some way to keep the dragon out of his mind. There was something indecent about the way that his private thoughts weren't private around Ellegon.

You need not worry so much. The dragon snorted, a gout of flame that would have crisped the six of them had Ellegon not craned his long neck to one side. *I find no pleasure at all in looking deep into what passes for a human mind, and avoid it as much as possible. Your deep, dark, and dirty secrets are safe from me, Pi-rojil.°

The dragon banked sharply, and Pirojil's head spun. It didn't feel like the dragon was turning as much as it felt like the whole world had turned on its side, the greenery below now a wall instead of a distant carpet.

°That is the clearing where you killed the assassin?°

Either it wasn't, or they were coming upon it from a different angle.

Why ask me? Pirojil wasn't the woodsman, and didn't pretend to be able to—

°Because even when he isn't busy puking, Kethol can't keep a map in his head, unless it's practically a tree-by-tree map of some place he's been on the ground. And because Erenor has me thoroughly blocked out of his mind, which disturbs me not at all, because if he meant the family any harm he would have committed that harm by now.°

Pirojil tried hard not to think about why Erenor would have blocked the dragon out—

°And I shall try, although not very hard at all, to care about why, or about why you or he wish to keep your little secrets—such puerile little secrets—but I think I shall fail utterly, and shall end up caring not one little bit.°

The dragon leveled out for a few moments and then banked sharply, again. Even over the rush of wind, the sound of Kethol's retching carried, although, thankfully, the smell did not.

This time, Pirojil could easily make out the buildings of Kelleren's farm—and even the tiny forms of the people out working in the fields. He could imagine that he saw wide eyes and open mouths as the dragon passed overhead, but that was surely just his imagination, as they were far too high for that.

"There." Jason Cullinane's voice carried, although just barely, over the rush of wind. "You can't see it from the ground, not until you're just on top of it, but there's an old road over there."

Hold on. The dragon banked even more steeply than before, and went into a dive. The pressure of the wind against Pirojil's face increased, and covering his eyes with his free hand—to free both hands would have been to trust the harness straps far more than he had any wish to—he tried to look out between two barely parted fingers . . .

But it was no use. The dragon was falling—flying, he hoped—too fast for him to be able to see.

And if you want to take the chance of archers waiting, their arrows' heads dipped in extract of dragonbane, you are welcome to it. Me, I've come more than too close to that of late, and I'm not terribly eager to repeat that.

Pirojil smiled. It wasn't everybody who would admit to what sounded like cowardice. Pirojil had a strong streak of it, himself, although keeping it under control was simply part of the job. Truth to tell, one of the reasons he thought Kethol was not the brightest of men was that Kethol appeared to have little or no fear in his makeup, and would rush in without thinking of the danger.

Facing danger was often—too often—part of the job, but not-thinking wasn't.

Thank you so much for the faint praise.

Well, there was no sign of any archer—or anybody else—along the old road, but it made sense to check it out. All they had to show there, right now, was one dead body, rotting away in an un-marked grave. There wasn't much you could do to make a dead man talk.

It would be convenient to know who had sent the killers, and why. But in a fight for your life, fighting for your life was more than enough to occupy the mind; leaving an enemy alive was something to muse about later.

Are you willing to make a quick drop-off? Pirojil thought.

Yes. As long as it's not Jason. I promised his father I'd look out for him, and his mother.

That wasn't a problem for Pirojil. The last thing he wanted at his side was somebody he had to protect. With any luck the assassins would be long gone, leaving behind nothing that could be used to send Pirojil, Kethol, and Erenor on their trail—but it would be foolish to count on luck.

Particularly when you are using yourself as bait.

Pirojil hadn't wanted to think of it that way, but there was that. If he and the other two could draw attention to themselves, maybe even draw an attack, that would give Ellegon an opportunity to drop Ahira and Toryn in behind the attackers, and surprise them.

Very well, he thought. *Let's make it quick.*

The dragon dropped into a steep dive that left Pirojil's stomach somewhere high in the sky.

Ask and ye shall receive, although not necessarily just what ye ask for. Ellegon came to a bumpy landing at a wide spot in the road. Pirojil didn't bother with the knots that tied him to the rigging on the dragon's back; he drew his belt knife and slashed himself free, then did the same for Kethol, who was too busy with his dry retching to focus on anything. That wasn't his fault, any more than it was Pirojil's fault that women shuddered at his face. It was just the way he was.

But Kethol would stop being airsick shortly.

"What is—what are you—just wait a moment," Jason Cullinane's fingers scrabbled at the knots on his own safety line.

Be still, Jason. The dragon was already rising to his feet, as Pirojil landed heavily on the ground, Erenor and Kethol beside him.

Ellegon took three lumbering steps, then leaped into the air, his wide, leathery wings beating air so hard that the dust from the road would have blinded Pirojil if he had not covered his eyes.

And then the dragon was climbing away, heading east.

Kethol straightened himself, wiping his mouth with the back of his hand. It wasn't cowardice that made his fingers tremble visibly; he could no more control the shaking than he could have the vomiting that left him weak.

"Well," Erenor said, "here we are."

The road had been built of stones, either flat or with a flat cut into one side, long ago. The spaces between the irregular stones should have been overgrown with grasses and other plants, and surely there was enough room for a tree seed to have found purchase.

But, just as on the Prince's Road, either the construction or more likely some spell had prevented that from happening.

Kethol, despite his weakness, already had his longbow strung, an arrow nocked, and his quiver slung hunting-fashion over his shoulder, leaving the sword on his left hip free of obstruction.

He sniffed the air.

"Do you smell something?" Erenor asked. "Besides me, that is—I'm more than due for a bath, and—"

"Shut your mouth," Pirojil said. They were already a target; there was no need to be a babbling target.

"Nothing." Kethol shook his head. "If there's anybody within a solid league of here, I'll be surprised." He sniffed again.

"It must take quite a good nose to be able to smell nothing," Erenor said, smiling. His tone was ever so slightly mocking, but the lack of tension in his shoulders said that he was relieved. And, for that matter, it said that he believed Kethol.

"It isn't that," Kethol said. His brow furrowed. "Follow me." He un-nocked the arrow and set off down the road at a quick jog, Pirojil quickly catching up, Erenor unsurprisingly trailing far behind.

The road to nowhere—although it obviously had gone from somewhere to somewhere else—twisted, snakelike, through the woods, lifeless but surrounded by forest. A thicket of blood-red fundleberries grew right up to the edge of the road; when Kethol dropped from a trot back to a slow walk, Erenor reached out and snagged one.

Pirojil slapped it out of his hand. "We're not here to graze like a bunch of cattle," he said. "Pay attention to what we are supposed to be doing."

"So. It's 'pay attention,' is it?" Erenor rubbed the back of his hand against his chin, and for a moment his smile left him. "It's not my fault I'm not Durine, Master Pirojil," he said. He ran his hand down the front of his tunic until it rested on the hilt of his sword, a vain and empty boast if ever there was one. "I make no pretense—none to you, that is—that I'm anything but what I am, but I do the best that I can," he said. "As you've had occasion to see, more than once, Master Pirojil." Slowly, deliberately, he reached out and picked another berry. "Call me swindler, illusionist, deceiver, and trickster, if you'd like—but you've no cause to call me faithless, sir." He drew himself up straight.

Kethol stood between them. "Would the two of you please just stop this?" His eyes didn't meet Pirojil's; they were too busy scanning the surroundings. "There's a smell of woodsmoke up ahead, and while I'd swear that there's no scent of horse or human, I'd rather not bet my life on my nose, and hope both of you would have more sense."

There was a slight emphasis on *both*.

Pirojil grunted. They were both wrong. He was irritated with Erenor because Erenor was irritating. Too clever by half; too pretty by more than half. And more smug than pretty.

"Let's get going, then," he said. He reached out and grabbed a handful of berries, ignoring the way the thorns bit at his fingers.

He bit into one. It was sweet, and cool, almost meaty in its intensity. And the fundleberry brambles would make it impossible for anything larger than a small mouse to make its way through to the road, at least there.

He felt some of the tension drain from his shoulders. Pirojil trusted Kethol's abilities, certainly, but he trusted thorns even more.

Pirojil shook his head. That shouldn't have made him feel disloyal.

Should it?

Pirojil stood over the remnants of the campfire. It was wet and cold, easily a day dead. Over on the other side of the road, three sets of hoofprints showed that there had been three horses, although he could have worked that out himself from the three places that soft grasses had been laid down for bedding.

Three men, there had been, the second part of the ambush. But they were a day gone, and you could go far in a day, if you were of a mind to.

Pirojil shook his head. "I don't suppose you want to try to trail them."

Kethol shrugged. "We could."

The three of them, on foot, trying to catch up with three men on horses? Three men with most of a day's start, at the very least?

And what if they did find them? To make that worthwhile, they would have to capture at least one, and hope that he was one who knew who had sent them, and why. You didn't put up three against three and expect to be able to capture—just winning would be quite difficult enough.

Yes, they had been sent to kill the baron, and Pirojil was willing to put his body in between the baron and any sword, arrow, bolt, or bullet seeking it, if need be.

Erenor shook his head. "I don't think so," he said.

Pirojil turned quickly, and started to say something, but stopped himself. "Very well," he finally said, his jaw tight. "Why don't you think so?"

"Because I think there's a danger to the baron—if we take him with us, and another to him if we let him go to Biemestren alone."

Pirojil was inclined to dismiss Erenor out of hand, but Kethol cocked his head to one side.

"What do you mean," Kethol said, " 'let him'? The baron does what he will, without any permission from us."

"What I mean is obvious, even if it isn't obvious enough for the two of you," Erenor said, shaking his head. "You two—to you everything is always so simple and straightforward. Either somebody is your friend, your ally, or your enemy. People are either utterly trustworthy, or ready to sell you to the nearest slaver at their next opportunity. Something is either magical, or mundane." He shook his head and made a *tsk*ing sound. "Pirojil, give me a gold mark, please."

"Why?" Pirojil shook his head. "I don't see the point."

"You will," Erenor said, his palm outstretched. "A gold mark, if you please."

"Enough of your games," Pirojil said. "If you have something you want to say, then just say it. If you don't have anything—"

"Could we do with a little less bickering, please? Here." Kethol produced a gold coin and thumb-flipped it to Erenor, who snatched it out of the air quite easily.

"Thank you, friend Kethol," Erenor said. He held his fist in front of Pirojil's face. "I have a coin in my hand here, correct?"

Pirojil frowned. "No, you don't. You switched it to the other hand."

"Really?" Erenor smiled. "Then this," he said, opening his hand to reveal the coin lying flat in his palm, "can't be here, can it?"

Pirojil nodded. "So? It *was* in your hand."

"And it isn't now." Erenor pocketed the coin with his right hand—and why did he ask for a coin if there were coins enough in his pouch to jingle?—and brought both hands, palms up and out, in front of Pirojil. "Correct?"

"I suppose so."

"And now," he said, reaching his left hand past Pirojil's right ear, touching the ear lightly with his fingers and then returning the hand, the gold coin once again in the palm, "it isn't here, either, correct?" This coin, too, went into his pouch with the click of metal on metal.

"Yes, yes, yes, but what of it?" Pirojil was unimpressed. "So you can do magic, and hide and reveal a coin. I've seen you do better illusions, but—"

"But the illusion is the point. It's not the hand that you think holds the coin that you should be worrying about," he said, reaching his hand once again past Pirojil's ear. Again, he touched his fingers against the side of Pirojil's head. "The one thing you can be sure of is that whatever you're being shown isn't being shown for your benefit, but for somebody else's." He withdrew the hand, and this time it was holding a small, pointed knife.

Erenor smiled as he considered the edge of the knife as it gleamed in the bright sunlight. "And while you are trying to spot the coin, an enemy has just slit your throat. Perhaps it wasn't so clever of you to keep your mind fixed on where the coin was, eh?"

Kethol smiled. "He has you there, I think."

Pirojil grunted. "I don't see the point."

"Well, then," Erenor said, reaching out his other hand and producing another knife. This one was—

Pirojil's hand went to his belt sheath of its own volition, and found it empty.

Erenor's superior smile was maddening. "So you see, the real game was for me to take your belt knife from you," he said, offering the knife, properly hilt-first, to Pirojil, who accepted it with bad grace and clumsily resheathed it, not taking his eyes from Erenor's hands for a moment.

He reached out and produced yet another knife, this time apparently from Pirojil's left ear. "Let us agree, shall we, that I could not possibly beat you in a swordfight or a knife fight, but—"

"You'd best be sure of that."

"—But I didn't have to. I've just had three easy chances to open your veins to daylight. Even somebody as clumsy as I could have slipped the blade through your neck," he said, and flipped the three knives end-over-end into the air, adding a third in an impromptu juggling exhibition, giving the lie to his claim that he was clumsy. He threw first one, then a second, and then the third knife high into the air, and by the time he caught the last knife, the other two were gone—Pirojil had been watching the third and didn't see where Erenor had put them.

Erenor held the remaining knife between his thumbs and fore-fingers. "Now, would you care to bet me that I can't make this disappear while you watch?"

"Bet what?"

Erenor pretended to consider the matter. "Oh, perhaps, one of my spell books? The minor dominatives one would be quite handy, and—"

Kethol held up a hand. "You can have another one of your spell books." He looked over at Pirojil. "Well, we're not going to keep them forever, and he's made his point."

Pirojil shook his head. There was something seriously wrong here. It wasn't just coins and knives that were appearing and dis-appearing right in front of his eyes; it was their roles. He and Kethol were supposed to be in charge, not Erenor. And most of the time, that meant that Pirojil was in charge.

To make it worse, Kethol apparently understood what Erenor was getting at, and Pirojil's mind felt all fuzzy, as though he was a dullard who couldn't understand what was right in front of his face.

Pirojil had too much pride to pretend otherwise. "I don't un-derstand what you're getting at," he said.

"The point is, friend Pirojil," Erenor said, "that what informa-tion you're given can determine what you do. If I show you one hand, you look there, and not to the other. If you're watching knives tumbling through the air, you're not watching me sheathing the one in my hand."

"And if we tell the baron that there's evidence of somebody— the assassins—having been here, he'll go after them." Pirojil frowned. "Or even if he listens to reason—as much as Cullinanes ever listen to reason, which isn't a lot—he'll send us after them, when he should be in Biemestren, and we should be at his side." It wouldn't be the attack on himself that would anger Jason Culli-nane so much—but an attack on his mother, and his Uncle Ahira?

Cullinanes acted like they, themselves, were invulnerable, not like people they cared for were.

It took maturity to do the right thing when your fire was up, and even then . . .

He shook his head. It wasn't wrong to be angry, but it was wrong to thoughtlessly act out on that anger, and in his dreams, the screams of people in a burning house would remind him of that until the day he died.

Erenor's smile seemed warm and genuine as he spread his hands wide. "You see? Even I can be wrong—I thought you a slack-wit who wouldn't take the point of my little demonstration."

The flapping of his huge leathery wings sent a covey of grouse flapping noisily, explosively, into the air—Pirojil had been wrong; something was hiding in the brambles—as the dragon came to a bouncy landing on the road. Kethol and Erenor quickly scrambled up his scaly side, Pirojil behind them.

He slipped on the fourth rung of the rope ladder, and would have slammed his crotch down on the previous rung if Jason Cullinane hadn't grabbed his hand.

Which would have been not only painful, but embarrassing.

"There's no reason to hurry," Jason Cullinane said, as he lifted Pirojil up. Pirojil tried to rely as little as he could on the baron's grip to bring him up the rest of the way. It wasn't that the grip was weak—in fact, the younger man's hand was awfully strong for one so smooth—but there was something . . . inappropriate about the likes of Pirojil relying on a noble. It was supposed to be the other way around.

"After all," the baron went on, "you wouldn't have signaled for a landing if there was some problem."

Toryn smirked. "It's one thing to rely on loyalty, and another to rely on competence."

Jason Cullinane eyed him coldly. "I'll rely on both, thank you for the concern." He clapped a hand to Pirojil's shoulder. "Ignore him. Please."

The dragon settled down on all fours and craned its neck to munch on the fundleberries, brambles and all. The thorns didn't seem to affect the dragon a bit.

"So." Jason Cullinane looked to where Erenor and Kethol had already fastened themselves into their positions on the dragon's back. "I take it you didn't find anything interesting."

°Speak for yourself, young one,° the dragon's mental voice said over the crunching sounds as the dragon snaked its neck farther into the brambles. °Or, at least, try some of these before you speak quickly. Yum.°

Pirojil tried very hard not to look at the smug smile on Erenor's face. It would have left him almost unable to prevent himself from using his fist to pound that smile into a bloody red paste. He would, of course, have controlled himself, but it was easier not to look.

"There's nothing of any interest, my Baron," he said, the words tasting of salt and ashes in his mouth. "I don't see any reason we should look any further. If there were other assassins, they are long gone by now."

It was all he could do not to vomit in self-disgust. Yes, it was the right thing to do. Loyalty took precedence over honesty. But lying to the baron made him feel cheap—and disloyal.

The only reason it was tolerable was that Erenor *was* right: the loyal thing to do was to lie to the baron with a straight face, and if that made Pirojil's stomach want to rebel, then so much the worse for his disloyal guts.

The dowager empress—*the* dowager empress, Andrea Cullinane—unbuckled her straps and rose, concern creasing her face.

There were women who aged poorly, and repulsively, like the other dowager empress, and then there were women like Andrea Cullinane, who wore each year with dignity and beauty. Wrinkles at the corners of her eyes and lips spoke of both laughing and worrying, but her jawline was still firm, and her hair, tied back behind her like a young girl would, held only a trace of silver here and there. "Are you unwell, Pirojil?" she asked, rising gracefully, balancing easily on the dragon's wide back, stepping tentatively toward him, each step a movement in a dance. "You look pale."

"He looks as ugly as usual," Toryn said. "He—" Toryn stopped himself at Ahira's glare.

The dowager empress reached out a hand to touch Pirojil's. "Do—are you ill?"

He pulled back. It wasn't fit that somebody like her should touch somebody like him, someone who couldn't even find a way to tell her, or the baron, the truth. He could do that, of course, but Erenor was right. Loyalty was more than simple obedience, just as friendship was more than blindness to faults. And if Pirojil was sickened by the very thought of lying to the dowager empress and Baron Cullinane, well, then, what of that? His life was expendable, after all. What was a little nausea or guilt?

"It's nothing, my lady," he said. "It's just been a long couple of days, and I'm a little tired." And that was true enough.

She frowned. "If you're sure . . . ?"

"Leave it be, Andrea," the dwarf said. "Leave it be."

Ahira's gaze was steady, and his expression stony. Pirojil hadn't fooled the dwarf for a heartbeat.

So why hadn't Ahira exposed him? Or at least questioned him?

°Because he trusts you, you ugly, short-lived fool.° The dragon craned his neck to look back at Pirojil. The huge eyes, as wide as Pirojil's arm was long, stared at him, only the nictating membrane blinking. °As do I, in my way, for that matter.°

His fingers seemed distant and clumsy as he buckled himself in, then sagged back against the straps as the dragon leaped skyward.

°Your loyalty, if not your judgment, that is,° the dragon went on. °All three of you let your own personalities influence how to deal with a problem. Kethol likes solutions that are plain, straightforward, and heroic: dash in, sword in hand, and let the bones and drops of blood fall where they may. Erenor likes it complicated and tricky: lie by telling the truth, or get somebody who likes to tell the truth to lie, and multiply complication upon complication until everything is so knotted that only he can untie it.°

Pirojil didn't want to know what the dragon thought about him. °You? You should know: You like to solve things in ways that punish yourself. If it isn't putting your body between a knife and somebody you protect, hoping to get cut, it's throwing your face in front of a young woman who will recoil in horror, and then flagellating yourself for being ugly. If danger or rejection isn't available, you mope about, as though you are weary of life, until it arrives.°

Pirojil shook his head. Truth to tell, he was tired, at that.

15

A Matter of Succession

Walter Slovotsky found himself almost nodding off as the discussion of financing the railway between New Pittsburgh and Biemestren droned on.

". . . I estimate, roughly, a cost of a thousand marks every league, and that's just for steel and wood. The steel will get cheaper as time goes by, but the wood surely won't." Ranella shuffled through her notes. "There are four major stands of oak and two minor in Adahan, two and three in Cullinane, and six and five in imperial forests that I've had surveyed, and all are reserved. That should see us through the first year, but we'll need to buy more widely, after."

What? You going to tell me that oak doesn't grow on trees?

That wouldn't have gone over well; Other Side humor didn't translate. Either that, or folks around here were a bunch of humorless sourpusses.

Or both, of course.

He looked across Thomen at Beralyn Furnael's pinched face. Which president was it who Will Rogers said looked like he had been nursed with a lemon? Twenty-odd years on This Side and he was starting to lose much of his memory of the Other Side. Senility was only months away.

No, tendays. Not months. They didn't have months here. For months you needed a moon.

He missed the moon.

He let the conversation drone on around him. The details of imperial finances were—thankfully—the business of the baron minister and not—even more thankfully—that of the imperial procter.

". . . and I'm frankly tired of spending as much silver and gold— yes, and pig iron, if the truth be known—on the salaries of these so-called engineers," Arondael went on. And on. "For what we're paying just one of them, I could pay two regimental captains."

"Ah." Young Verahan smiled as he raised a finger in gentle protest. "But could your two regimental captains build a railroad?"

Arondael threw up his hands. "Perhaps not, but perhaps so. It seems little more than putting down a road made of iron instead of stone, and while I wouldn't make any claims for Holtun, in Bieme we've been building roads—and good roads—for some time now."

Verahan was starting to snap out a response when Bren Adahan, signaling him to be quiet, leaned forward. "If necessary, most of the financing can come from Adahan. But if that's so, then I don't see why you shouldn't pay what rates I set for iron and steel when it comes from my barony."

"If you please, slow down a little, for my benefit, if none other, Baron Minister." Tyrnael appeared surprised. "The Crown sets the price."

"Of the iron, and of the steel," Bren Adahan nodded. "But of transporting it? It's not just a matter of what we have to sell, but where it is. When the line is finished, I'll be able to put as many sheep, as many cows, as many swine, as much flax, and as much steel as we can sell right here, in Biemestren, within days of bringing it to market." He shrugged. "But if the building of the lines is paid for *by* me, well then, it seems only proper that the profits from the lines will be paid *to* me."

Beralyn leaned over and whispered something in Thomen's ear. Probably something derogatory about Walter Slovotsky and/or the Cullinanes, although she was probably, as usual, giving Bren Adahan a pass. Their families were hereditary enemies, but by her husband's time, that had become less personal than official—Zherr

Furnael and Vertum Adahan had been, in their way, friends.

Thomen nodded. "I think that would be only fair, but the rail-road lines are not going to be either paid for, or built by—or pro-tected by!—Barony Adahan alone. The question I've put to Parliament is as to *how* the costs will be divided, not whether." He steepled his fingers in front of his face. "I was a great admirer of the Old Emperor. I served him, loyally and faithfully and happily, as baron, and as a judge.

"But I've never thought that loyalty should make me blind to his faults, and one of his faults, as emperor, was to make too many decisions out of improvisation, rather than principle. It's been my wish to be—no: I'm speaking not as the senior baron, but as em-peror, so . . . it has been our wish to be more consistent than our predecessor was.

"It's our intention to use Parliament and our office to set policy, to establish principle and law, so that all may know what to expect, from the peasant who works his fields with dirt between his toes, to—" his gesture encompassed the room "—those here, and to our neighboring countries, as well. Unpredictability certainly has its place, but we prefer to hire unpredictability," he said, with a smile at Walter, "rather than exercise it ourself."

Tyrnael tapped his aide on the arm, and the slim young man next to him left the room quickly.

Walter Slovotsky wasn't sure why, but he didn't like that at all.

"If I may." Tyrnael leaned forward, his eyes not leaving the emperor's. "Your point, my Emperor, is most well-taken," he said. "It's one that's been of concern to me for many years, particularly during the reign of the Old Emperor—who was my friend, and whom I greatly respected."

Walter Slovotsky didn't recollect hearing about a whole lot of warmth between the two, but he hadn't around for much of it, so perhaps his skepticism was unwarranted.

In a fucking pig's fucking eye.

Tyrnael stood, leaning on the table in front of him with both hands. "I'm . . . worried about some of the discussion we've had here today," he said. "The absence of Baron Cullinane has been noted, but yet no one has advocated taking away his title, his lands, his treasure, or his home because of it." He nodded judiciously, agreeing with himself. "That is entirely as it should be. Should it not? Or shall we sit and discuss who shall take on Barony Cullinane, as well?"

"Of course not." Niphael grunted. "That seems obvious; I'm sure the baron has some less than obvious point he wishes to make."

Tyrnael walked over to where General Treseen sat, and put a hand on the general's shoulder. "Indeed. But—with permission of the emperor and this Parliament—let me make it in my own way. I only ask for a few moments' indulgence." He patted Treseen's shoulder. "We do not believe that guilt flows from person to person, do we?

"Oh," he went on, making it clear that the question was entirely rhetorical, "it can, of course, in whispered conspiracies, in dark corners, where promises and gold can be exchanged.

"But not simply by association or by blood." Again, he patted Treseen's shoulder. "The good general, here, was governor of Keranahan while the Baroness Elanee not only thought treason, but plotted it. He saw her almost daily—yet nobody here has suggested, and nobody should suggest, that he is a disloyal governor." He removed his hand from Treseen's shoulder and returned to his seat. "That is as it should be." He looked from face to face. "There are those—I have heard them—who speak of Governor Treseen with less than the respect he is due, and while I can disagree, surely they have as much right to their opinions as I do to mine.

"But the principle is what is important."

"Yes, yes, yes," Claressen said, "we all believe in principle, Baron Tyrnael, and even if that were not the case, not one here would admit otherwise," he said, with a booming laugh, "and—while I think it is easy to criticize Treseen for missing a plot—governing a barony is not an easy thing, and relieving a governor is something that should be done only with careful deliberation."

"Exactly." Treseen slammed his fist down on the table with a loud bang. "Let me ask you this: if that is so for a governor, how can it not be so for the rightful and proper heir to the barony of Keranahan?"

The uncharacteristic violence of the pounding on the table must have been a signal, Walter Slovotsky decided.

Quite quietly, with Tyrnael's aide at one side and a soldier in Keranahan livery at his other side, a slender, well-dressed young man in his late twenties walked quickly but gracefully into the room, and took up a position just inside the doorway.

He was too pretty, Walter Slovotsky decided, although there was a ruggedness in the jaw and in the gymnast's shoulders. The eyes were blue, their chilliness softened by the friendliness of the full mouth above the well-trimmed beard.

He was familiar, of course. Walter Slovotsky had been careful to check out the Tyrnaelian captain that Bren Adahan had given a pass to, and the gifts that the captain and his servants had brought.

This was one of the servants. *And some damn fool has been living the easy life among nobility far too long because he didn't think to question that a wide-shouldered man carrying a captain's bags was his servant.*

Yes, he could make excuses—the nobleman's hair had been rough-cut, and his beard untrimmed—but excuses didn't count, except by the ton, and even then they were cheap.

And there was something familiar about the face. The young nobleman looked sort of like—

Shit.

It was Elanee's son. Miron.

Shitshitshitshitshitshitshitshitshitshitshitshitshit.

Walter Slovotsky looked at Tyrnael, who was carefully not meeting his eyes.

"My name," he said, "as some of you know, is Miron. I am, by custom and law, heir to Barony Keranahan. I have been in hiding, these many tendays, as people of whom I do not pretend to know anything have accused me of conspiring with my mother to do horrible, treasonous things.

"I have come here today to ask that those who would accuse me be brought before this Parliament, so that I can swear, on my sword, that all that I have been accused of is untrue. I loved my mother, as a son should, but I am here today to say that she loved me enough to keep me uninvolved in anything wrong, anything traitorous she was involved in.

"There is no man alive, or dead, who could swear otherwise. As to my mother . . . well, as she lies dead in her grave, may I say— and not be thought disloyal?—that she has been punished enough?" He raised a palm. "But that is not why I am here. I have come here today to claim my barony, my inheritance, to be given the title I am due and to assume the responsibilities that are mine by birthright."

He—overly dramatically, Walter Slovotsky thought—crossed his arms over his chest. "Or if that's not to be, surely, this Parliament will want to know the reason why."

Walter Slovotsky looked over at Tyrnael.

I think we've just been suckered, he thought. *By an expert.* He would have liked to applaud that expertise with a twenty-one-gun salute, but he doubted he could get Tyrnael and Miron to stand in front of the guns.

Shit.

The silence was deafening as Walter Slovotsky rose to his feet. "Thom—Emperor. I think we ought to have a recess," he said.

When you don't know what else to do, stall, he thought.

And I'd probably better add that to Slovotsky's Laws.

Thomen nodded. "It's been a long day, and looks to be a longer evening." He looked over at Miron. "Lord Miron," he said, "we will have much to discuss, I think. Welcome to Biemestren."

———————

Aiea smiled at him over her glass of wine. "You always take this sort of thing too seriously, Walter," she said.

Her hair, long and honey-brown, was tied in what Walter insisted on thinking of as a Psyche knot—although he didn't know where he had picked up the name—leaving her neck bare. For some reason, he found the fine hairs at the base of her neck remarkably erotic.

I know the reason, Walter Slovotsky decided. *I'm a guy.*

The cut of her gown—low in front, thigh-high on the side—had what he thought of as a French flavor, in contrast to the barely perceptible epicanthic folds of her eyes.

She laughed, lightly, the sound of silver bells. "And you should know, by now, not to let that show on your face," she said, her voice low, her breath warm in his ear.

Aiea's expression sobered. "What concerns me is that we haven't seen any sign or had any word of my baby brother." That Jason was Karl and Andrea's child by birth while Aiea had been adopted didn't seem to have affected the relationship that the two of them had. "I'm starting to get worried about him. I'm not surprised that he's late, but . . . I'm worried."

"I'm not," he said, lying.

There was no point in worrying her. He carefully didn't look over at the two empty seats next to her, where Bren Adahan and Kirah were supposed to be. Bren Adahan had taken a patrol out on the road to Cullinane, and while that couldn't be kept secret very long, the story that he and his new wife were having dinner in their rooms might hold for a while.

If Aiea knew that, and knew that Walter hadn't stopped him—and Bren would, they both knew, defer to him on this sort of thing—she would know that he was concerned, as well.

Her smile broadened. "Did you know that your eyes have trouble meeting mine when you lie?" she asked.

He matched her own smile. "No, I wasn't aware of that." He

glanced over to where Miron was holding forth at the Tyrnael table, across the room. He was regaling half a dozen entranced faces with some no doubt entertaining story.

Probably something about the stupid Polack who had let him into the keep.

She drew a slim finger up his thigh. "Well, they don't, but I thought it was worth a try, you being so easy to put something over on today." With her free hand, she picked up a sweetmeat from the table and fed it to him. Too much honey, but not bad at all. "But at least you're not letting it show," she said.

"Well, it sounds like I've done something right."

"Well," she said, her finger still high on his thigh, "right about here—on the inside of my leg, not the outside like you like to carry yours—I've got a small, sharp knife." She brought her hands up to the table. "Would you like me to solve your little problem for you?"

She probably wouldn't—she probably would have more sense—but there were times when she was anything but sensible, so he shook his head. "No."

"And why not?"

"Because that would make it worse. Worse for you, worse for me, worse for your brother, and worse for Thomen." Better for Tyrnael, of course—if Miron was murdered while here, while under the protection of the Crown, it wouldn't affect him adversely. By weakening Thomen, in fact . . .

Damn. Even an accident would militate to Tyrnael's advantage. Nobody would believe that it hadn't been arranged by somebody close to the emperor, or at least close to Walter Slovotsky.

How long had Tyrnael had Miron under wraps? Long enough to make some sort of deal, some sort of arrangement with him. As Holtun/Biemish hard feelings went, there was no particular vendetta going on between the baronies.

Whatever the result of his machinations, Tyrnael had achieved at least one success: he had established himself as a power in his own right, beyond the rest of the barons, and that would augment his power regardless of how Miron's claim on the Keranahan throne worked out.

And, perhaps, regardless of whether or not Miron marrying Tyrnael's eldest available daughter was part of the deal.

Shit.

"I should have lined things up," he said. "He was in on his mother's plans—that's why she sent him after Kethol, Pirojil, Durine, and Leria."

Aiea made a face. "He could have been kept in the dark."

"You don't believe that, do you?"

"No. But others might. Barons who've had more than a few thoughts themselves about how their noble rumps should grace the throne won't want to see one of their own convicted on anything but solid evidence of treason."

Governor Claressen rose from his chair and more staggered than walked over. He never drank much wine, but servitors kept a tankard of beer full for him with much effort, and between trips to the garderobe he had managed to put away a gallon or so, and seemed to be waddling his way on another such trip.

"Good evening to you, Imperial Proctor," he said, his words slurring, his voice a booming basso. "Or is it such a good evening for you, now?"

"I've had better," he said.

" 'I've had better,' he says. 'I've had better.' I like that." Claressen threw back his head and laughed. "I suspect you have, at that." He clapped a hand to Slovotsky's shoulder. "I suspect you have, at that," he repeated.

He bent over and whispered, "Do you think, perhaps, that an imperial proctor can afford to have such a fool made of him?"

He staggered off without waiting for an answer. He hadn't sounded drunk at all when he had whispered.

———

Walter Slovotsky caught up with Leria outside the Great Hall. "I think we'd best talk, Lady," he said.

The decurion running her guard detachment—which was up to five now, although Walter Slovotsky was becoming increasingly sure that any threat to Leria was a sideshow—gestured him toward a door that led out, and down a set of outside stairs to the courtyard below.

The tents and pavilions of the guests were an ocean—well, more of a pond, really—of noise and light to their right; he led her off to the left, into where a large maple shaded them from the flickering lights of the wall-mounted torches.

But it wasn't completely dark; he could read the accusation in her eyes. "You said—"

"Everybody said," he said. *And if I'd had the brains that Stash and Emma's baby boy is supposed to, that alone would have been enough of a warning.* "If I'd needed to, if I'd thought I needed to, we could have had Treseen round up enough of his mother's servants. Nobles talk too much in front of the servants—some of them would have heard something." Anything that they could use against him.

"But I saw him kill—"

Slovotsky raised a hand. "You saw Miron have a farmer killed in Adahan, and he'll say that he was trying to locate you—for your own safety, of course—and that he feared that the farmer meant you harm." Besides, the barons weren't going to turn on one of their own for killing a commoner. It wasn't so long ago that it wasn't against the law for anybody who was allowed to call himself "lord" or better to kill anybody who wasn't, after all.

"The problem is that he's the heir presumptive," Walter Slovotsky said. "He was the acknowledged son of the baron, and—"

"No," she said. "Not the acknowledged son. *An* acknowledged son. The baron had two sons, one of them by Becka, his first wife—Miron was the other one, by Elanee."

"Yes, but Forinel's dead, and—"

"No, but—" She sighed. "No, I think I would know. I loved him, and he loved me, you know. Elanee charmed him into going out into the world to prove himself."

Walter Slovotsky had not had direct experience of the baroness's charms, but he had had some discussion of it with Kethol, Pirojil, and Erenor. It wasn't just that she was a lovely woman—she had some raw magical abilities that expressed themselves sexually. Erenor had spotted them, although it sounded like she had given both Kethol and Pirojil embarrassingly serious woodies, as well as them all a much worse kind of hard time.

She smiled fondly. "Forinel was, well, he wanted to be something in his own right, not just the baron's son and heir."

"You've never heard anything from him?"

She shook her head. "He—he promised he'd return to me." Her hand started to move toward her throat, then stopped.

"He gave you a keepsake." Walter Slovotsky tried to keep all hope out of his voice. It was a long shot anyway, but . . .

"Yes. His ring. The one with his father's crest carved into it."

Walter Slovotsky nodded.

Well, as one of Slovotsky's Laws says, "If you're drowning and somebody throws you an anchor, grab it." What he needed was something like—

Good evening, Walter, sounded in his mind, distantly.

Well, it's about damn time.

Yes, everyone is well, thank you for asking. I just wanted to be—

Shh. Don't land here.

With all the strangers around, it was too dangerous, particularly now. It was unlikely that whatever Tyrnael had going on included maneuvering an attack on Ellegon—but it wasn't impossible.

He felt paranoid, but even paranoids had enemies.

Meet me at the crossroads off the Prince's Road, just south of the bridge. Midnight.

I assume there will be some explanation, then?

Yeah.

°That would be nice.°

Walter Slovotsky looked for a shadow passing over the stars above, but with—

°You've got this new invention blocking your line of sight. They call it a 'wall'° Ellegon's mental voice was fainter and fainter.

°Later . . . °

Go.

"Lady," he said, "go put on some riding clothes, and wait for me in your rooms. We're going to quietly ditch your guard, sneak out of the castle, and go for a ride." Horses wouldn't be a problem; he could pick up some at the barracks in Biemestren. Tipping his hand, on the other hand, would be a problem. Sneaking out made more sense, and never mind that sneaking out came more naturally to Walter Slovotsky than walking out the front door would have.

She shook her head. "I don't understand. There are more patrols—"

"Don't worry about the patrols." It was good to feel confident of something, for a change.

And it was a change.

16

"I'm Not a Bad Man..."

I don't like it at all," Pirojil said, quietly. "Meeting outside of town?" He sucked in air through his teeth. "Why can't the baron just walk up to the front gates? It doesn't make sense."

"Not to me, either." Kethol shook his head. Yes, they were late for Parliament, but surely that wouldn't put the baron in danger of arrest when he showed up at the castle gates?

Would it?

"If somebody tries to arrest him, do we let them?" he asked.

"I don't know." Pirojil spat. "I'm not of a mind to let a bunch of imperials arrest the baron, not if there's another choice. Not without orders." He was silent for a long moment, then raised his head and beckoned to Erenor, who obediently trotted over.

"Yes, Master Pirojil? What is it that this unworthy wretch, deserving of your condescension and scorn, can do to help you?" The mockery was only in the words: his tone and manner seemed sincerely humble.

"Shut your mouth and listen," Pirojil explained.

"I live but to obey."

The temptation to slap Erenor, his hand moving back and forth until Erenor's face was spread across the landscape, was almost irresistible, but Kethol had always been able to resist the almost irresistible. After all, he had kept his hands to himself around Leria . . . except, perhaps, for that one time, that one night, that probably was just a dream.

In the dim light provided by the twinkling stars and the blue-and-green pulsating Faerie lights, Kethol could more hear than see Pirojil smile. "Does sarcasm spoil?"

"Not that I am aware of, Master Pirojil, although this unworthy one knows so little and is so totally worthless that it—"

"Then perhaps you can save it for later? We wouldn't want to have you run out, of course."

Kethol would have tried to figure out what was going on between the two of them, but it probably didn't matter, and both of them seemed to have quicker wits than he did, about most things. Not gambling, or woodcraft, or bowmanship, or fighting—Pirojil might be a touch better defensively than Kethol was, but Kethol was better on the offense, at least most of the time—but in everything else, he felt like he had been born with a few too few wits when he was around Pirojil, and more than a few around Erenor.

"As you wish, Pirojil," Erenor said. "What is it that you want, then, if it's not to abuse me? Are there any chamberpots hidden about that need emptying? Horses that require currying? Heavy bags that need to be transported from one place to another, and then back again?"

"No." Why Pirojil was putting up with this was something that Kethol would have to ask him about later. "It's a question of magic. How much preparation would you need in order to be able to make the baron invisible? How much time?"

Erenor laughed. "Ah. I see where the sudden lack of disrespect comes from." He played with his beard with the tips of his fingers and thought about—or, knowing Erenor, pretended to think about—the question.

"It depends on what you want. True invisibility is rather difficult, and making it so that the subject can still see is even more so. The classical approach is to bend light around the subject, and then modify the behavior of the spell so that light comes in at the eyes. That takes three fairly difficult spells, working together. I've done all the spells before, but I don't think I could keep all three in my head at the same time.

"There's a simpler approach, that makes the eye of the viewer tend to go by the subject, but that won't work on somebody who has already seen the subject until he moves, and I don't know if I can work the dominatives all at once, although—"

"Could you possibly, just this once, answer a simple question? If there are troops being set out to arrest the baron, can you make him invisible quickly enough so that he can get away in the dark?"

"Well, that's another matter entirely." Erenor had dropped the false humility, and now the pedantic tone of security had gone, as well. "Quite easy, for that sort of purpose. All I'll do is make his cloak more light absorbent. A quick distraction, and he can wrap it about himself as he runs—darkness in the darkness is invisible enough, particularly if I add some distraction in another direction." He considered it for a moment. "The problem, I think, would be persuading the baron to run."

Yes, that might well be a problem. But it was worth knowing what their choices were. Not that Kethol's preferences would likely have much to do with what happened. As usual.

Ellegon, his legs tucked underneath him, looking like one of those ridiculously oversized snakes that had slipped out of Faerie not all that long ago, had slithered down the riverbank and into the river, and hidden himself mostly under water. Only the top of his head and his eyes showed, and when the inner membranes were shut, he looked like a not particularly large rock sticking up out of the water.

Kethol wasn't sure why Ellegon had done it that way. Yes, the dragon probably wanted to stay out of sight while remaining nearby, but at night, it would probably have made more sense for the dragon to be circling high overhead, invisible except as an occasional shadow against the stars . . .

Haven't you ever gotten tired? sounded in his head. *I certainly have.*

. . . and it would have been nicer if Kethol could have had some privacy in his own head.

He looked at the road, as it twisted up toward where the castle was hidden by the tree-covered ridge.

Leria was there. He had been about to see her; he had been sure of that. But not now—they hadn't been told to stay out of town in order to be put back in charge of her guard detail.

Which was just as well. Just looking at her made him hurt. She was lovely and gentle and . . . and a noble lady.

. . . and he was just an ordinary soldier—in rank, if not necessarily in abilities—and a better than ordinary woodsman, and he knew that if he remembered it accurately, their fleeing from Miron and his companions had been a scary time, and not the best time in his life simply because he had rarely been more than a few quick steps from her side.

If nothing else, if he had fouled things up, or if he had been unlucky, she could have been hurt, or worse.

So it hadn't been as good as he remembered it.

And remembering her, in the doorway, wearing—

No. He wouldn't remember that, not with the dragon peeking at his every thought.

You know, while I'm sure that you were quite . . . adequate, I doubt that you invented anything new. Although—no, Kethol. Be still and listen to me. I don't really like peeking into minds, and most of the time I just sort of let the noise wash over me. You have the bad habit of thinking about me, and that attracts my attention. The dragon snorted, sending bubbles and steam up from the river. *So try real hard not to think about me, and I'll try real hard not to tell you that again, as that will surely make you think about me again, which will . . . *

Kethol looked over to where the dowager empress was in quiet conversation with Ahira. Ahira would understand how Kethol felt. The dwarf was in love with Andrea Cullinane—anybody could see it—and she was just as far out of his reach as Leria was out of Kethol's.

The very idea was laughable, but Kethol wasn't laughing, either at the dwarf or at him—

There was a triple hoot that sounded vaguely like a hairy owl, and then another.

That made Kethol smile.

Toryn didn't quite have the sound right—it took some practice—but he was trying, and it was likely that anybody who could be sure enough that that wasn't the sound of a hairy owl probably knew that hairy owls always hooted twice, not three times.

Hoofbeats sounded in the distance. At least two horses, possibly three.

"Everybody," Pirojil said, quietly, "off the road." Like Kethol, he already had his sword in his right hand, a pistol in his left.

°Your caution is commendable, but unnecessary, in this case.° The dragon's head rose out of the water. °It's Walter Slovotsky and another.°

Well, good. Kethol put his flintlock pistol to half-cock and stuck it back in his belt before he resheathed his sword. He would have thought that Walter Slovotsky was self-confident enough to brave the dark by himself, but on horseback, it was—

Leria.

"Good evening," Walter Slovotsky said. "Would somebody give us a hand?" His horse shied and pawed at the ground as though it was about to bolt, and Leria's wasn't much better.

His fingers trembled as he grabbed at her horse's reins, settling it down with firm hands and soft words.

It snorted and pawed, but settled down, and he was glad that it was Pirojil who helped her down to the road.

"You folks set up a campsite near here?" Slovotsky asked.

"Why would we want to do that, Walter?" the dowager empress asked, letting the irritation show in her voice. She must have been very tired, or upset about something that was none of Kethol's concern, as she usually had more control than that.

"Because we need to talk, and I'd just as soon not stand out on a windy road in the middle of the night," Slovotsky said.

"There's a wartime campsite just the other side of the river," Kethol said. "It was a mustering ground during the war for baronial troops."

Pirojil grunted. "Doubt it's being used right now with all the baronials in soft beds in the city."

Erenor leaned close and whispered in Kethol's ear, "Some of them even alone."

"Sounds good."

Walter Slovotsky liked to pace while he thought, and Pirojil didn't like the way he kept pacing. "Well, we're up against it," he said. "Tyrnael's maneuvered everything quite neatly. I'm not sure what deal he has with Miron, but—"

"It doesn't matter what deal he has," Jason Cullinane said, his jaw tight.

Pirojil warmed his hands in front of the fire. It wasn't cold enough that he couldn't have gotten by with just his cloak, but there was something about a fire that warmed you more inside than outside.

In the flickering firelight, Jason Cullinane's sweaty face was grim and stony. "I'm of suitable rank, I think, to deal with him."

His mother rolled her eyes. "Which would, I'm sure, irritate Miron—assuming, of course, that you could beat him in a fair fight—"

"I can. I've—"

"—never seen him fight, and you don't have the slightest idea," Ahira said. "So stop bragging and start thinking. You can't go around challenging every lord or baron who gets in your way." The dwarf picked up a stick and poked at the fire as he talked. "There's at least two involved. The other barons wouldn't put up with it, particularly since you can't prove any offense. What happens if you and Niphael disagree on a matter of, oh, taxation or quartering? Does he have to worry about you calling him out?"

"This isn't the same thing at all," the baron said. He took a pull from the waterskin. "Miron tried to have me assassinated."

Toryn wagged a finger at him. "Oh, I don't think you should be making accusations without proof," he said. "Particularly not against a fellow baron."

"He *isn't* the baron."

Toryn's smile was wicked in the firelight. "I wasn't talking about Miron. Tyrnael is in a much better situation to recruit and hire soldiers." He shook his head. "I wouldn't even care to wager that it's him. You Cullinanes have made enemies far and wide, and I've no doubt that the Slavers Guild would still like to see your head, and if it weren't attached to your body anymore, why, that would be all the better."

Pirojil eyed him coldly. The baron said that Toryn was trustworthy, but the baron was as capable as anybody else of being wrong.

—But no, if Toryn had intended to kill Jason Cullinane, he surely could have done so by now. A simple knife in the back in the night and he could be far gone by morning.

"Do you think it's a coincidence that this happened just in time to be to Miron's advantage?"

"No." Toryn shook his head. "I don't believe in coincidences. But unless you're prepared to prove it—"

"We could put them in front of Ellegon," the baron said.

Once. Maybe.

Walter Slovotsky shook his head. "I think I'd better work up a long lecture for you that we'll call Politics 101."

"Don't you patronize me, Uncle Walter—"

"Then don't you act like a child, Jase. Every one of the barons has had thoughts and done things that they wouldn't want the emperor—or Ellegon—to know about. You threaten to start using Ellegon as some sort of fire-breathing lie detector on a regular basis for them—the way your dad used to do to keep Guild spies out of our raiding teams—and you're going to stimulate conspiracy and rebellion, not put an end to it." He shook his head. "Bad idea. If you can imply that you suspect Tyrnael, you might get him to swear on his sword, and if he's lying that ought to make him nervous about the idea of having to actually use it some day . . ." He shook his head. "But you can't. Ellegon?" He addressed the dragon, as though Ellegon was right in front of him, although the dragon was still down at the river.

I agree. If I start doing that sort of thing, I'd best not make any appearance in Holtun-Bieme at all. Any baron who has ever—

"—committed a thoughtcrime," the dowager empress said, "is going to turn that into a real crime."

Slovotsky had started to bristle at the interruption, but instead smiled and touched a knuckle to his forehead. "She's still pretty and she's still bright."

"And," she said, her voice too light, "you are married to my daughter, so treat me with some respect."

"Always, Andrea. Always." For a moment, the mask dropped, and Walter Slovotsky seemed serious and older than his years, rather than younger. "As long as you don't mind if the respect is mixed with a little lust."

Pirojil had never heard the dowager empress actually giggle before. Laugh, certainly. But giggle?

She definitely giggled. "I'm sure you say that to all the dowager empresses—well, come to think of it, I'm not sure you'd say that to Beralyn."

Ahira grunted. "If you two could save the flirting for later, I'd appreciate it. I'd rather pay attention to the issue at hand: what do we do?"

Walter Slovotsky spread his hands. "Two obvious possibilities:

one, we accept defeat. It wouldn't be the end of the world or even the end of the empire if Elanee's son ends up getting the barony, or if Tyrnael manages to put one over on not only the emperor's proctor—that would be me—and his baron minister . . .

"But it would be a start in that direction. Thomen doesn't even have a wife and son, and—"

"—which means that if he dies, the succession is in doubt, Tyrnael has the best claim—assuming that the Biemish barons are senior—although there's a few Euar'den nobles around. There's some Furnael cousins around the capital and in your barony."

"The best thing," Ahira said slowly, carefully, "might, in that sort of situation, be for Jason to take the crown."

Slovotsky spat into the fire, a gobbet of spittle that sizzled and died in the coals. "Don't even think that, much less say that out loud." He fingered the leather thong about his neck. "Which brings me to the other idea. Back during the raiding years, Karl and I started wearing these amulets—supposedly makes it difficult-to-impossible for locations spells to work." He looked to Erenor.

"Yes, I've seen it." Erenor nodded. "It's a fairly simple set of spells—it just keeps changing, while magically part of you. It may not be impossible to solve the pattern and eliminate the confusion—it's usually foolish to claim something is impossible—but I've never heard of it being done."

Jason Cullinane's brow furrowed. "What would you know of such things?" He looked from Walter Slovotsky to Erenor, and then back again. "And why would you be asking him, instead of, say, Mother?"

"Now, now, now." Walter Slovotsky held up a hand. "Well, kiddo, there's a few things that you haven't been told. Need to know, and all that, and—"

Ahira seized the young baron's hand with his massive one. "I've known Walter since long before you were born, Jason, and there's never been any point in getting upset with him being sneaky."

"Hey, it's what his imperial emperorness pays me for, no?" Slovotsky waited until the baron settled down. "Now, would an ancestral ring that Forinel used to wear constantly be enough for a location spell?"

Erenor nodded. "Absolutely. It's one of the reasons family heirlooms are so closely guarded. You can do all sorts of interesting things to somebody with something so meaningful to him. With some limitations, it's better than hair, or nail clippings, and almost as good as blood. Far better than stools."

Pirojil fondled the ring on his hand, the signet stone, as always, turned inward. That was true enough, and it would probably be best if he destroyed the ring. Smash the stone to powder; melt the gold in a hot fire and throw it into a river, or the Cirric, or just bring it to a goldsmith and have him melt it down with some gold coins, diluting it until it was just metal, and not the ring Pirojil had worn.

Pirojil should have seen it coming. Of course—that's what the three of them were for.

"Well, then," Slovotsky said, "that's what we'll do." He gestured to Leria. "Give the ring here."

"But—"

"You're the one who said she is sure he's alive. Let's give Erenor the ring, let him locate Forinel, and then he and Pirojil and Kethol and Ellegon go pick him up." He looked over at Andrea and Baron Cullinane. "We can stall things here for a while, and if he's alive, and can be found, that'll give Tyrnael a setback, put Miron out in the cold, and—"

"And help secure Thomen on the throne while improving our position," Jason Cullinane said. He nodded. "Better than my idea."

"Well, it does have its virtues," Erenor said as he stood. "It's a brilliant idea, Walter Slovotsky. With the proper spells, an heir's ring should be able to lead somebody toward Lord Forinel, assuming that he's not tried to protect himself against such things—"

"Why would he?" Jason Cullinane asked. Pirojil didn't know whether he was more irritated with the baron for interrupting or with Erenor for not having answered the obvious question without it having to be asked.

Or maybe he was just irritated. It was obvious who was going to have to go haring off after Forinel.

Which was, all in all, reasonable.

The Katharhd, though. A tough land to work. Not tamed, like the Middle Lands were—too many magical creatures about, even before the Breach.

Forinel, so Pirojil had been told, had gone off to the Katharhd to make a name for himself, and while there were places Pirojil would have been less eager to go chasing around in . . .

That was the thing to do when you were up to your chin in a sewer: be glad the sewage wasn't up to your nose. The Katharhd would be bad, but there were worse possibilities. Pandathaway, for a variety of reasons, came instantly to mind, followed closely by Faerie and preceded by Ther—by another country he had left a long time ago, riding away at night to the sounds of fire and screams.

So: the Katharhd. So be it.

At least it wasn't Therranj.

"Wait." Erenor raised a palm. "Leave that for a moment. I don't know that he is, and I don't know that he isn't. But, even if he is not protected, there are still two problems."

Walter Slovotsky snorted. "Wizards and lawyers can never make anything simple. Well, what are they?"

"The first one is the lovely Lady Leria," Erenor said, bowing in her direction in a way that would have been overtheatrical to the point of mockery if anybody else had done it. Pirojil ignored the way Kethol glared at Erenor, and wasn't at all surprised to see that Kethol's hand had a knuckle-whitening grip on the hilt of his sword. Kethol probably didn't even know he was doing it.

"What is the problem?" Walter Slovotsky asked. "She doesn't seem to be a problem to me." His grin was disarming. "She's bright, brave, and remarkably decorative, as well, if you ask me."

Nobody had asked him. Particularly Kethol, whose grip on his sword was even tighter. Pirojil reached out and tapped him on the hand. "Just take it easy," he whispered, low enough that nobody else should have been able to hear it.

Erenor ignored the byplay. "It's the conditions. She's been holding it as a keepsake from Forinel, and unless I miss my guess, he was wearing it in," Erenor paused, "intimate moments with her."

In the firelight, Pirojil couldn't see the redness in her cheeks that he was sure was there.

"All of which makes it as much part of her as part of him, if not more so," Erenor went on. Off to the west, the sky was dark, save for a solitary Faerie light, dashing into and out of the approaching cloudbank, as though it was playing with invisible friends. "If," Erenor said, "if I could put a location spell on it, the ring could guide one toward Forinel—or to where he's buried, most likely—until it was nearer him than her, and then," he said with a shrug, "all it would do is point back to her."

"What do you mean, 'if '?" Jason Cullinane had contained himself as long as he could. Pirojil could have waited. Erenor would have gotten around to it sooner or later, if only for the joy of hearing himself speak.

"*I* can't do those spells." Erenor spread his hands in a gesture of helplessness. "I flatter myself that I'm a better than average illusionist . . ." he waited, probably for somebody to offer a word of praise.

Erenor shrugged apologetically. "I'm not a bad man; I'm just not a very good wizard."

Pirojil shook his head. "You might have mentioned that right away," he said.

"There's the obvious solution," Andrea Cullinane said as she rose. She walked around the fire to where Leria sat and held out her hand. "The ring, if you please."

"But . . ."

"Give me the ring," she said.

Erenor's mouth twitched. "Begging your pardon, Lady, but while I may not be much of a wizard, I can see flames just fine. You may have had some magical fire burning within you, although if you did it was likely little more than a spark, but the spark's long since gone out."

She extended her right hand, her fingers cupped and pointing toward him. "There was a time, Erenor, when I could have reached out and struck you blind, deaf, impotent, and lame with one syllable. I . . . was something of a wizard, once, and for some time."

Pirojil knew that, and he knew how and why she had given up her magic, and if he had needed more reason for loyalty to Andrea Cullinane, he could have looked to that.

But he didn't, of course. "Shut your mouth, Erenor," he said, rising. "You'll speak to her with respect on your tongue, or you'll have no tongue in your mouth."

Erenor turned back to him, his usual smile firmly in place. "I was perfectly respectful, Pirojil. But I was truthful. This dowager empress—just like the other—can no more work a spell than you can."

"But she was a wizard, and when she was a wizard she had an apprentice," Walter Slovotsky said.

Andrea Cullinane nodded. "He's been a journeyman, working his way through to mastery for a long time now. He should be able to work the spell. His name is Henrad."

17

✠ Henrad

Andrea Cullinane took Walter's confidence that he could get
her inside on faith.

This time it made sense.

Oh, she would have taken his word that he could *do* it, but
under other circumstances she wouldn't have taken his word that
it was the *right* thing to do. Too often, in her opinion, he liked
things complicated for their own sake. No wonder he and Erenor
seemed to get on so well.

That tendency probably explained Walter's affair with Aiea
while he was still married to Kirah.

—and never mind their own encounter on the way to Ehvenor.
She kept her grin to herself. There was something about Walter on
a slowly rocking boat . . .

But that was the thing about Walter Slovotsky: he was full of
boast and brag, but he could be counted on, almost all the time, to
do what it was that he actually had promised to do—if you could
correctly parse what he *said* he would do.

His word was good; it was just, well, complicated.

It would have been simpler now, if she would have joined the
others walking up to the main gate, but that would have the draw-
back of everybody in the castle prematurely knowing she was there.

Walter's style was to prefer it complicated, but he was right.
Once she had made arrangements with Henrad, she could turn her
attention to politics. The politics were important, and she should

still have some influence here and there, from her days as empress, and then as dowager empress and mother of the heir.

But the sooner that Kethol, Pirojil, Erenor—and Leria; Erenor was right that she had to go along—were on their way, the better. She didn't have much hope that they would actually turn up Forinel—the late Elanee would have had no compunction in having him killed, after all—but perhaps the threat hanging over the heads of Tyrnael and Miron could be turned to some immediate political use.

Politics.

Fooey.

She took a deep breath. Walter Slovotsky liked juggling half a dozen things—and women—in his mind, but Andrea Cullinane had always preferred to keep things simple, to concentrate on one problem at a time.

"This one is pretty easy," Walter had said. "It's why magicians— Other Side magicians, not real wizards—always have pretty assistants in scanty outfits. While the girl bends over to flash a little cleavage, it's no problem at all for the guy in the black suit to slip a pigeon into his pocket, or a coin out of it."

He slapped Jason on the back, perhaps with more force than was absolutely necessary. "For purposes of this discussion, Baron Cullinane, you're the pretty girl assistant, Ellegon is the magician, and Andrea's the pigeon." His all-is-well-with-any-world-clever- enough-to-hold-Walter-Slovotsky smile was firmly intact. "And me? You can think of me as the stage manager." He clapped his hands together, twice. "All right everybody: places please."

The chill night air whipped her hair behind her as Ellegon circled high above the castle, his massive wings beating more quickly but much more shallowly than usual, which made for a quieter, smoother ride, and probably explained why Kethol wasn't making gagging sounds from behind her, which no doubt pleased Erenor and Ahira and Pirojil to no end.

Poor dear.

He wasn't meant to fly, and if everything went right, he would be doing a lot of it in the near future, having to protect that Leria girl at the same time.

Up here, everything below seemed remote and unimportant, like a doll house with impossibly finely crafted features. It was easy not to care about the destinies of those tiny, ant-sized people far below.

°The morality of altitude.°

Karl used to talk about that.

°I know.°

She closed her eyes for a few moments. It was true what they said, about grief going away, bit by bit. Sometimes you could hardly measure the progress, but she could now look back fondly—yes, missing him—but without any ache at all. It just didn't hurt anymore, which felt somehow disloyal.

°I won't tell if you don't.°

Fair enough.

Guards walked the parapets of both the inner and the outer walls, but the watches weren't properly staggered, Walter had said. She couldn't see them walking their tours—it was far too dark, and they were too far below—but Ahira's darksight could, from his position slung below the dragon's belly, like a baby in a carrier.

A mental chuckle echoed in her mind. °I just might tell him you thought that.°

Ahira wouldn't mind. He had a sense of humor.

°He's not overly thrilled. Something about how there are times when he wished another one of you could see into the infrared, and he could tell the difference between blue, indigo, and violet, and—it's time. Here we go.°

The only question in her mind was as to how much of a fuss

Walter would make at the front gate, and the answer to that came as the party wound its way up the hill toward the gate: a signal rocket hissed off into the night, shattering the quiet with a loud boom and a shower of green sparks.

Silly question, really: How much of a fuss would Walter Slovotsky make? Why, as much as possible, of course.

°Hold on.°

Ellegon spread his wings widely, and the world tipped on its side until he was in a steep bank that became more of a fall than anything else.

She closed her eyes as she fell, her fingers clenched tightly in the straps. She didn't need to see the ground rushing up toward her, to hope and pray that Ellegon would brake in time, to—

G-forces mashed her down against the cushioning blankets beneath her, and her breath came out in a whoosh as the dragon snapped from a dive into horizontal flight, then cupped his wings to brake their speed before he landed on the parapet more quietly than Andrea would have thought possible.

Helpful fingers tugged at her rigging from behind, but she slapped them away and unleashed herself from the harness, then slid down one of the ropes, glad of the thick leather gloves that protected her hands from rope burn.

She was the last one; Kethol helped her down to the walkway, with his usual clumsiness that came from a delicacy about where he placed his strong hands. She would have made fun of that, but he was so uncomfortable around her that the slightest comment would probably have made him impotent for years. She had learned more years ago than she liked to remember how careful you had to be when teasing boys, and then men.

It wasn't by accident that Ellegon had landed near one of the stairways that led down from the parapet to the outer bailey. With Pirojil in the lead, she followed Erenor down the stone steps to the calf-high grasses, Kethol and Ahira following along behind.

°I'm gone,° Ellegon said, as the dragon slipped, snakelike, over the far wall. It was only a hundred or so yards to the woods from here, and once in the woods Ellegon could quickly get far enough away that the flapping of his wings wouldn't draw unwanted attention to the rear of the castle complex while the arrival of Jason and party was drawing wanted attention to the front of it.

Unless, of course, the dragon drew attention to himself by breathing fire.

°I'm a young dragon, but I was hatched centuries ago, not yesterday, and I'm perfectly capable of controlling myself at both ends, thank you very much,° he said, sounding just a little irritated. You would think he would have developed a sense of humor about himself in his first couple of centuries.

°Yes, you would, wouldn't you?°

While there were stone stairways at several places inside each of the curtain walls, of course—making it easy for defenders to get onto the wall was part of any castle's design, just as much as making life difficult for attackers was—the only place that the inner wall had any outside stairway was at the front gate, to permit soldiers to cross the outer bailey as they went to and from the outer wall.

But that stairway—built of well-aged wood that could have been torched in a moment, should the situation have warranted— was always guarded. In wartime, there would have been a soldier with a lantern and a bucket of lantern oil posted on the wall next to it, but even now it was seen as a weak spot in the fortification, and defended.

Castles weren't well-designed to keep people in, but they were intended to keep people out.

If the rope wasn't where Walter had left it, they would have to try lassoing an outcropping on one of the ramparts, and such things were made deliberately wide not only to support a wartime additional structure, but to prevent that very thing. She didn't think much of their chances of doing that, although Kethol and Pirojil seemed to think it likely, and Erenor, unsurprisingly, presented it as little less than a fait accompli.

He thought a lot of himself and his companions, that one did. With any luck, he'd be right.

Well, if nothing else, they always had the option of walking up to the wooden stairway and calling attention to themselves.

There would be some sort of fuss, no doubt, but . . .

Walter had chosen the place well; it was well-shadowed by one of the corner towers, so much so that Andrea couldn't see the rope at all, and only knew it was there when Kethol started climbing up it, Pirojil steadying the rope below.

Alternately pulling with his arms and locking the rope with his crossed legs, it took him an inordinately long time to make his way up to the ramparts, and when he did he had to hang there, just below the level of the walkway, as a pair of soldiers marched by, chattering some gossip about one of the decurions and a lady from Arondael that Andrea would have liked to have heard more of. It wasn't just that it was often politically useful to know who was sleeping with whom—although it could be—but one of the things that Andrea missed about Biemestren was gossip.

Out in the barony, there just wasn't any, except for what went on among the servants and some of the townspeople, and U'len's rendition of that just wasn't satisfying. If you were interested in people, you pretty much had to be interested in at least listening to gossip.

Finally, Kethol reached the top and dropped the end of the rope he had carried down for Erenor, then pulled from the top while Erenor half-walked his way up the side of the wall, reminding her of that silly *Batman* show that she used to watch on reruns.

Ahira went up at the same time, every bit as quickly, using Walter's rope and going hand over hand, disdaining to grip with his stubby legs.

The outside of the wall had a slight inward slant—the idea, so she understood, was to make it possible to drop rocks or pour boiling oil down the side and have both splash outward at attacking troops—which helped some, although the stones had been angled and the gaps mortared to avoid leaving any real purchase for fingers and toes.

Then Pirojil knelt and extended the loop at the end of Kethol's rope. "Just hold on, my Empress," he said, "and let them pull you up." He tightened it around her foot, then gave three quick pulls on the rope.

She would have been insulted at the insinuation that she couldn't do it herself, but she had tried climbing a rope before, and it was much more difficult than Kethol made it look, much less not as easy as Ahira did. Women didn't have the upper body strength that men did. More strength of will and character, much of the time, certainly, but when it came to transporting a weight, even one's own weight, from one elevation to another, men were superior.

Hmmm . . . men were better at lifting weights, and at pissing on fires to put them out. Andrea Cullinane figured that that was a fair trade for women's longer lives, the ability to keep the species going, and multiple orgasms.

Strong hands, both Ahira's and Erenor's, helped her the last few feet up to the walkway atop the ramparts. Erenor's hands lingered on her just a second more than absolutely necessary before letting go. That was an easy man to read, although she was privately frustrated that she hadn't been able to tell that he was a wizard herself. She had lost the ability to see the inner fire when she had sacrificed her own magical abilities.

That wasn't what she missed most, of course. What still ached was the missing magic itself: just the using of magic, the electric, almost sexual vibration that coursed through her body and mind, washing over her in an embrace more intimate than any other passion could be—her nipples hardened at just the thought.

But that was gone from her, forever . . .

There was a reason wizards were called magic users, after all: using the magic was pleasure, in and of itself. No wonder so many overused it, finding themselves addicted, getting more and more addicted and more and more insane with every passing year.

So being without it was probably all for the best, all things considered.

But why did she find herself missing the magic more than she missed her dead husband? Did that make her a shallow person? That wasn't something she would have confided to anybody, not even Ellegon, and she was grateful that he was out of range now and wasn't fond of reading her mind anyway.

She followed along behind Ahira and Kethol, Erenor following her, conscious of his eyes on her. Pity that high-heeled boots were so impractical except on horseback; while she felt the tug of years, she knew that she still looked awfully good, from any angle, particularly in her traveling leathers. It was remarkably pleasant to be looked at with barely concealed lust.

Hmmm . . . perhaps she should be doing more sit-ups, and try to tone her belly just a little more.

They reached the base of the southwest tower, and started up the steps.

"Halt there!" sounded from behind. "What are you doing here?"

She turned to see a soldier approaching, his thick face sweaty in the torchlight, his mouth opening to call out again.

Pirojil had already spun around, his sword in hand—

And Erenor muttered a single syllable, and the soldier dropped like a puppet with its strings cut, his head hitting the stone with a solid thunk that made her wince just to hear.

His smile was infuriatingly self-satisfied. "He'll be fine, when he wakes up," he said.

She had used the trick herself, and remembered the technique, if not the details. You spoke all of a spell except for the last syllable of the instigator, and held it in your mind, waiting, like a phone where you've dialed all but the last digit. Then all you had to do was release that last syllable. It was tricky—if you needed to use another spell instead, you couldn't use any of the same dominatives without sacrificing the memory of this one—but it gave you the ability to quickly use the one in your mind with no notice whatsoever.

"Bind him," she said, "and stay here." She shook her head and continued up the stairs, two steps at a time. Yes, it was more elegant to put the guard to sleep with a sleep spell than it would have been for the others to knock him down and out—or kill him—but it created the same problems for them. There were a series of timing glasses at the main guardpost, and unless this one made his circuit in time to turn his upside down before the sand ran out, the decurion on duty would sound the alarm.

And, worse: any wizard—probably any apprentice—in the vicinity would have seen the flare of Erenor's inner fire as he used his spell. Unless Erenor was a lot better than he said he was, he wouldn't be able to hide his flame from the likes of Henrad, not even when his magic was quiescent.

"That's quite so, my old teacher," a voice sounded beside her ear. "It would seem to me that the lot of you have committed rather a solecism by bringing another wizard into my domain, unbidden and unasked, and entirely unwelcome. Even if he is," a sniff, "little more than an illusionist with delusions of grandeur."

She reached out, and felt only air.

"No," the voice went on, "it's not invisibility. I can do invisibility quite easily, mind. This is different. It's one of my own spells—I enjoy letting my senses walk about the castle, leaving my body behind, as a nightly constitutional."

Nightly?

"Yes, nightly," he said, "and if you will stop subvocalizing and simply talk, it will be simpler for both of us. I'd rather not try to actually read your mind; I'm afraid that I couldn't help but tiptoe through the parts of your memory of me, and, well, Mistress Lotana-that-was, I'm entirely afraid that I would not find a pleasant picture of that dirty, uneducated stripling boy whose inner fire you noted, and whom you took on, all those years ago."

She had stopped climbing, and found that she was breathing

and sweating more heavily than just the exercise should account for.

"Be still for a moment," the voice said, this time from directly behind her. "I shall return."

"Henrad, I—"

"Be still, I said."

She leaned back against the cold stone of the tower. Her progress around the spiral staircase had brought her all the way around the tower, hiding the base of the staircase where, presumably, Pirojil and the rest had the guard secured.

But it did give her a view of the front gate, and of the assemblage surrounding Jason and his party.

It was hard to make out individuals in what little light there was, but it was easy to see that there had been no bloodshed—at least, not yet—and if something were going to go horribly wrong, it would likely have happened already. It would have been preferable if they could have simply slipped inside the inner ward as though they had entered with the rest of the party, and then presented themselves to the majordomo for quartering.

General Garavar was not going to like the idea of anybody being able to sneak into Biemestren castle unobserved, and would have a proper fit.

That might work well for castle security, but it would make life difficult if Walter had to sneak anybody else inside again. It had been tricky enough this time.

"You can come up now," Henrad said. "I've taken care of the guard matter. I informed the guard captain that one of his soldiers was making enough noise that I was bothered enough to deal with it, and I've told your companions that they should do as you originally planned, and just climb down to the inner bailey and mix with the rest."

She was surprised that Pirojil and Kethol had agreed to that, but Ahira had likely persuaded them, and if Erenor had had the sense to keep his mouth shut, Kethol and Pirojil would probably have seen the wisdom of going along.

After all, if Henrad was going to do any harm to her, there wasn't anybody in the Middle Lands who could prevent him from doing so in his own place, surrounded not only by his spell books and whatever magical implements he had created, but by protective spells of all sorts.

She had expected something dark and dreary, but when she rounded the final turn, the archway to Henrad's aerie was filled with light that, strangely, seemed to stop at the arch.

He stood in the doorway, hands on hips in a deliberately dramatic pose, his gray robes belted about a slim waist with a golden cord that appeared to be a gilded snake biting its own tail, Ourobouros-like. His robes fell open to his navel, revealing a well-muscled chest, matted with thick curls of black hair.

"Hello, my teacher," he said, smiling reaching out a hand. "Come in, please." He waited patiently, making no move to touch her until she stepped forward and took his hand in hers.

He led her inside, tucking her hand under his arm. "Welcome to my home," he said.

The tower wasn't more than a couple of dozen feet wide, but the room inside was immense, at least in appearance. Acres of green marble, veined with silver and black, stretched off into the distance, surrounding a circular island of thick carpet perhaps fifty feet away.

Her boots made hollow sounds in counterpoint to the slapping of his sandals as they walked, and she couldn't hear any returning echo.

The carpet/island grew as they approached, until it alone was large enough to contain a huge arc of workbench, cupping the living quarters. Retorts burbled merrily over alcohol flames, while wisps of smoke moved vessels from place to place, adjusting the drip of a spigot here, adding a powder from a stone urn there.

Henrad touched a finger to a portion of the carpet, and two

armchairs extruded themselves. He seated himself tailor-fashion in one, and gestured her toward the other. "It's good to see you looking so well," he said.

"You, too." This wasn't the man Walter Slovotsky had described. Henrad looked and sounded not just well, but vibrantly healthy. His eyes were clear, his teeth white and even, and his beard neatly squared off. It was hard to tell under the golden light over the glowglobes that floated overhead, bobbing like balloons, but he even seemed to have a tan. "Or is this just a seeming?"

He smiled. "Ah. You've been listening too much to the great Walter Slovotsky, and to others. A reputation for being a sick and crotchety old man gives one a certain, well, isolation that's useful for someone who wants to do more with his magic than kill bugs and relieve insomnia. Don't you think?" He brushed a hand down the front of his robes; in an eyeblink, he was the shriveled sick man that Walter had described: frightened, bloodshot eyes looking out at her from sunken hollows, teeth gapped and green, skin sallow and broken, sores leaking a horrid yellow pus. "I could appear to you like this," he squeaked, in between horrid wheezes, "if you'd prefer." He struggled to get out of his chair, leaning on the crooked stick he used as a cane, and just as she started to rise to help him, in another eyeblink he was young and vibrant again, eyes twinkling in amusement.

"Now, which is it, teacher mine? Which is the seeming?" he asked. "The young and virile man you see before you, or the withered, spent husk?" He plopped down on his seat and folded his hands in front of him. "Can you tell?"

She shook her head. "I . . . I don't have the spark, anymore, Henrad. I burned it out, in Ehvenor."

"Did you, now?" His tone mocked her. "Rather foolish, that, leaving you mundane and powerless, having to come to me, your former apprentice, to beg a favor, to ask me to attune that ring you have hidden in your garments to its former bearer." He shook his head. "Such a trivial favor. Why not ask me something, well, something grand? I could take twenty years off your age, if you'd like. Or make a magical sword for your son, if you'd rather have something more traditional." His smile was warm and entirely false. "But such a little thing," he said. "It hardly seems worth the bother, to you or to me." He brightened. "I know—would you like me to rekindle your fires?"

She frowned. "If you're saying what I think you're saying, that's not possible. I burned those abilities out, in Ehvenor, and—"

He held up a palm. "Oh, yes, and so bravely you did, sealing the rift between Faerie and reality, I'm sure it was wonderful. But I am quite serious—I haven't been working for nothing, you know. I can't restart your abilities at what they were, but I could, if you'd like, oh, relight the fires, bring you back your ability to work magic." His smile broadened. "Then I could do for you what you did for me," he said. "You could be my apprentice." He reached out his hand, and there was a mug in it, steam licking up. He took a tentative sip. "Have we an understanding?"

Yes, she wanted to say, *yes, do it, do it now. Give me back my fire.*

To be able to work magic again, to feel power flow through her veins and nerves, to have harsh words of power sweet on the tongue again, her mind and body and spirit all afire . . .

His smile broadened. "Yes, I know. You miss it, don't you?"

"But . . . but what would happen in Ehvenor? Would the rift open again?"

"I couldn't tell you." He spread his hands. "If it did, it could be sealed once more. Even Vair the Uncertain could tell you that." He rose and walked across the carpet toward her. It should have taken him half a dozen steps, but it took only two. He took her hand, wrapping both of his hands around hers, and drew her to her feet. "The preparation has taken much time, but the doing of it would be but the work of a moment."

"One syllable left?"

He shook his head, his eyes never leaving hers. She didn't remember him as having gold flecks in the brown. And it was strange: as she looked into his eyes, the irises seemed to spin.

No.

She had pushed her magical abilities too far, bringing them past the point of wanting, well into addiction. "Henrad . . . I can't."

"Of course you can," he said, raising her hand to his lips. "It's a question of will, not of can."

It was tempting, the way a drink of ice water would have been tempting to someone just in out of the desert; like food would have tempted a starvation victim.

No.

She had made her bargain with the world: closing the rift between reality and Faerie had been worth the price she had paid, and she was an Andropoulos by birth and a Cullinane by marriage, and the Cullinanes kept faith.

That was how she had raised her son, and it was how she would live.

And never mind the hunger inside her. She could live with that. Moment by moment; day by day; year by year.

"*No,*" she said. "I want you to make the ring locate its owner, Forinel." She pulled away from him. "But that is all, Henrad. I won't be your apprentice, or whatever else it is that you want."

His expression went dead and lifeless. Not angry; not sad. His eyes seemed vacant, and his mouth hung slightly open. "Very well," he said. "Just this once. But the offer stays open, and the next time you come to ask me for a service, you must accept it."

"Then there won't be a next time."

The smile returned. "So you say . . . now." He stretched out a hand for the ring, and as she laid it on his palm he closed his eyes for a moment, then uttered a single word, three syllables in a harsh language that could not be remembered, three sounds that could only vanish on the ear like three sugar crystals on the tongue.

" 'Tis done, Andrea," he said, tying a leather thong around the ring.

He dangled the thong between thumb and forefinger, and the ring slowly rose to one side, the thong still taut, as though the golden ring had been drawn by a magnet. "I think you'll find the lovely Lady Leria that way," he said. "As to Lord Forinel, well, of such matters I shall not claim to know either much or little."

"Henrad, I—"

He silenced her with a finger to her lips. "Shhh. Not now. Until next time, my old teacher." He snapped his fingers and murmured a quiet word, and in an eyeblink she found herself out on the windy top of the tower, facing an inky black doorway, the ring's thong clutched tightly in her hand.

Pirojil waited silently as the ragged steps descended down the stone staircase. There was, of course, the temptation to run up to the dowager empress's side, but if she had wanted his help, all she had to do was whisper.

Even in the dim light of the overhead stars above and the flickering torches on the walls below, she looked ghastly: she leaned against the wall more for support than for guidance, and her fingers and knees trembled visibly. Her hair, stringy with sweat, had come loose from the band that had held it back, and it clung wetly to her neck and face, like tiny tendrils.

He was wary of touching her without permission, but he grabbed hold of her hand and helped her down the last couple of steps.

"Thank you, Pirojil," she said, her voice ragged. "The others—?"

"We decided that the others should take the wizard's advice, and make their way down to the bailey, and mix with the crowd. Ahira wanted to wait for you, but we decided that I could probably sneak in alone better than he could." Erenor had been the obvious candidate, but Pirojil didn't like the idea of leaving him alone with the dowager empress. His eye tended to wander, and while Pirojil didn't think his fingers would—and was sure that Andrea Cullinane would put him in his place if they did—he didn't want to risk it, unless necessary.

Kethol, of course, could have done that better than Pirojil. Would it have been more cruel or more kind to have let him have the job of waiting for Andrea Cullinane instead of joining the others, including Leria? Pirojil didn't know, and didn't like to think about it.

Are you unwell? he didn't ask. Any damn fool could see she was unwell, after all. "Is there anything I can do?"

She leaned back against the base of the tower and shook her head. "Just give me a few moments. If you can."

"Of course." He turned away from her. It wasn't proper that he should see her so disheveled. She was the dowager empress— let others call her the Dowager Baroness Cullinane, but to Pirojil she would always be *the* dowager empress—and he was just an ordinary soldier, after all.

"I don't understand it," she said, so quietly that he wasn't sure whether she was talking to herself or to him.

"Your pardon?" He didn't turn back. She hadn't told him to face her.

"It's hard, sometimes, Pirojil, trying to figure out when things are and aren't as they seem," she said. "Even when magic isn't involved."

That seemed to call for a response. "I've often found that true, if you don't mind me saying so."

"Yes," she went on. "Take yourself. You're not what I would call a handsome man . . ."

He made himself laugh. "That, my Empress, is beyond doubt." Too gently put, that. He was ugly enough that women turned away.

". . . but, as I was saying," she said, her voice louder, but somehow more gentle, "you're brave, and you're faithful, and you manage to be loyal to my house and to your companions, even when some would find conflicts—even, I suspect, when you find conflicts between the two. That's the reality of you, soldier. The looks are deceiving."

He nodded, accepting that as his due, every bit as much as the silver quartermarks he received in pay.

If by being brave she meant that he did what was necessary, despite any fear, well then that was as much a part of a soldier's equipment as his knife, or his knowledge of how to use it.

But loyalty? Why praise him for loyalty? That was like praising him for eating. At the end of the day, when he lay down to sleep and closed his eyes, what else was there to comfort him in the dark?

The softness of a woman? Hardly.

Children? Let's not be silly.

The memories of the screams of the dying? They were cold comfort, indeed, no matter what a younger man had thought.

"I can't figure it out, Pirojil, and I'm not sure I ever will. Which is the real Henrad? The young, strong, well one who tempted me with that which I'd given up? Or the sick, twisted one, so far gone in his own addiction that he needs to bring others into it, as though sharing it makes it better?" She shook her head.

"Or both," he said. "The opposite of a lie isn't always the truth, my Empress. Sometimes—not always, mind you, but sometimes— it's just another lie."

"Yes, Pirojil, there is that." She was silent for a long time. "But sometimes both can't be lies. He held a finger to my lips, and it looked to be a young man's finger, smooth and straight, but it *felt* all wrinkled and bent. Tell me, Pirojil: how can both be untrue?"

He thought that maybe she wanted an answer, although he hadn't any, but when he turned to look at her, she was looking away.

So he didn't say anything at all.

Part Four:

Forinel

18

The Search Begins

It's easier to get forgiven than to get permission.
—Walter Slovotsky

It was all Kethol could do to keep his voice calm and level. "No," he said. "It's a bad idea." It was important to persuade them, or else *she* was going to be endangered, and—

No. He sighed. You can't persuade somebody who has already made up his mind, and Walter Slovotsky and the rest of the nobles had already made up their minds.

Pirojil didn't meet his eyes as he checked the straps on one of the rucksacks, then tossed it to Erenor, who stacked it with the others—there was much to be said for a bag that you could carry on your back as well as on a dragon's.

Walter Slovotsky shook his head. "I don't see a better choice." He sighed. "Wish I was going with you."

Erenor snorted. That was the first time Kethol had heard Erenor snort. He wasn't sure he liked it. "So, you think this is going to be easy?"

"Not at all. No, hey, I didn't mean it that way." Walter Slovotsky held up a hand. "I was thinking that I'd rather have somebody else explain *this*," he said, looking pointedly at Leria, then back to Erenor, "to Thomen."

The emperor would likely have the same objection to sending Leria that Kethol did. As far as Kethol was concerned, it was better to let Miron have the barony than risk her, again—and perhaps even end up having to let Miron have the barony in any case.

He was the heir, after all, if Forinel was dead.

Why did the idea of Forinel being dead seem so pleasing? It wasn't as though Kethol had any chance with Leria in any case. She was a lady, after all.

Truth to tell, in the privacy of his own mind, he was looking forward to this. Some more time with her, away from Castle Biemestren, away from it all, where she would need him, again.

For a while.

He felt obligated to try to talk the nobles out of it, but since he couldn't, he would just do the best he could. Some time alone with her was something he had idly daydreamed about, and if he had to share her company with Pirojil, Erenor, and the dragon, well, so be it.

Storm clouds smeared the western sky, and lightning flickered on the horizon, too far away for the thunder to reach their ears.

Yet. The storm was moving in along with the dawn, and the wind on top of the ramparts had a decided bite to it. Leria shivered in her mannish traveling clothes, and Erenor opened up one of the rucksacks, producing a Katharhd-style jacket without looking.

It was made of a sheep's skin, a hole cut in the center for the head, and fastened at the corners with ties, and at the waist with a belt, leaving room enough for her to tuck her arms inside.

Jason Cullinane looked from Kethol to Erenor and Pirojil, and then back to Kethol, as though deciding something, although Kethol didn't have the slightest idea as to what.

The baron stepped over to him and beckoned him to one side. "I'm sorry I can't come with you. I know my father would have, and . . . and there are no excuses, but Walter, my mother, and Ahira say that I'm needed here." His tone was almost pleading, as though it was important for some reason that Kethol understand him.

Which it wasn't. What Kethol understood was that he, for one, was glad that the baron wasn't coming along. No matter how good

Jason Cullinane was with a pistol, flintlock rifle, or sword, he would be a problem: Kethol, Pirojil, and Erenor might have to, at a moment's notice, choose between protecting him and protecting Leria, and Kethol feared that any one of them might choose wrongly.

How many backs did this baron think he could watch at one time?

"I understand, Baron," Kethol said.

"I wouldn't want you to think me a coward."

"No. I'd not think that."

There was a twinkle in Pirojil's eyes as he watched the conversation. No, they might think the Cullinanes to be foolhardy, but not cowards.

"Take this, please." Leria gave a folded piece of paper to Walter Slovotsky. "I don't know that this will do much, but I've done the best I can: this explains that I'm going along at my insistence, not yours."

"Yeah." Walter Slovotsky tucked it in his tunic. "I'm sure that will persuade Beralyn not at all and Thomen only a little. You did push the Forinel angle?"

Her smile was genuine, and warmed Kethol. "There's nothing to push, Walter Slovotsky," she said. "I simply said Forinel was the first boy I loved, and that I had to know why he hasn't come back to me."

" 'Boy.' I like that. Nice choice of word."

"Why, thank you, Walter Slovotsky," she said, too sweetly. "I'm so glad you approve."

Let's get going, people, sounded in Kethol's mind. *I don't think that hanging around here is going to lead to any productive discussion, do you?*

Ellegon swooped up from behind the treeline, vast leathery wings beating the air as he set himself down on the ramparts.

A cry went up from the northwestern tower, and the alert bell started ringing. The dragon's arrival was always cause for an alert, if only for the Home Guard to be sure to keep people away. Accidents could happen, and dragonbane was being cultivated in far too many places for far too many reasons to be controlled.

Erenor, a bundle of thongs held in his mouth, scrambled up the dragon's back, lithe and agile as a boy half his age, and secured the rucksacks to the rigging almost as quickly as Kethol and Ahira could throw them up to him.

Beralyn is awake, and she's having Thomen awakened at this very moment, and I'd just as soon we be gone before he manages to stumble out of his bedchamber and inquire as to what is going on, wouldn't you? the dragon asked, wisps of steam coming from between his scaly lips as his mouth parted long enough to snap up the pig carcass that Ahira had hauled up to the ramparts.

The bones crunched merrily in the dragon's mouth.

"Would you help me up, Kethol?" Leria asked, extending a hand.

It was all he could do not to take that hand and pull her to him, her mouth warm and wet on his—

But he stooped to make a stirrup of his interlaced fingers, and lifted her up high, until Pirojil and Erenor, each taking an arm, brought her the rest of the way.

Kethol let Pirojil check her straps as he made his way to his usual place on the webbing across the dragon's back, and fastened himself in with just a safety line around his waist.

He sat down, hard, and gripped the webbing tightly with his hands, slipping each boot under it for additional security.

"Good luck," sounded from below, and "Be careful," and "See you soon," and, finally, in the dwarf's gravelly baritone, "Ta havath."

Ta havath. Stand easy, it meant. Relax. Don't worry.

Easy for him to say.

Hold on.

A roaring gout of flame ending any pretense of quiet or subterfuge, the dragon leaped skyward.

19

✠ Thomen

It's easier to get forgiven than to get permission.
Usually.

—Walter Slovotsky

I learned a lot from my father, and more from your friend Karl," the emperor said, his voice seething with calm. "Now you've taught me another lesson."

"Yes, Emperor." Walter Slovotsky stood at the position that he would have called "parade rest" rather than "at ease," back during his abortive six weeks in ROTC, a few lifetimes ago: back straight, feet shoulder width apart, hands folded behind his back, eyes looking straight ahead, not looking down to meet the emperor's.

Thomen sat back against his fluffy pillows, thin, warm-weather blankets piled about his bed. He still wore a silken nightshirt, as though he hadn't gotten out of bed, yet, although Walter knew from Ellegon that he had. Having Walter Slovotsky attend him in chambers could be either a sign of friendly intimacy or a deliberate insult, and Walter really didn't have much of a doubt as to which this was.

"Aren't you going to ask me what that lesson is?" Thomen's voice was silky smooth, more reminiscent of Tyrnael's than of any Furnael's.

I sort of thought you were going to tell me anyway, Walter thought. "Yes, I would like to know, if the emperor would be kind enough to share the thought with me."

"Never trust *anybody* who isn't blood," Thomen said. "You went behind my back."

There wasn't any obvious answer to that. Yes, he had gone behind his back. No, he wasn't sorry, particularly.

"Don't you have anything to say for yourself? I mean, other than offering me your resignation."

"The emperor can have my resignation at any time that he wishes it," Walter Slovotsky said. "My family and I can be on our way before nightfall."

"That might be a good idea," Thomen said. "Where do you think you'd go?"

Walter dropped his gaze and met the emperor's stony look squarely. "I think I'd be more than welcome in Home, for one place. Or in Barony Cullinane, for another," he went on, ticking it off on another finger. "Or Endell, for another—His Majesty wasn't overly eager to lose my services when we made the move here, and I've always gotten along well with the Moderate People."

"You'd leave your daughters here with Kirah and Baron Adahan?"

There was a threat in that question, and it took Walter Slovotsky a moment to decide how to handle it. "No, I don't think that would be a good idea," he said, quietly. "I think that things are unstable enough around here right now that I'm worried about their future—"

"Pfah." The Emperor snorted. "Essential to the empire, are you?"

"No." He shook his head. "Or maybe yes. We'd only know that in retrospect, wouldn't we?" He shrugged. "I'm sure the emperor and the empire could get along perfectly well without me—but I'd just as soon have my family far away, in a more stable situation, if I'm not going to be here."

The door behind him eased open, and Walter Slovotsky forced himself not to spin around—humility might be called for, here and now, but not a sign of weakness or of fear—as a dumpy young serving-girl arrived with the imperial breakfast on a wicker bedtray that looked exactly like one he had seen once in a J. C. Penney.

Well, when it's wicker bedtray time . . .

She set it down in front of Thomen, and left without a word.

Thomen removed the silver dome from his plate, and picked up an eating prong. The smell of the smoked trout and fried onions on his plate made Walter Slovotsky's mouth water.

"So, you're ready to leave my service, is that it?"

"Not eager, no. But ready, yes."

Thomen Furnael smiled around a mouthful of trout and onions. "This humility doesn't suit you, Walter."

"Thomen, I—"

"I'm talking. You do it well, but I know you: It's utterly false and not believable for a moment." He pointed at him with the eating prong. "You're thinking, while I'm berating you, that you're still the great Walter Slovotsky and I'm just the boy that you and Karl Cullinane rescued, and that if you got angry enough with me, I'd be lying here, dead, for hours before I was found, long enough for you to get away."

Walter Slovotsky didn't answer.

"Well, aren't you thinking that?"

"No," he lied. He shook his head. "It's not just that I don't mean you any harm, Emperor—although I don't," he quickly added, his voice raised. "It's also that I'm sure you've got guards behind some hidden panel here, and that if I made a move they didn't like, or if you dropped a secret password in casual conversation, they'd be all over me like ugly on a dwarf."

The emperor nodded. "But that wouldn't save me, not if you wanted me dead—I remember waking up in this room with your knife at my throat, not so long ago."

"Well—"

"—and was it not this very bed that Prince Pirondael died in, of a knife thrown by you?"

Walter Slovotsky nodded. "Yes, it was. Moments after he murdered your father, if you'll recall." He frowned. "No, actually, it wasn't this bed, come to think of it. Karl had the bed removed, and a new one put in, for some reason or other. And I'm sure you've had the feather mattress changed more than a few times, but—"

"Be quiet, Walter," the emperor said. "It's hard for me to stay mad at you while you're chattering so." He smiled, for just a moment. "As I should be, shouldn't I?"

"You're worried about Leria?"

The Emperor's mouth twitched. "Yes. I am. I don't know much about love, Walter, but I do know that I find her company pleasant, and that she's of good lineage, and fertile, and that one of the problems my mother is right about is that I need an heir."

Fertile?

"I had the Spider examine her," Thomen said, answering the unasked question.

It was probably his mother who had ordered that, but it was a good idea nonetheless. Good ideas didn't spring only from the minds of good people. And the tastiest food was grown in dirt, dirt with manure mixed in.

I'm getting old. Years ago, I wouldn't even have thought "manure" when what I meant was "shit."

"Well, with all this preparation, what does the lady say?"

Did Thomen color just a little at the cheekbones? It wouldn't have been politic to stare, and probably worse to ask. "I haven't asked her, yet. I haven't even decided to ask her. But there have been rumors enough going around, and you've seen the two of us together enough—didn't you think for a moment about asking me before sending her out into danger?"

Walter slowly—careful of the audience; accidents could happen—reached two fingers into his tunic and pulled out Leria's letter, and tossed it to the bed. "This will explain that it wasn't me who thought of it, that it was Leria's idea, and her idea alone, and probably that I tried to talk her out of it, and that if things go wrong she has no one to blame but herself—except, I hope, Miron and his dead mother, and you should save your anger for them."

Thomen fingered the wax seal. "Whose thumbprint is this? Yours? Aiea's?"

"Don't break it—save it. It's Leria's. Unless, of course, she's setting me up for some unknown reason, which I doubt." Walter leaned up against the bedpost, folding his arms in front of him. "You might next want to accuse me of having her signature and her handwriting forged, as long as the accusations fly."

The emperor had broken the seal already, and scanned the letter quickly. "She doesn't seem to blame anybody, except perhaps herself, and that only for not talking Forinel out of such a bad idea." He looked up. "But she couldn't have talked him out of it, could she?"

"An impressionable kid? Under the influence of Elanee?" He shook his head. "To listen to Pirojil talk about her," there was no particular point in mentioning Erenor, "she apparently had some raw magical gift, some sort of sexual compulsion thing, and you can just see how that would have worked on a kid, particularly if Elanee seduced him in the process."

The emperor nodded. "So, it wasn't your idea; it was hers, is that it? I ought to apologize to you, I suppose, for having suspected you of instigating it, since it was her idea, after all, and—"

"No, it was my idea. She went along with it willingly, not quite eagerly, but it was my idea."

The emperor nodded, again. "I'm glad you said that. I didn't believe for a moment that it was her idea, or that you would let any young girl push you into anything you didn't want to have happen."

"Your mother's choosing your servants again, eh?"

Thomen raised an eyebrow. "Oh? You've been listening to gossip, again, I take it."

Walter smiled. "I always listen to gossip," he said. "That's part of what you pay me for, Thomen," he said.

The emperor smiled, and took another prongful of his breakfast. "Well, then, Parliament meets at noon, and you've no doubt got things to do to prepare yourself and Jason Cullinane for that," he said. "Do I have to tell you that we don't need any duels with Miron?"

"Probably not."

"Good." Thomen waved him away. "Then be about your business, Imperial Proctor," he said, lightly.

Walter turned to leave.

"Oh, just one thing. I wouldn't want you to think your charming me out of being angry means that this is all forgotten and over with." He chewed thoughtfully. "I guess before I decide quite what to do with you we'll just have to see how things turn out with Forinel."

And particularly with Leria, Walter thought.

"And particularly with Leria," Thomen said.

20

The Waste of Elrood

Erenor held up the leather thong and flicked a trimmed fingernail at the dangling ring, one more time.

Ting.

It orbited rapidly, tethered by the thong, slowing only gradually until, once again, it hung not quite straight up and down.

Kethol hacked a point on the stick with his belt knife with half a dozen quick strokes, then hammered it into the hard ground with the flat butt of the knife, which had been made flat for just that sort of purpose. He picked up the other stick and walked a few dozen paces away—the farther, the better, but there was no point in making a hike out of it—and whittled a quick point on that one, too. He stuck the point tentatively in a crack in the hard-baked ground, and looked up at Erenor.

"No, that's not quite right." Erenor held the ring over the first post, and waved Kethol to the left. "A little bit over—just half a pace, no more," he said. "Not that it should matter much, but we may as well get it right." Which made sense.

We may be sure tomorrow, Kethol thought, *but either the Katharhd stretches farther north than I thought it did, or we are heading more toward Therranj than the Katharhd.*

The good part of that was that it might make a side trip to Home not only possible, but a good idea. The Engineer had no particular reason to be generous where Kethol, Pirojil, and Erenor were concerned, but as they were on Baron Cullinane's service, he might be prevailed upon for at least the loan of a couple of those revolving pistols that the baron had.

Kethol preferred relying on the sword, himself, but the truth was that Erenor would be, even if he worked very hard for many years, at best an indifferent swordsman, and perhaps an adequate crossbowman.

The bad part of that was Pirojil. He wouldn't talk about it, but the clearer it became that they were heading toward Therranj, the less he liked it, and if he didn't want to discuss it, there must be some good reason.

It wasn't something you could ask about, though. If Pirojil had been willing to talk about it, he would have.

Pirojil squatted in front of the fire, poking at it with a stick, sending sparks high into the still air. Not the sort of thing you wanted to do in the woods—forests would burn often enough by themselves; you didn't need to help them any—but out here in the Waste, there was nothing to burn except the wood they had brought with them, cut down at the edge of the Waste. Plenty of wood, though—that was one of the nice things about Ellegon as a form of transportation: weight wasn't a problem, not for four people and their gear.

As long as you're not the one carrying the four people, and all of their gear, that is. The dragon eyed him from where he lay a bowshot away, stretched out lazily on the hot-but-cooling ground from nose to tail.

Think of me as a lizard. Lizards like lying around lazily in the heat, and there's something . . . luxurious about sun-warmed dirt, rather than having to flame it into pleasant warmth myself. Ellegon sighed, steam and smoke issuing from his huge nostrils.

As the steam and smoke dissipated, Leria walked around the dragon's head. She was dressed in a long, flowing, but utterly opaque white nightdress, her traveling clothes rolled in a bundle and clutched to her chest.

"Lady," Kethol said, "if we have enough water, we should wash out your clothes, and then let them dry while it's still warm out, or at the very least spread them out to air in the hot sun."

She nodded. "I can spread them out myself," she said, looking around for some place to do just that.

°Use my tail,° Ellegon said. °Just hang them over the scales; I'm not planning on going anywhere for some time.°

"Thank you, Ellegon," she said, as she unrolled her bundle of clothes. "Oh, Kethol? I refilled the billy," she said, as she shook out a white blouse and bent over to drape it over Ellegon's tail, her back to them. "It should be warm enough to be comfortable by now."

Rather than watch the way her bottom strained against the cloth of her nightdress as she bent over—there was no point in torturing himself any more than necessary—he glared pointedly at Erenor until Erenor stopped watching the way her bottom strained against the cloth of her nightdress as she bent over. "And put it back on the fire," she went on. "It should be warm enough to wash with shortly."

She turned around. She had been less careful in drying herself after her sketchy ablutions than she should have been, and Kethol felt his cheeks burning as he looked away from where her nipples showed through.

Erenor smiled at her. "That's very gracious of you, Lady." Kethol didn't like that smile, but there was a lot about this whole thing that Kethol didn't like, and it was kind of surprising that he wasn't used to it by now.

"Erenor," he said, "you take the next turn."

"No," Pirojil said, rising. "I will." He looked, long and hard, at the two stakes, his face studiously blank, and walked around the dragon toward where they had set up the privy and a small fire to warm the billy, only to return a few moments later to snatch up his rucksack, and, not meeting Kethol's questioning gaze, jogged back around the dragon.

Erenor cocked his head. His raised eyebrow asked, *What is that all about?*

Kethol shook his head. "Maybe he's just tired of the way you use up all the hot water. I know I am." He held Erenor's eyes with his own gaze, and wasn't sure whether or not he was doing it to punish both of them because he had been tempted to give Erenor an honest answer, or just to keep Erenor's roving eyes away from Leria, at least for the moment.

Therranj. Pirojil saw it, too. They were heading toward Therranj, not the Katharhd. Kethol didn't know what there was about Therranj that bothered—frightened? No, not frightened: bothered—Pirojil, but there was something.

Well, if Pirojil wanted him to know about it, he would have told him about it. Let the man have his secrets, and if his secrets weren't all that secret, well, then let that be Kethol's secret, and not Erenor's.

"We have plenty of water," she said, "and I tried to use as little as I could, so as not to waste it."

One corner of Erenor's mouth turned up. "He wasn't criticizing you, Lady. Friend Kethol has had to use my cold, overly dirty bathwater on, I blush to admit, far too many occasions, in situations less . . . luxurious than the one in which we find ourselves." His broad gesture encompassed the empty Waste about them.

"I hadn't thought of a vast, empty stretch of flat, broken ground as luxurious," she said, smiling, as she stretched out on her sleeping blankets, after decorously tucking the hem of her nightdress under her legs.

"Ah, Lady," Erenor said, rising to his feet, his arms outstretched as if to embrace the whole Waste of Elrood, "then you don't appreciate the nature of true luxury, if you don't mind me saying so."

Well, she apparently didn't mind him saying so, judging from the smile and the beckoning gesture that invited him to go on, but Kethol did.

Erenor had no more business flirting with a lady than Kethol did, after all.

"Well, Lady," the wizard said, rising, "look about us: privacy and solitude, as far as the eye can see, and in the Waste of Elrood, the eye can see far, indeed.

"No annoying clomping of horses in the street, much less the offensive smells being wafted to our delicate noses.

"No nobility—I mean, of course no *decurions* and troop *captains*—seeking to interrupt a quiet conversation or a few moments of rest with tasks that are likely to be unpleasant and possibly even, from time to time, dangerous.

"No servants, flitting about, here and there, ostensibly working, but in fact carrying gossip up and down every staircase in the castle.

"No cooks, seeking to rid their coldcellars of every bit of gristly meat, suspiciously limp carrots, maggoty bread, and turned turnips, preferring to feed it to the soldiers rather than to the compost heap.

"Again, I say, look about us. Leagues and leagues of, well, leagues and leagues—neither walls, nor doorways, nor alleyways, nor forests, nor covered bridges sheltering large, hulking men with sharp swords in their hairy hands and unkind intentions on their simple minds. Instead, we have pleasant company—at least, I certainly do, and I'm quite sure that Kethol and Pirojil do, as well, and hope that you find the company not unpleasant—an unsleeping dragon to keep watch, and, if my skills as a cook have not utterly deserted me, we shall have a dinner I hope you find fit for a lady, and which is more than fit for the likes of the three of us."

Squatting—and how Erenor managed to look graceful while squatting was something Kethol would never understand—he reached a long stick into the fire, and pulled the hot coals off the clay pot, then gently slid it across the hard ground until it was free of the fire. He knelt over it, and carefully blew every last ash and cinder from the cover, and then, protecting his hand with the sleeve of his tunic, he removed the lid with a typically Erenor-like flourish.

There was only the lightest of breezes on the Waste at the moment, but, cruelly, it brought the meaty smells of roasted chicken and garlic, the rich, earthy smell of cooked turnips, and a half-dozen other tantalizing aromas that had Kethol's mouth watering, and his stomach in sudden pain with hunger that he had barely noticed before.

Erenor ladled out a generous helping into a wooden bowl, and brought it over to Leria, waiting patiently until she tasted it.

"Mmmm. That's really very good," she said. Then her forehead wrinkled prettily, and her lips twisted into a frown. "Does it really taste this good? Or is this just another one of your seemings?"

"*Just* a seeming? Just a *seeming*? I should be insulted, although I am notoriously reluctant to take offense." Erenor laughed as he returned to the pot and served first Kethol, and then himself. "Tell me this: what difference, my Lady, would that make?" He lifted his bowl to his lips and sipped at the broth.

"Only the difference between appearance and reality," she said. "Are you going to tell us, Wizard Erenor, expert in seemings and deception, that there is no difference between appearance and reality?"

Kethol would have expected a return, a flirting sally, but Erenor was still capable of surprising him: he considered the question for a long moment, not even covering the fact that that's all he was doing by raising his bowl.

"I guess," Erenor finally said, his tone unusually serious, his smile atypically genuine, "that would depend on what the illusion, what the appearance, and what the reality is." He dipped thumb and forefinger into his bowl, produced a piece of meat, and put it in his mouth, licking the sauce from his fingers. "In this case, this stew consists of fresh chicken and vegetables, cooked in their own juices with just a sprinkling of water, some salt and Kiaran brown pepper, with nothing more than some roux to thicken it. Quite tasty, is it not? But if, perhaps, I made the chicken meat just a trifle more flavorful, reduced the taste of the salt if I had added too much—

just a little too much, mind you, not enough to make you terribly thirsty—or took away a harmless but metallic taste that the clay pot had picked up, somehow, somewhere, would that be a bad thing? Would it even be a false thing?"

He shook his head, answering his own question. "I think not," he said. He stretched out his arm toward Kethol. "It's been suggested, and there may even be some truth to it, that I am willing to swindle my companions out of the odd coin here and there. That may be true, and it may be false, but it's something that they understand about me, just as I understand that Master Pirojil will keep hold of my spell books, at least for the time being. There may be deception in what I do, and there may be coercion in what he does, but there is, in no real sense, any betrayal, as they know what I truly am and I know what they truly are.

"Now, were I to truly betray them, to steal their hidden coin, to reveal their private secrets, well, then, that would be another reality, and not merely a harmless illusion and deception."

His eyes bored in on Kethol's. "There are lies we tell, and there are truths we don't speak of, and we are not false in the speaking of lies nor in the silence of those truths, because sometimes—not, my dear Lady Leria, when we would have it so, but when the world would have it so—lies are loyalty, and fidelity, and honor, and friendship, and more, and spoken truths—even truths that *should* be spoken, by others, or at other times—are betrayal, and infidelity, and worse."

"Very good." Two meaty hands smacked together in loud applause from behind Kethol. He had heard Pirojil's footsteps in the back of his mind, but had paid them little heed while Erenor had commanded his attention.

"Very good, Master Erenor," Pirojil said, as he wiped his hands on a towel, then flicked it across his shoulder to dry. "A lecture on honor and fidelity and friendship and truth from a swindler and illusionist. I find myself impressed, and even moved."

After all these years, there were times when Kethol didn't understand Pirojil at all. It was impossible to tell from his expression-less, ugly face or his even tone whether he meant what he was saying or not, or what he meant if not.

Sometimes, sometimes around Pirojil he felt like his mind was all numb and fuzzy.

Leria's eyes caught his, and she nodded.

He didn't know what that meant, either. But he returned the nod, and she smiled.

Well, apparently he didn't do quite everything wrong.

21

✠ Miron

The talk in Biemestren was all about Miron, and ascension, and if Walter Slovotsky had had any real choice in the matter, he would have been somewhere else while others sorted it out.

Politics *was* a swear word, after all.

Jason Cullinane caught up with him just outside the Great Hall. "Uncle Walter, have you a moment?"

Uncle Walter, it was, eh?

"Sure, kid." That sounded strange coming out of his own throat—for just a moment, he was tempted to look around for Big Mike, his father's best friend.

But Big Mike was on the Other Side, and Walter hadn't seen him for more than twenty years.

"So, what is it?" he asked. "Thomen tear you a new one?"

"No." Jason shook his head. "Although I think he's going to spread the rumor that he did, but—"

"Good."

"*What?*"

"Shut up and walk with me, please."

Walter Slovotsky forced a smile as he linked arms with Jason, and walked down the corridor with him, studiously ignoring the way Governor Claressen tried to catch his eye. Claressen was important, yes, and so were half a dozen other lords and barons who were trying to get his attention, but there was something about Jason . . .

Walter tried to figure out what it was.

They turned the corner, and walked out into the bright sunlight, down the wide stone steps.

In the great tradition of locking the barn after the horse has been stolen, the guard had been tripled along the inner ramparts, and while he was too far away from them really to make out any expression, he imagined he could see at least a couple of them glaring down at him as they walked their rounds, sure in their own minds at least that it would be somebody else who was drawing the duty if it wasn't for that sneaky imperial proctor who had so embarrassed the lot of them by being able to come and go—with and without others—from a supposedly secured castle.

Well, let it be their problem, for now.

No, no, no, he was going to have to figure out some way to soothe the irritation, and better sooner than later, but not right now, dammit.

How many eggs could a juggler keep in the air at one time? Particularly if everybody seemed to be going for the juggler.

There was another joke that wouldn't sell to a This Side audience, and it was just as well that Walter Slovotsky was always his own best one.

As they walked down the steps, Toryn, who had been standing under one of the trees, resting on one foot, with the other foot up against the bole of the tree, his arms folded, his back up against the solid bole, straightened.

Walter didn't like him, and if it wasn't for Ellegon and Jason—particularly Ellegon; Jason was still a kid, in more ways than not—vouching for him, he would have followed the basic principle that had seen him safely through the raiding years: the only ex-slaver is a dead slaver.

But if pigs had wings, they'd be pigeons.

"Jason and I are looking for a place for a private talk," he said.

"I know." Toryn's smile was too wide. "That's why I had him—I asked him to go get you." He bit his lower lip for just a moment. "I like to show you something."

Oh? Like your back, leaving, permanently?

"Very well."

With Parliament in recess—and how long that could be stretched out was an interesting question, and like most interesting questions, probably had an unpleasant answer—the barons had spread out around various parts of the castle and the capital. There were two hunting parties, one gone west for deer, and the other north after a particular bear; both mixed Holtish and Biemish—and both a heavy drain on Home Guard troops to keep the barons company, and make sure that ancient grudges didn't break out into an accident. Bren Adahan was with the northern party, and the emperor with the western—the forces of sanity and reason were spread too thin for Walter's taste.

It would have been nice if Miron and Tyrnael had decided to go hunting, as he could always have hoped for an accident—with enough noble witnesses that it was an accident, of course.

But they hadn't, and under Tyrnael's watchful eye, Miron—stripped to the waist in the hot sun probably to display his flat, youthful belly as much as to keep cool—was engaged in a fencing match with one of Tyrnael's satellite nobles. It was hard to tell just who was under the mask, but from the build it could have been Lord Esterling as easily as Lordling Verken.

Miron, on the other hand, wore no mask, and seemed to be relying on his skill rather than any restraint on his opponent to protect his head and eyes. Most likely, of course, one or more of Tyrnael's minions had a flask of healing draughts ready for an emergency or error, and damn the possible expense—that a handsome young would-be baron would risk a little pain and a few gold marks to look good in front of the ladies and gentlemen wasn't exactly a huge surprise.

Both were good. The blunted blades flickered in the bright sunlight, sometimes faster than the eye could see.

Fencing was hard work—Miron's chest was shiny with sweat as he moved quickly, a gasp of applause from some of the watching ladies his reward when he lunged in full extension, underneath the other's blade, to touch home.

"Watch this, Uncle Walter," Jason said, as Miron parried a tentative thrust, then backed up a quick step before reversing into a lunge that came close to scoring.

Walter Slovotsky frowned. Yes, there had been a hesitation there. Not much of one, but certainly the sort of thing that a good swordsman could exploit.

Just a question of timing, and of having noticed it. It would be tricky to pull off, but the usual principle applied: if you knew what the other guy was going to do next—not suspected, but knew—he was yours.

He watched the sparring for the next few passes, gratefully accepting a tall glass of cool water from a tall cool serving-girl who was passing among the crowd with a tray, who returned his casual smile with what appeared to be real interest.

He hadn't noticed Aiea until she shouldered her way out of the crowd and joined him and the other two up against the stone railing. She must have been hidden behind some taller people, or more likely under the shade of one of the multicolored canopies that protected many of the watchers from the heat of the noon sun.

She was, of course, spectacular, even though the shift she wore was far less ornate and decorative than most of the ladies' relatively sedate daytime apparel. There was something about the way that the whiteness of it set off her olive skin, and the occasional flash of leg from the thigh-high hemmed slit up the right side that had Jason frowning.

She was Walter's wife, yes, and she was older than he was, but Aiea was still Jason's sister, and while adoption meant a lesser relationship in Holtun—fostering was a different matter, of course—

it was fully understood in Bieme, and, more importantly, by the Cullinanes.

She kissed her brother lightly on the cheek before taking Walter's hand.

Yes, he had made mistakes in his life, but Aiea wasn't one of them. They had been kindred spirits for years, and he easily could read the smile in her eyes that she kept from her lips to mean that she was amused at the way Jason was restraining himself from commenting on the way the high, wide, tight cotton belt—more of a girdle, almost; it was a new style that Walter, for one appreciated—emphasized the swell of her breasts as well as the slimness of her waist.

She stood between Walter and Jason, and watched the fencing. "He's quite good, isn't he?"

Jason nodded. "Yes," he said. "He is that. With a blade in his hand." His eyes never left the swordplay. "Or in helping his mother try to get Ellegon killed. Most likely me, as well."

That was possible, of course, but unlikely. That would mean that Tyrnael was behind it, as Miron, with few friends and connections, in hiding in Barony Tyrnael, would hardly have been able to make any of those sorts of arrangements without Tyrnael's sponsorship.

It was unlikely, though, that Tyrnael would have involved Miron in that, even if he was the source of the would-be assassins. Why tip his hand—even to an ally?

"Which didn't happen," she said, quietly. "Nor is it proven that he is involved, and if it were—"

"We wouldn't have a problem," Jason said. "Maybe we don't. Have a problem, that is."

Well, Walter could see where this was going. If Miron could be provoked into challenging Jason—presumably in some way that left Jason clear of any real suspicion that he had provoked the provocation, so to speak—it would be a simple matter to have a duel, and no matter how minor a duel it might be, a single strike that went under the armpit and deep into the chest could easily kill a man dead before any waiting lackey with healing draughts or even a talented healer could do anything about it.

There were some obvious problems with that, but it might be manageable. It would have to be beyond question that the impetus was Miron's, and not Jason's, as the latter case would be read as the emperor's favorite baron having removed a disliked candidate from succession, and there were more than a few barons and other nobles who had reason, good or bad, to fear that it could happen to them, as well.

But even a Cullinane could defend himself from an unprovoked challenge, and if in that defense he managed to be more successful than was likely for a typical duel, well, that could be managed.

There was still one problem with it.

Walter Slovotsky looked at Toryn, unable to read his expression. It would be nice to know if Toryn had worked out the problem. Jason was like his father—too straightforward, most of the time. Too honest, really. He could use a devious companion—which anybody who had left the Slavers Guild could reliably be counted on to be—as long as the companion was smart enough.

Aiea was. She shook her head.

"It's an interesting thought," she said. "But no. Don't."

"I liked Durine," Jason said, quietly. "He was—"

"He was a fine man, a loyal soldier, and a remarkably . . . durable lover," Aiea said.

Well, there was a surprise. Walter tried not to show it.

". . . but Miron didn't kill him, not directly; you can't prove that he was involved in what his mother did; and this just isn't going to work."

Jason Cullinane's mouth twitched. "Perhaps you're right," he said, after a long pause.

Well, the boy still had a lot to learn about deception. He had given in far too easily.

"Stay here," Walter Slovotsky said, as he stripped off his vest and handed it to Aiea, taking the opportunity to remove a few of his weapons and hide them in the folds.

It would have been nice to know if Toryn had figured it out, as Walter would have preferred to delegate this, but . . .

"Lord Miron," he said, gently elbowing his way through the crowd. "You seem to be quite the swordsman."

Miron didn't turn his head until he had managed to slip past his opponent's defenses and score an easy touch on the sword hand, one that in a real fight would have disarmed his opponent instantly.

The masked man saluted and stepped back. "Very nice, sir," he said, his voice muffled.

Miron turned to Walter Slovotsky. "I thank you, Lord Proctor," he said, his smile seemingly sincere. Maybe it was. For the moment, at least.

"Perhaps I could take a lesson?" Walter deliberately turned his back as he selected a practice sword from the rack.

"I don't think that—"

"Oh, please," Walter said, turning around, "I insist." He examined the hilt, and nodded—ever so slightly—to himself as he did, then tugged overly dramatically at the welded-on button that served as a tip. "I'm far too far out of shape, and besides, if you're going to assume the barony, it would probably be best if we get to know each other, and I can think of few better ways than a friendly bout or two. And if you're not, then what's the harm?"

"Oh, Lord Proctor," Miron said, "you think I've no case?"

"Well, there is the matter of your brother."

"Half-brother."

"Forinel?"

"Years gone, fled his responsibilities." Miron shrugged. "Were he coming back, surely he would have returned by now."

Well, if Forinel was dead, then the spell wouldn't have worked. Perhaps, just for once, Miron meant just what he said.

"If he could be located . . ."

"Possibly," Miron said. "My mother, a few years ago, said she had made a search for anything of his that remained in the castle. A garment, a lock of hair—his baby teeth; anything that a good wizard might be able to use to help us find out if he still lived."

Translation: she scoured the castle, and had anything that might lead somebody to Forinel burned.

Walter had suspected as much, but it was nice to have some confirmation. And nicer to have further confirmation that Miron didn't know that Leria had Forinel's ring.

Well, then, let's see how good he is, on half a dozen levels.

Disdaining a helmet—Aiea had his vest with its hidden vial of healing draughts, just in case—he squared off against Miron.

Their practice swords crossed, and it didn't take more than a moment for Walter to realize that he was facing a better swordsman than Walter had ever been. Miron's blade moved like quicksilver, never quite where Walter thought it would be, and while in their first pass Miron didn't—quite—touch him, it was just a matter of the younger man playing with Walter.

It was just as well that they were just using practice swords.

Except, of course, for that strange hesitation. It was just a moment, just a hint of robbed time, but it was there whenever Miron did that particular high-line parry on retreat. A good swordsman— Jason Cullinane for certain, Walter Slovotsky as well—could go right through that hesitation and into the heart.

With a real sword.

So: Walter Slovotsky had a real sword. He had planted it here, a sword with a slightly loose tip, not quite welded on properly, and while he was by no means a match for Miron, he could thrust right through his hesitation and into his heart.

Miron scored easily, with a touch on Walter's sword arm.

"Another point," Walter Slovotsky said, fiddling with the tip. "If you please."

"I am rather fatigued—"

"Another point, if you please," Walter repeated as he saluted, and advanced without waiting for Miron to return the salute. He was rushed, as this would be his only chance at Miron—yes, he had planted the sword, and his having loosened or perhaps removed the tip was the reason that he uncharacteristically kept his sword in constant motion.

A slight widening of Miron's eyes was his only reaction.

Their blades crossed, yet again, and Walter tried the high-line attack, just as he had done before, and just as he had seen Miron's sparring partner do before.

It would be simple. All he would have to do was renew the attack on the low line, and go right through Miron's hesitation and into his—

Miron parried the thrust smoothly, then ended the point with a solid touch on Walter Slovotsky's chest that stung.

Miron stepped back and dropped his own sword to the ground, his palms raised, fingers spread. "Enough, Walter Slovotsky, if you please," he said, panting more than he had to. "You're too good an opponent for me to take on when I'm so tired. Perhaps I can give you another match, some other time."

Walter Slovotsky nodded. "That would be nice," he said.

Miron smiled. "Oh—you might want to have that practice sword seen to? If my eye doesn't betray me, the tip seems a little loose."

"Really?"

Even Jason would have had to have seen it: the whole hesitation had just been a maneuver, a gambit, intending to trap Jason into a fight that he could not win, not when he was planning to exploit a weakness that wasn't there.

Was it Miron's intent to kill Jason in the fight? Or just use the misbehavior of the former heir apparent to the imperial throne as evidence of imperial betrayal, evidence that could only be washed away by the obvious concession?

Walter knew which way he would bet.

It was probably best to be underrated by an opponent, but perhaps there was some virtue in letting Miron know that he wasn't the only person around here capable of some subtlety. There was an argument to letting Miron think he had won more in winning this match than he had, and an argument in having him know that he had won less.

So Walter Slovotsky furrowed his brow, looked carefully at the thoroughly welded tip of the sword, and shook his head. "I think it's just fine," he said, and tossed it, hilt-first, to the younger man. "I don't know what would make you think it otherwise."

He walked back to where Aiea, Jason, and Toryn were waiting.

Jason nodded. "Point taken, Uncle Walter," he said, quietly.

Aiea looked up at him and shook her head.

She was probably right: he shouldn't have given anything away. Miron was dangerous enough—and so was Tyrnael. But Miron was good enough to tempt Walter Slovotsky into the weakness of showing where his strength lay.

Had that been the purpose of this all along? Did Miron play a deep enough game that his little maneuver with the hesitation was intended to see if he could get Walter to reveal Walter's own ability to look through something that subtle?

Shit, shit, shit. The fact that Walter was even considering such wheels within wheels within wheels was the sign of a bad situation getting worse. That was the trouble with layering subtlety on shade on nuance—it would be easy to be so busy reaching for a fine distinction that you would be wide open for a simple club across the head.

It was a politician's trap, and Walter Slovotsky had, willy-nilly, become a politician.

It had happened to St. Thomas More, after all, too caught up in fine distinctions of what silence could mean to notice that the game was rigged or to realize that the only thing that stood between him and the executioner's axe was the Channel.

Hurry up, you folks, he thought. *This one's not just slippery, he's smart. Too smart.*

But what if Forinel couldn't be persuaded to come back? What if they couldn't even find him? Well, they had the ring.

And if he *was* alive . . . *what if* he couldn't be persuaded to come back?

That was easy. It wasn't accidental that Walter Slovotsky had sent Pirojil and Kethol: they would drag Forinel back by the scruff of his neck if they needed to.

They needed him badly.

It needn't be for long, after all. If Miron was no longer the heir apparent to the barony, that made him far more expendable, and maybe he could even be expended.

Hurry up, guys. We need him, and now.

22

⚜ Therranj

The elven city spread out below them, although Erenor could see only a small part of it, and he was sure he could feel only a small part more.

Still, it raised the sort of question that Pirojil would probably like to think about: was it a city embedded in a forest, or a forest embedded in a city?

Tall, thin spires, sparkling like diamonds in the morning sunlight, reached up above the leafy canopy that concealed Therranj below, but they looked, well, more grown than built, as though they were crystalline frameworks that had grown up along with the ancient trees. A single road led from the forest only a short way, until it vanished into the grasslands, where a herd of antelope grazed, heedless of the dragon cruising far above. These days, in these times, cougars were more of a threat, and humans far more so.

They wouldn't have been so heedless before, not while Kethol was busy vomiting, over the side, Erenor thought, unable to smile about that anymore. He tried to keep a sense of humor about others' problems, but it was hard to maintain a proper detachment over gagging sounds.

Ellegon banked into a slow, wide turn.

Beyond the far ridge of hills was the Home settlement, what the Therranji called the Vale of Varnath. It was a noisy place, filled with sounds of laughing children and working engines, and while those sounds were far too distant, a smudge of smoke on the horizon spoke of something belching smoke up into the air. A different sort of magic, this *engineering* thing, and Erenor wasn't sure he approved of it.

Here, though, it was quiet—save for the rushing of air—and the only smell at this height was a distant reek of humus from the forest.

He closed his eyes to filter out the rest of the world, leaving him with only his inner sight.

Powerful fires glowed below, some in familiar colors—a flaming doran threatening in one place; a cool owgre, darker but more sallow than the green of the trees over there; a lush, patterned digovi far away—others in shades and hues that he had never seen before, with inner or outer vision. Erenor sensed other fires, somewhere, powerful enough to hide not only their location, but their nature, and that made him feel for a moment like he did during sword practice with Kethol: clumsy, useless, beyond hope.

Elves.

It was a mistake to see them as the tall counterpart of the Moderate People, or perhaps it was a mistake to see the Moderate People as being as simple as they appeared to be, as well. It wasn't just a matter of power, but of much more subtle difference, as though what you saw and felt—even with your inner sight—of elves was only part of what they were, as though the rest was embedded in Faerie itself.

Maybe it was like a worm felt as it lay next to another worm. Yes, you could see one end of it, and you could see that the other end stretched out into the distance. Perhaps it was as long as you were, just differently positioned. Or perhaps it was much longer, and you were only equipped to see part of it. Or maybe it was infinitely long.

Perhaps it was something that a simple hedge wizard, even one with a fairly advanced specialty in and skill at illusion, was never going to understand.

Check the ring, Ellegon's mental voice commanded. *Are we

still going in the same direction, or have we passed over where he is?*

Lady Leria had kept the ring hidden on her—exactly where, Erenor could only enjoy speculating, and thought that he had better not do so aloud, all things considered—until this morning, when Ellegon and Erenor had prevailed upon her to give it to him.

He was probably the right choice. Pirojil and Kethol were simultaneously both too suspicious and too trusting of magic. Enchanted rings had a legendary way of disappearing when you needed them, so this one was trusted to two separate thongs—both tied to the ring, not merely looped through it—each knotted separately around Erenor's neck, so that the thongs would have to be not merely lifted over his head, but untied or cut in order to remove it.

It still left enough play for Erenor to hold the warm golden ring in the palm of his hand—why *did* a piece of gold seem to hold more warmth than its size and weight justified?—and while wizards were legendarily clumsy, Erenor was no legend, and his fingers could as easily feel a slight tug in one direction or another as they could prevent tugging on a purse while the slim blade concealed between index and middle finger of his other hand sliced the bottom out of that purse.

There was the slightest of pulls to the left, to the east to—nowhere.

Nowhere?

That couldn't be. The spell had been put on the ring by Henrad, and even Erenor could see that the wizard's flame burned hot and deep, a blazing redor that would probably consume Henrad's sanity, eventually, if not much more.

Nowhere?

Another circle, please.

His pulse raced, and he tried to slow it, and calm himself.

There had to be a reasonable explanation. If they were directly over Forinel, well, that would explain it. The pull would be down, and with the way the dragon bumped up and down with every pulse of a wingbeat, it would be difficult even for hands as sensitive as Erenor's to feel the added weight, and compare that with what it had been but moments before.

Hang on. I'm going to climb, and then glide.

Erenor had never quite figured out how Ellegon could pull his huge bulk into the sky faster than his beating wings would justify, but it probably wasn't important, or at least not to Erenor.

Wizards are supposed to be curious.

Well, I am curious. Just not about everything, all the time. I'm fond of women, but that doesn't mean that every time I meet one I feel the immediate need to unbutton my trousers, either.

Ellegon eased the climb into a shallow glide. Far below, the forest slid by beneath, until they were once again over the grasslands, and the ring was tugging back, toward Therranj.

But . . .

But they were leagues to the south of where they'd left the forest—either that, or the herd of antelope had skittered north further and faster than any such beast could run.

And it still pulled, just north of east, as though . . .

This is not good.

Back to where the ring stopped working?

The dragon's head was strained forward, into the wind, but it felt in Erenor's mind like Ellegon nodded.

*There was a plaza . . . *

Erenor nodded.

23

Ti'een the Messenger

His leather wings beating fast enough to make a deafening buzz, the dragon landed with a more than usually hard thump.

Be thankful it wasn't harder, Ellegon said. *I'm trying my best.*

"I am." *Really, I am.*

Kethol was thankful, just not *very* thankful. He *was* very thankful that he wasn't flying, at least not at the moment. It was all he could do to keep his fingers from shaking as he disengaged the harness and quickly made his way down the dragon's side in order to be able to be the one to help Leria down to the ground.

The dragon had landed on a circular stone plaza, a dunam or so of unpolished marble surrounding a fountain in its center. The tall, vine-wrapped, huge-boled trees that lined the edge of the plaza shielded them from any direct sunlight, as well as most of the breeze that had flattened the plains grasses. Even so, as a stream of water shot up high into the air before splashing down into the high-rimmed bowl of the fountain, a fine mist was dispersed into the air, alternately cooling and ignoring Kethol, as the whims of the changing winds led it.

Hmmm . . . , Ellegon ducked his saurian head and sipped at the water in the fountain. *Quite good. Where does the rest of the water go?—this tastes of a spring, and ah . . . I see.*

The dragon curled himself around the fountain, like a cat

around a ball. °I don't see how I can do much of anything except wait here,° he said, °unless you want me burning down the whole forest to make a path, and I think that might get us talked about, even if I could do it. It would take a while.°

The trees . . . you couldn't see the tops of them, not from here; canopies of leaves made it difficult to see any farther than where limbs branched out, some as low as a manheight or two in the air. Ancient scars, most partly covered by the thick vines that twisted up the sides of the trees, told of long-trimmed branches near ground level, and an occasional wide, flat arc of bark-clad root made him wonder if the roots went even deeper below the ground than the branches went above it.

There were only hints of anything beyond the plaza: three cobbled paths that bent quickly around one of the leafy giants, disappearing into the forest; a few shiny crystalline edges peeking through the leaves.

But the forest was alive. Something small rustled through the vines around the base of the nearest tree, and while Kethol couldn't see any birds, the throaty warble of a yellow thrush called out from high above, answered—or, at least, so it sounded—by the braying of a jackdaw.

He sniffed the air. Off in the distance, there was the vaguest reek of skunk—pleasant, at the distance—and that seemed to cover any other smell, save for the pleasant, musky background of rotting humus on the forest floor.

"Which way?" he asked, as he turned to Erenor.

The wizard shrugged. "I don't know."

Kethol took a step toward him. "You didn't lose—" He stopped himself as Erenor produced the ring from inside his tunic, still tied to both thongs.

"No, I didn't lose it," Erenor said, grinning. He dangled the ring by its thong, held between thumb and forefinger. "No, I didn't lose it." The ring simply hung there. "It's just stopped working, or, at least, it seems to have just stopped working."

Kethol looked down. That meant that Forinel was buried under this plaza, as the ring—

"No, no, no," Erenor said, "if that was the case, it would have drawn us here, not merely have stopped doing anything. And were he dead—which he isn't, Lady Leria, I am willing to bet much on that—I find it a strange coincidence that he would have died just as we were flying over the plains, toward Therranj."

"Then what do you attribute it to?" a new voice asked, from behind him, high and reedy.

Kethol spun, his hand going to the hilt of his sword, stopping the motion when Pirojil covered Kethol's hand with his own.

"Be still," Pirojil said.

An elf stood in front of him, easily a head taller than Kethol himself was. Tall, his almost preposterously slim form more mocked than disguised by the gray cloak that he held loosely closed in front of him with one hand. His ears certainly came to a point under the shock of white hair that concealed them, and his chin was sharp, and pointed, as well.

It was impossible to tell his age, not even on an if-only-he-had-been-a-human basis. While his hair was white, it was the gleaming white of fresh snow, not a graying of age, and the skin of his face had neither the glow of youth nor the thinness of aging to it.

"Erenor, wizard, former student of the late, lamented Descobar, greets you," Erenor said, formally, his hands clasped in front of him in a bow.

"Ah." The elf smiled. "If you wish to know my name, why not merely ask? It's not a secret, and unless I miss my guess entirely, you're not master of sufficient dominatives or instigators to do any sort of naming spell under favorable circumstances, much less here, much less now." The elf ducked his head, fractionally: a bow, yes, but one to an inferior. "I am Ti'een," he said. "No real wizard, nor one with any pretensions to such. I'm known as Ti'een the Messenger, and I bring you a message from Lord Forinel—"

"Forinel? He's well?"

Kethol found himself hating the breathlessness in Leria's voice.

"—if," the elf said, looking at Leria with visible distaste, something more than mere irritation, "if I may be permitted to speak without interruption. Lord Forinel says: 'We shall arrive shortly, having been delayed by illness. Please wait.' "

They knew we were coming.

°Duh,° the dragon said. °If there was some reason to hide it, you might have wanted to mention it by now. Not that it would have done any good, of course.°

"In the meantime," Ti'een said, "I have another message, for another of you. It goes: 'You left not so long ago, leaving behind death and pain and misery—though not solely of your own making.

" 'It is not right that you come back here, now or ever.

" 'Blood does not seek blood, and pain does not seek pain, for that is not the way either of the elven or of the humans who have lived among us, but do not linger here, nor return.

" 'You are what you are, and if you have come here to ask that you become something else, leave now.' "

Kethol was waiting to see Erenor's reaction when he realized that the elf was facing Pirojil.

"I don't know why you're talking to me." Pirojil's lips where white. "I haven't come here to ask for anything, not from you, not from anybody else," he said, his voice too calm, too low, too even.

You work with somebody for long enough, you eat and sleep and shit and fight with him, and one day you find that you can, sometimes, read his mind. Not through any magic, but through the way he stands, or speaks, or breathes.

Kethol had long been that way with Pirojil, but now the facility abandoned him.

Was Pirojil going to attack the elf?

If so, were any of the elven soldiers that Kethol only now could see out of the corner of his eye, at least a dozen of them, gathered around the edge of the plaza, going to try to stop him? Kethol was a good longbowman, sure enough. But the prowess of the elves was legendary—

—and there were at least three bowmen among them, their bows strung and arrows nocked. Kethol's bow was still strapped to his rucksack, at his feet.

But his sword was loose in its sheath, and even if he hadn't had the sword, he still had hands and feet and teeth.

A tension he hadn't known was there went out of Kethol's scalp.

Well, perhaps the elves could get their retribution, and perhaps they could even stop Pirojil. But if Pirojil decided that his companions' deaths were worth the killing of this Ti'een, well, then, that was the way it was.

He didn't have to look out of the corner of his eye to see Erenor's nod, not one whit more than he would have had to see Pirojil's, or Durine's, and he would not shame Erenor or himself with any doubt.

And if that meant that Leria died here, too?

No.

She looked at him, and nodded, once. *Yes.*

"No." Pirojil held up a hand.

No?

What was this no? No: meaning *I'll not put up with this insult?* Or no, meaning *Don't kill the elf, don't pay attention to how angry I am, don't—*

"No," he said, again, quietly. "My name is Pirojil," he went on. "You must be mistaken. As for me, I'm just an ordinary soldier, fealty-bound to Barony Cullinane of the Empire of Holtun-Bieme."

Kethol looked over at the elf soldiers—at where the elf soldiers had been. They were gone, either having moved back into the trees as silently as they had emerged, or never having been there at all.

"Ah." Ti'een smiled, and as he did, his pointed canines reminded Kethol that the Therranji had a reputation for, if not cruelty, a certain viciousness. Therranji garrotes, after all, would tighten by themselves, their barbs digging into the flesh of the neck as they did so. "The Empire of Holtun-Bieme, is it? Two tiny countries, welded together under a usurper, and they are an empire. I shall have to remember that."

Do. Ellegon's nose issued steam. *Do remember that.*

"Of course, noble dragon." Ti'een's head bobbed toward the dragon. "I shall." He turned to Kethol, pointedly ignoring Pirojil. "You are . . . ?"

"Kethol," he said.

"Well, Captain Kethol—"

"Just Kethol." There had been a time when Kethol had been mistaken for an officer, that he had let the mistake go. Leria had been there, and he had often wondered why she hadn't objected, or protested. Had it amused her? Or had it flattered her that the Adahanian officer had assumed that her escort must be a captain of some sort?

But that had not been here, not in front of Pirojil and Erenor.

"Very well, Just Kethol," the elf said. "If you, Just Kethol and your . . . companions will follow me, I will take you to where you can wait for Lord Forinel."

24

Playing for Time

What's the secret of comedy?
Err . . . timing?

—Walter Slovotsky

I see no great reason to wait on this matter," Baron Nerahan said,
his voice echoing hollowly through the Great Hall, "but hardly
one for any haste, either." Robald Nerahan toyed with his bristly
mustache, twirling the ends of it enough that Walter pretty much
expected him to break into a Snidely Whiplash-style "nyah-hah-hah"
at any moment. "Why do we need to rush?"

Saint Dymphna, save me from my allies, Walter Slovotsky
thought.

"I agree with Baron Nerahan," Tyrnael said. "My barony is being run by men I trust, and while I certainly am eager to get back—
there are some matters I'd rather handle myself—I think this is the
sort of decision that should be made judiciously, by the whole Parliament."

*And, Saint Dymphna, as long as you're listening, please con-
sider preserving me from allies who talk like melodrama villains,
and enemies who voice insincere support, trying to make a weak
case in my favor.*

Was that going to fly? It was a transparent attempt at manipulation, but—

"Not I." Selahan went for it—well, Walter Slovotsky had long ago concluded that he was, in fact, as stupid as he looked. Any noble who spent enough time out in the sun to burn through any tan was probably not spending enough time tending to affairs of state.

"I'm eager to return home, myself," he said. "There's only so much I'd like to see the governor's deputy doing in my absence, and . . ."

Walter Slovotsky turned his ears off as the Holt rambled on. The fact was that it was the Selahan governor who was in charge in Barony Selahan, and the Baron Selahan was likely to be one of the last of the Holtish barons to assume control of his barony.

"I think it would be wrong of me to delay any decision." Treseen knew whom he was working for. "I'm certainly willing to serve as long as necessary," he said, his fingers idly playing with his belt knife. There was no threat in that; Treseen was just one of those people who needed something to keep his hands busy, and if he wasn't fiddling with his knife, he'd probably be playing with himself.

At least he wasn't twiddling his mustache.

"But if this Parliament confirms Lord Miron as baron, we could at least start to move toward the day I'll retire." He smiled. "I've thought about buying a small holding along some main road, somewhere, and sitting on my front porch, watching the world go by."

He didn't look over at Tyrnael, and Walter didn't wonder at all whether that small holding was not so small, and was in Barony Tyrnael.

He didn't wonder for a moment.

A pity, that—after the near disaster in Keranahan, Walter should have not only figured out how crooked Treseen was, but inquired as to his price.

Niphael and Verahan weighed in next, both eager for their own reasons to end the Parliament and get home, while Benteen and Arondael just seemed to want to argue for the sake of arguing.

Jason Cullinane stood. "I'd like to settle this now. Perhaps Miron isn't provably guilty of having been involved in his mother's plotting—but does that mean that we have to give him the barony?"

Well, yes, it probably did, and half a dozen of the older barons, concerned about their own heirs, immediately called out, while Beralyn Furnael simply smiled at the way the hated Cullinane had just helped make the case for her.

No, she didn't particularly want Tyrnael and Miron to win—what she wanted was Walter Slovotsky and the Cullinanes to lose.

"Excuse me." Thomen's voice wasn't loud, but it cut through the babble like a sharp knife through a neck. "We have not yet decided that the succession is a decision to be left to the Parliament."

Bren Adahan smiled at that. The royal *we* neatly ducked the question of whose decision that was.

That was something to trade off on:

"The emperor is, of course, quite right," Walter said. "Is it an imperial decision? Or should it be left to Parliament? Or is it one that the emperor should propose and the Parliament dispose?"

Political deals had to reflect the reality on the ground, and the reality was that the Biemish barons could, collectively, take on the Home Guard quite easily, and with Holtun occupied largely by baronial troops under imperial command, there wouldn't be much to stop them.

On the other hand, the barons would have to reach some sort of consensus that that was the thing to do, a consensus that they'd not easily reach with their heads—and the attached necks—under the emperor's roof.

Parliament had to be seen by them, though, as every bit as much of a chance to exercise collective power as scheming to overthrow the Crown was, and that meant that their decisions would have to count.

In the long run, a parliamentary imprimatur on imperial nominations for succession probably made the most sense, and imperial nominations ought to, except under extreme circumstances, stick to the usual rules of inheritance.

There were times when you had to roll the dice, and hope they'd fall where you wanted them.

"I think," Walter Slovotsky said, "that the emperor should propose Baron Keranahan's son and heir as the next baron, and I think that the Parliament ought to endorse that choice, and freely, after some due consideration, of him and of other possible claimants to the barony."

Tyrnael's mouth twitched. "Just how much consideration should be needed? We have Lord Miron here; there are no other claimants—"

Now or never. "Yes, there is," Walter Slovotsky said. "The wizard Henrad has put a location spell on an old family heirloom."

Tyrnael was good, but he wasn't good enough to keep the surprise off his face. Miron had told him about Elanee having destroyed all the possible traces, a long time ago. "How—I mean, how wonderful," he said. Faked sincerity came easily to the baron. "I had heard rumors that you'd sent Ellegon and others off to Keranahan to look for such items, but . . ." he shrugged. "But that's but a few days ago—could they have located something so quickly, and . . ."

Walter had always preferred limit poker, rather than table stakes. In a limit game, you could take each hand as it came, knowing that if, in the long run, you made better decisions than the other folks did, you'd end up with all the chips.

But in table stakes, there came a time when you had to push all your chips to the center of the table, and hope and pray that either you had the best hand or nobody else would call.

"It was an old ring of Forinel's, Baron Tyrnael," Walter said. "He gave it to Lady Leria the night he left, years ago, under the influence of Lord Miron's mother." Walter Slovotsky forced a smile to his face. "No, I'd not send Lady Leria and the Cullinane soldiers to look for some distant possibility—they already had what they needed, despite Baroness Elanee's very thorough scouring, I've no doubt, of Castle Keranahan.

"No, I've sent them to find Lord Forinel. He should be here within a very few days. Shall we give it another, oh, tenday? Shall we, Baron Tyrnael?"

"Ten days," Tyrnael nodded, looking around. "Are we all in agreement?" he asked, his gaze finally settling on the emperor. "Within the next ten days, either Walter Slovotsky will produce Lord Forinel, or Lord Miron will be confirmed as Baron Keranahan?"

Walter Slovotsky was not the only one who could push all his chips into the pot.

"Ten days." The emperor nodded.

25

✠ Forinel

Kethol had been in worse jails. Come to think of it, he had never been in a nicer one.

Mostly, being locked up meant being stuck in some dark hole with—if you were lucky—a chamberpot to keep you company. Escape was always the issue, and in practice that had usually meant waiting for Pirojil and Durine to figure out something—as he had never seen, much less been in, a prison that you couldn't get out of, not if you had enough wit and help.

Here, he and the others were free to wander not only in Visitors' Tree—a misnaming for a dwelling that was more than half that crystalline construction that the Therranji built or maybe grew around the Named Trees—but down the winding staircase cut into bark of the tree itself and to the ground below.

There were no walls, except for the forest itself, and while that probably wasn't impenetrable, every time he tried to leave one of the paths he simply found himself crossing and recrossing them, over and over again, until he finally gave up and took the paths.

And all paths that he took seemed to twist through the forest to the fountain plaza where Ellegon still lay, and then back to Visitor's Tree.

The dragon seemed utterly unbothered by the notion of simply sitting in place and resting for days, or even longer—

*We're a patient lot, we are, except when we're, oh, chained in a Pandathaway sewer, forced to flame foul feces into smoke and

ash, or have it up to our noses. After a century or two of that, even
a patient dragon like myself can tire."

Kethol tried another path and found himself back at Visitors'
Tree.

It was a comfortable imprisonment.

Human servants, their pale skin and light hair generally speaking of Salke ancestry, brought food and drink at regular intervals.
There was always more than one could possibly eat or drink—so
much so that it was understandable that at each delivery, leftover
portions were unceremoniously scraped from their trays and plates
into an oubliette in the circular inner wall of the wedge-shaped
apartments, sliding away down the impossibly slick crystal tube inside.

But the human servant engaged in conversation only to the least
extent possible, and answered no questions, referring everything to
Ti'een.

"Care to try again?" Leria asked, one eyebrow arched.

"Eh? I mean, 'Excuse me, my Lady?' "

"No," she said, with that giggle that made her seem to be a
little girl, "you meant 'eh.' "

She didn't look like a child, though. Her traveling clothes had
been replaced, at least for now, with an elven dress that appeared
to be little more than a long, wide, embroidered bolt of silk,
wrapped several times around her at bosom and hips, but only once
on its way from breasts to hips, then twisting around her left leg
down to that ankle, leaving her right leg bare from sandals to mid-
thigh.

He couldn't see any pins, and there was always the feeling that
the whole garment was about to fall off, like a hawk's jesses wound
too loosely around its spool—but that would have been undignified,
and the Therranji elves would hardly have provided her with their
own formal clothes if embarrassing her had been their intention.

*Whatever they've done with—or for—Forinel, he's obviously
earned some respect here, and I'm sure they're not going to em-

barrass her,° the dragon said, from off in the distance. °Worry about the other things.°

"You haven't answered me, Kethol," she said.

He shook his head. "I'm sorry, Lady. I was caught up in thought."

"Well," she said with a smile, "uncatch yourself, and let's see if we can walk ourselves free of this leafy prison, or at least discover where the walls and the bars might be."

He nodded. "I'll get—"

"No." She laid her hand on his. "Pirojil is sleeping off whatever it was that he drank last night, and he's foul enough company these days."

He was about to protest when she put a finger to his lips. "Shh. I don't mean to criticize him. He's obviously troubled. This is where he comes from, isn't it?"

Kethol shook his head. "I don't know."

Her eyes met his. They still had that strange quality of interfering with his breathing.

"Very well," she said. "Let's walk."

Their apartments were far enough up the tree that Kethol would have been concerned about how long the climb would have been, although as they exited through a crystalline door and onto the circular staircase cut into the bark, he wouldn't have sworn that they were as much as halfway up the tree's trunk.

The woods were quiet, at least at this level, despite the breeze that rattled the leaves against each other, hard enough that, for just a moment, Kethol could see flashes of crystal through the leaves.

"I've been thinking about Pirojil," she said. "It begins to make sense. Remember when Erenor tried a seeming on him? To make him look less, well—"

"Ugly is the word you're looking for, Lady," he said.

"Ugly it is." She nodded her agreement. "It didn't work, and Erenor is rather good at seemings, if nothing else.

"That sounds like what I've heard about elven magic. There

used to be an elven presence in Tynear, back during the Euar'den days." She sighed. "He's been made not just to look ugly, but to be ugly, in a deep and profound way that makes a seeming impossible. Or so Erenor thinks."

"He said that?" When would Erenor have been alone with Leria, anyway, and—

"No." Her eyes met his. "If you spend enough time with some-body, if you talk and listen to him about things important and trivial," she said, "you find that you know what he thinks about some things without him saying it. Haven't you found it so?"

Kethol nodded. "Yes, I have."

Whether her hand rested on his arm for physical support or for something else he couldn't have said.

Hoped, yes, but said, no.

Besides, it didn't matter. It was only a matter of time.

Forinel was on his way, and the two of them would, shortly, be on their way back to Biemestren. All in all, it was just as well, although she would have made a lovely empress. Better she be with Forinel.

The ring was, after all, the heart of it. She could have taken the ring off and secured it in a jewelry box, somewhere. But if she had kept that ring on her person, next to her heart, for years, she must have loved him very much, indeed, enough that the pain of missing him was less important than the familiar warmth of it.

The stairway led down to the trail, and half a dozen branches of the trail led off in different directions. He had taken all of them, but explored the least beyond the one that curled around behind a massive white birch.

The birch was just too large. A birch should not grow so tall that you could not see the top, nor so wide that half a dozen people could not have joined hands around its base.

He reached out and pulled off a small piece of bark, idly tucking it in his pouch.

"Why did you do that?" she asked.

"An old habit, Lady," he said. "Birch bark burns easily, even when wet. You learn to gather a little here and there, so you'll have it in a time of need."

"Just a little?"

"A little is usually enough."

Once, years ago, during the Old Emperor's Last Ride, he and Pirojil and Durine, along with the Old Emperor and a few who had not, yet, died on that ride, had been caught in the woods during a horrid rainstorm, and spent a horribly wet night, at best half-sheltered by an oiled canvas tarpaulin, in front of a birch-bark fire that even the Old Emperor had been surprised Kethol could light.

You had to be careful, though. If you peeled the bark all the way around the circumference of a birch tree, it would kill it. Not quickly, but surely.

You could cut the heart out of it without ever going more than a finger's-width deep. Amazing how much damage you could do through ignorance, without any maliciousness intended.

She should have known that. She should have known how her smile stripped the bark from around him.

He smiled at her. "I'm surprised you didn't know that," he said, then raised his hand in apology. "I'm sorry, Lady; it's not my place—"

"Don't be silly," she said. "After . . . after all we've been through, together, you and I?" For a moment her smile vanished, as though it had never been there, but then it flickered back to life. "Oh, let's try this way," she said, taking his hand to urge him down the left-hand path.

He had been down the left-hand path before, but not with Leria pulling on his hand, so, like an obedient little puppy, he followed.

No; there was no point in being hard on himself. The world could do that for him just fine.

°Forinel is here,° Ellegon said. °At the fountain.°

All things come to an end, and—

°If you can take a momentary break from pining for the lady, we've got a problem.°

Kethol's hand dropped away from Leria's, and to the hilt of his sword.

°Well, perhaps you can solve this problem with a sword, but I wouldn't advise trying it. The problem is that he isn't alone.

°He's with his wife.°

His *what*?

°Wife. The woman he is married to, and with whom he already has one child: his very pregnant, very elven, wife.°

"Kethol?" She looked up at him, concerned. "What is it?"

He opened his mouth, closed it, opened it, and closed it again.

26

Bargains

Pirojil wasn't sure why he wanted to separate Forinel's head from his shoulders, but he did.

Want to, that is.

Badly.

As if what he wanted to do had any damn thing at all to do with what he was going to do.

Besides, it wasn't as though it would be easy. Those eleven archers were always just barely out of sight—or, at least, that's what Ti'een had implied—and while Pirojil didn't have any particular moral objection to killing somebody in front of his massively pregnant wife and a young boy-child of three, perhaps four, that wouldn't have been his preference, either.

Forinel helped the woman to a seat on the stone bench. "It's not necessary, my dear, that you be—"

"Shh." She was more ungainly than a pregnant human would have been, moving more awkwardly: taller than any human and inhumanly slender, from the elongated head through the slim body and down to the too-small ankles that her white dress didn't quite cover, but her belly was every bit as large and round as a human woman's would have been. Elf babies weren't all that much different in size and shape from human ones. At birth, in fact, you could hardly tell one from the other, or from a half-elven, at least not to look at them.

The changes only happened in the growing.

That was apparent in the silent little blond boy who never strayed very far from his mother's skirts, his eyes moving from Erenor to Pirojil and the dragon, and then, always, back to Pirojil.

The tips of his ears peeked through his flaxen hair, and they had barely started to point. If it weren't for that, Pirojil wouldn't have been able to tell him from a human child, and if it weren't for the definitely human squareness of jaw and wide separation of eyes that mirrored Forinel's, he wouldn't have been sure that the child was half-elven, rather than being a purebred.

"You were delayed by illness," Pirojil said.

Forinel nodded. "Yes, we were. It's almost Erianne's time, and it's been a difficult pregnancy, even more so than the one that—" he glanced down, meaningfully, "—than others we've heard of. I am . . . ever so slightly concerned about the birthing," he said, although it wasn't clear to Pirojil how much the expression of concern was for the benefit of his wife, and how much the minimizing of the concern was for the benefit of the boy.

He would be a difficult man to figure out, all in all. It probably ran in the family.

He was half a head taller than his half-brother, Miron, and looked easily ten years older, although Pirojil knew that wasn't the case. Forinel's hairline, save for a prominent widow's peak, was far receded, although his black hair remained thick, and tightly curled, from the rest of his head down to his beard, and further, where it gradually turned into a black mat of chest hair, revealed by a white tunic slit open almost to the navel.

The tunic fit him too tightly across the shoulders, chest, and waist, as though the seamstresses who had sewn it for him had not been able to accustom themselves to the squat, overly broad measurements of a human. Either that, or he had recently put on weight in the shoulders, chest, and belly, and his lean form made it clear that he hadn't.

A short sword—a familiar length; elves tended to go in for

longer ones—hung from the left side of his waist, undecorated save for the single emerald embedded in the hilt.

Erianne reached a slim hand into one of her oversized sleeves, and produced a small vial, which she uncapped and sniffed at. The effect was immediate, if not overly dramatic: her too pale skin gained just a touch of color, and her shoulders relaxed, as though she didn't feel she had to hold herself stock still, for fear of falling apart if she moved.

"Erianne," Forinel said, "should you—"

"Shhh." She took his outstretched hand in one of hers. "A few moments of vanished discomfort will do neither me nor the baby any harm."

Erenor looked over at Pirojil and nodded. Whatever that nod was supposed to mean was a mystery to Pirojil, but, then again, a lot of what Erenor did and said and thought was a mystery to Pirojil, and what had ever happened to that gold coin he had borrowed from Kethol for a demonstration back in Cullinane, anyway?

Erenor apparently could read Pirojil better than vice versa. "She should know about that sort of thing, Pirojil," Erenor said. "She's quite a powerful wizard in her own right, and unless I'm very much mistaken, both of her children will grow to be even more so."

The blood grows thin, Pirojil thought.

Her face showed no trace of weakness, or of friendliness, as she turned to the wizard.

"That's true, Master Erenor," she said. Her voice was higher-pitched than it should have been, but there was no hint of weakness in it, no threat that it would break if it, or she, were too far pushed. "At least in potential. A child is like a seed, in some ways. You can see the possibilities, but until it flowers, those are only possibilities." She smiled, but the smile was not for him, but for the child and the man, as she took their hands in hers.

"Forinel."

Leria stood at the very edge of the plaza, Kethol to the side and behind her.

"Leria," he said, with a nod, his voice tight.

Erianne grabbed hold of his hand and tried to stand, although whether it was to comfort him or because she didn't like the idea of Leria looming over her was anybody's guess.

"Please," he said. "Sit. The trip has been too difficult for you as it is—"

"Forinel, she said, cutting him off. "Be still." She turned back to Leria. "My name is Erianne," she said. "This is my son—our son—Erinel." She ran her impossibly long fingers through the boy's hair.

Kethol listened with limited patience while Forinel talked. Forinel didn't want to go into details that nobody particularly wanted to hear, anyway.

He had ridden away toward the Katharhd, but a series of events—he called them "adventures," which visibly lowered Pirojil's opinion of him by another full step—had brought him to Therranj, and to Erianne. Word of his father's death had reached him via some Home traders, and—

—he hadn't had the courage or the integrity to face Leria, and he certainly didn't want to bring his wife and his child—children, now—into the Middle Lands in general, where they'd be despised outsiders instead of what they were here.

Kethol didn't know much about the Therranji, and the way that they'd been kept around Visitors' Tree made it clear that he wasn't going to learn much more.

Save that the bastard was breaking Leria's heart, of course.

". . . and I thought that, finally," he said, "that I should come here—"

"That we should come here," Erianne said, firmly.

"—that we should come here to meet you, and to apologize for having . . ." His hands seemed to grasp for some phrase that would make it all acceptable.

Leria's face was stony. No hint of tears, or of anger, or of anything. It was a mask.

"There's only one thing," Forinel said. "It sounds petty, I know. But the ring; I need it back."

"The ring?"

Erianne laid a hand on his shoulder. "The ring. I long ago realized what Elanee had done to him, and why, and that she would scour the barony for any thing that Forinel could be traced with. But the ring . . ."

"But the ring could be used."

She nodded. "Not just to locate Forinel, either. It's an heirloom, and there's a connection between it and his family." She let one graceful hand rest on her belly, the other on her son's head.

The little boy grinned up at her, but didn't speak.

"It could, perhaps, be used in various ways against his blood, as well."

Kethol took a step forward, desisting only when Pirojil held up a hand. "Stand easy, Kethol. You're not going to attack a pregnant woman, in any case."

"I believe you miss the point, Mistress Erianne," Erenor said, ignoring the byplay. "Lady Leria doesn't have the ring. I do."

"But you'd give her—him—the ring if I asked you to," Leria said.

Kethol nodded. "Of course you would."

"No, there is no 'of course' to it." Erenor shook his head, and his smile broadened. "No, I don't think so," he said. "I'm new to this soldiering thing, new to this notion of being sent off on missions, but as I understand it, returning empty-handed is not the objective of the exercise." He sneered at Forinel. "He may be a poor excuse for a baron, but I'd rather see him than Miron there. The people who sent us here—Walter Slovotsky and the Cullinanes—are better off without Miron becoming baron, much better off without Tyrnael having won one off the Cullinanes, much . . ."

Erenor let his voice trail off as he shook his head. "No. Perhaps we may return with nothing more than we left, but we'll not return with anything less." He tucked the ring back in his tunic. "Let the Parliament know that Forinel is still alive here, but doesn't wish to come home and assume his duties. Perhaps they'll send others out to find him, for whatever reason."

No, they would just give Miron the barony. Kethol opened his mouth to say that, stopped only when Erenor turned to face him.

Not one word, he mouthed. *Don't say anything.*

Erianne smiled genially. "Do you really think that you could leave Therranj with this ring, without our—my—leave?"

Erenor nodded. "Yes, I do. I think I could do just that." He murmured a quick phrase that could only be heard and forgotten.

And in an eyeblink, he was gone.

"Oh, I know," the air to Kethol's left said, in Erenor's voice, "it might be difficult for me to simply walk out, but impossible? No. I'm quite good at what I do, even if what I do is seeming not to be here." He muttered another quick phrase, and he blinked into existence—not where the voice had come from, but from next to Forinel, his knife near Forinel's throat.

Smilingly, Erenor took a step back as he sheathed his knife, then raised his palms. "No harm done, eh?"

"Master Erenor," Erianne said, "I've been involved with humans, in various ways, from time to time over the years, and I can tell when one is simply blustering, and when one is blustering to make a point. You have a point, and I assume it's the obvious: you want to trade for the ring."

Erenor spread his hands, palms up. "Lady Erianne, you are wise beyond your years, and I suspect that's rather many years to be wise beyond." He gestured toward Pirojil. "I tried a seeming on Master Pirojil some time ago, and found that it simply wouldn't stick." He shook his head. "That sounds to me like there's something there that's more than a spell. Pirojil said it to me, something about how his appearance isn't just what he was made to be, but what he is." He pointed to Forinel. "Make him look and sound like that—make it so that nobody, not even a wizard, can tell—and you can have this ring."

"No," Pirojil said. "It's not—"

"It's not possible," Erianne said. "I have some idea what—what was done to this friend of yours, and it's not like one of your little illusions, to be put on or taken off like a suit of clothes. You, now—"

Erenor shook his head. "You haven't thought that through, Lady. I'm little enough of a wizard, but I'd not extinguish my inner flame in exchange for a not nearly so handsome body," he said, with a sniff, "a few pieces of gold, and even a lady as lovely as Lady Leria. Even if you could somehow transform me, to make me really look like Forinel without putting that flame out, why, any wizard could see with one glance that the Forinel who returned had an inner flame that nobody had noticed before he left his father's home."

"Your point is well-taken, but—"

"My point is," Erenor said, his eyes no longer on Erianne, nor on Pirojil, "that if you want this ring, you'll have to send us back with a Forinel we can pass off."

Kethol was slow of mind far too often. For a moment, he didn't realize why everybody—not just Erianne and Forinel, not just Pirojil and Erenor, but Leria, as well, was looking at him.

Me?

Pirojil nodded. "We'll help, but it has to be you."

Me?

"No," he said. He spun on the ball of his foot and walked away.

27

Leria

Kethol stood alone on the veranda, an unrimmed lip of wood. It had been carved into the tree, not merely tacked onto it: the growth rings in the bare wood spoke of its age.

He had stopped counting somewhere around one hundred, as that hadn't even taken him off the veranda, and the rooms didn't go to the heart of the tree; he wouldn't be able to tell its age, anyway.

It had just been something to do.

He shook his head. It was something he *could* do. There were some things he could do, and some he was quite good at. A game of bones, say; a fight with a sword, or a bow, or bare hands, or a knife, or even a rifle. He could sit a horse better than most, and follow a trail as well as any. He could even fool the odd foreign soldier, every now and then, into thinking that he was an officer and not just an ordinary soldier.

He could, he hoped, die well, if he had to. He had seen enough do that.

But pass himself off as a noble? For the rest of his life?

No. It wasn't just that it was wrong—it wasn't him. He couldn't do it.

Yes, Pirojil and Erenor had come up with an explanation: Forinel had been badly injured in the head, and his health recovered, but some of his memories not. It had taken the appearance of Lady Leria to reawaken some of those, and he was helpless without her.

He needed to be reminded of things, from time to time, and while he was no slackwit—and his heirs would show no sign of his injuries—he would need help in governing Keranahan, indefinitely.

It was a good enough story.

That would make Treseen happy, and if after all was said and done, the emperor could be prevailed upon to find a new governor, that would be just as well.

Or, perhaps Treseen could be kept on, at least for a time, using him as a beater to drive Miron out into some public admission, if it was Miron who was behind the attempt on Jason Cullinane's life.

The worst part of it was how easily at least part of it would work: Kethol would be gone, and there would be nobody to miss him.

Kethol would be dead—and who would think it strange that an ordinary soldier was killed? What was strange, perhaps, was that he had survived so long. Who would miss him? Nobody, not really. Oh, the baron would find himself short a soldier who was rather better than average; Walter Slovotsky would miss being able to order Kethol to stick his hand into a hole to see if there was a badger hiding inside; the dowager empress would, for just a moment, grieve just a little.

But he would be gone, like a rock thrown into a pond, leaving few ripples to mark its passing, and those for only moments.

The golden ring that they would return with would now, with a proper location spell, point to him. That was easy to do, Erenor said. Just make a duplicate, heat it, and temper it in his blood.

Nothing more than that. Kethol shook his head. He didn't mind shedding blood, but this way . . .

It would be just like it would if he really died. That was the worst of it.

No, that wasn't the worst of it. The worst of it was her.

He couldn't have had her as himself; it would have to be as another man.

No.

Their footsteps sounded behind him, quiet enough on the thick carpets before they reached the bare wood of the veranda that nobody else would likely have heard them, much less been able to distinguish Pirojil's drumbeat walk from Erenor's irregular stride.

"You stand too near the edge," Pirojil said. "You could fall over with just the slightest of shoves."

Kethol turned. "I don't think so. Care to try?"

Pirojil smiled as he shook his head. "No, because I'd either succeed or fail, and I wouldn't want to do either. But you've got to learn to be careful."

"Why?"

"Because a ruler without caution is a like a bowman without arrows. He can strike a pretty pose, but that's all."

Erenor cocked his head to one side. "That's just about the silliest thing I've heard you say. How about 'A ruler without caution is like a horse with only three legs'?"

"That's—"

"—or 'A ruler without caution is like woman without nipples'? With clothes on, both look like the real thing, but you'd not want to trust a nursing baby's health to either, and—"

"Erenor, shut up," Kethol said. He was getting tired of the wizard.

Pirojil waved Erenor to silence. It didn't escape Kethol's attention that it was Pirojil that Erenor was listening to and not Kethol.

Pirojil eyed him thoroughly, the concern that creased his ugly face making him look all the uglier. "Me, I'd say no, even if I were offered the chance."

Erenor laughed. "Oh, me, neither. Marry the girl? Inherit a barony? Go from being an ordinary soldier to a rich man in a moment? Oh, I'd not do that, either," he said.

"I can't." Kethol shook his head. "I don't mean that I don't want to—I just *can't*."

"That, friend Kethol, is where you're wrong," Erenor said. "It would be easy. After all they've gone through together, it will surprise nobody if Lord Forinel and Lady Leria ask Pirojil to leave Cullinane service for theirs." His head cocked to one side. "And, no, an ordinary soldier like me won't be much missed, having gotten killed in the rescuing of Forinel—and that story will grow in the telling, let me assure you. In a dozen tendays or so, if it should happen that an aged wizard appears at your baronial door and asks to take up service with the barony, I think you'll have no difficulty finding a place for him, even if he's only a shadow of his former self, and barely able to do more than a weak seeming." Erenor muttered something under his breath, and in an eyeblink—and only for an eyeblink—he was an old man, bent with age, his long white hair a fringe around the periphery of his gleaming bald pate.

"I'll need my spell books back—all of them, Pirojil—to make a go of that."

Pirojil nodded. "Done. As soon as we get back to Biemestren."

"Do you mind telling me where they are?" Erenor asked. "I would just—"

"Well, yes, I would." Pirojil smiled. "It's not like I'm going to get into the habit of trusting you or anything."

"Excuse me." Kethol hadn't raised his voice, but both of them fell silent. "You're assuming that I don't mean it when I say no."

Pirojil shook his head. "Oh, I do think you mean it. I just think you'll change your mind. It's part of who and what you are—"

"What would you know about that?" Kethol said, instantly regretting it.

"—and what you always will be, under a seeming, or under a change that's so deep it makes you immune to seemings," Pirojil went on.

Kethol's jaw clenched painfully. "And what's that supposed to mean? That I'm such a lackwitted idiot that I can be talked into anything?"

"No, and I don't even mean that you're in love with Lady Leria, and have been since the day we took her away from Baroness Elanee—although there's that, too." Pirojil's eyes locked on his. "Because she's the woman who is going to make you do this. Elanee. Not Erianne, and not Leria. But Elanee, dead in her grave.

"The thing is, the thing I keep coming back to, is this: If you don't go through with this, the bitch wins. We killed her, and she still wins. It will be her seed that takes root in the barony."

He reached into his cloak and produced a mottled green bottle, pulled the wooden stopper out, and took a hefty swig, then wiped rubbery lips with the back of his hand before he passed it on to Erenor.

Maybe that was it. Maybe it was that Pirojil was more than a little drunk.

"That's the part that bothers me," Pirojil said. "What Elanee wanted—when she charmed Forinel into leaving so that Miron would become heir to the barony, when she tried to have Ellegon killed—was to establish her house, to raise Miron, and his sons and theirs.

"It wasn't just for herself that she tried to kill Ellegon—and Durine died in stopping her—it was for her House, for Miron, and for his children, when he has them.

"That's what you won't be able to face: her winning. Death? Shit, Kethol, we all are supposed to die in this soldiering we've taken up. It's just taken you and me a little longer than Durine, and him much longer than most." He put the plug back in the bottle, and pushed it home so hard that the glass neck shattered, splashing him with harsh-smelling whiskey.

He slapped at Erenor's hands, and threw the bottle away, over the side, ignoring the way what was left of the whiskey splashed down his arm.

"No. Leave me alone," Pirojil said. He twisted his fingers together, as though he would rend his own hands apart. "It's Elanee winning that bothers me, and you. That's what you can't stomach. Not dying. We're supposed to die." He shook his head, and his expression was a horror to behold. "Die, yes. But we're not supposed to *lose*."

Leria joined him out on the veranda. She was lovely in the torch-light. Somebody had done up her hair in one of those complicated knots that left her neck bare, save for a few wisps of stray hair that stroked at it, stirred by the light breeze. She shivered for a moment, although it didn't feel cold to Kethol.

"Well," she said, "I hear tell that you think I should marry the emperor." She folded her arms defensively under her breasts as she leaned back against the balustrade without pushing at it to test its solidity, the way he would have; he had to stop himself from reaching out to grasp her arm.

Kethol swallowed, heavily. He nodded. "Yes, I do."

"I don't recall him asking," she said, quietly. It was hard to read her expression.

"He will. Pirojil says that his mother sees you as a good choice, and—"

"Well, of course she does," Leria said. "I've spent more time and effort courting her than I have courting him. It's taken much more effort—he's far more pleasant company." She leaned her hands against the balcony rail. "He's a good man, Thomen is. Wise, kind, gentle—"

"You don't have to persuade the likes of me of the virtues of the emperor." Thomen Furnael was good enough a man and good enough a ruler that the Old Emperor's son had abdicated in his favor, and that had always been more than ample proof for Kethol that Thomen deserved to be emperor.

"The point," she said, "that you seem to be missing is that it's not him that I've wanted. I don't want to be empress. I've had my heart set on being Baroness Keranahan for some years now, and not by marrying Miron, either."

She looked up into his eyes. "I can't say that I could have been an ordinary soldier's woman, or a woodsman's wife; it's not what I was raised for; it's not what I know. I don't mind getting my fingers dirty, now and then, out in the woods or cooking over an open fire—but I'm used to a hot bath, if not when the day is done, sooner than later."

He didn't know what to believe. This all would be a lie, and while she may have been talented at lying to others, she had never lied to him before; he would have known.

"So in order to become a baroness, you'd go along with this, this craziness? You'd marry an imposter, knowing that if—*when* this all came out, it would be your neck as well as mine?"

"Yes," she said, smiling. "Just to be a baroness," she continued, her tone and smile giving the lie to her words. "I don't even care if you do it for the empire, or for the barony, or for me, as long as you do it."

That was a lie, too.

And then she was in his arms, holding him as tightly as she could, while he held her gently, for fear of shattering her to a thousand pieces if he used his strength, if he held her as tightly as he wanted to, and he wanted to tell whoever it was that was sobbing so loud to shut his mouth . . .

. . . until he realized it was himself.

"As you wish," he said. "Let it be so."

Afterword:

An Evening in Biemestren

The guard glared at him out of the corner of his eye as he passed Walter Slovotsky on the parapet, but didn't actually say anything.

You have a nice day, too, Walter thought.

Understandable, really, that Walter would be persona non grata up here. And it was even more understandable that there were two other guards, one between him and each staircase on either side, just so that a third could make twice-hourly reports to the new guard captain on where the imperial proctor was.

His slipping in and out of the castle without permission was professionally embarrassing to the Home Guard, and after Parliament was over, Walter intended to assign himself some proctoring in an outlying barony.

Tyrnael, maybe. It would be interesting to see if anybody there knew about the hiring of assassins. Most likely, of course, Tyrnael would have covered his tracks well enough, but you never knew.

If it even was Tyrnael.

He sighed. No matter which way you turned, you offered the rest of the world your back, and there were always knives out there, seeking it.

Some day, perhaps, one of those knives would find him.

Below, the inner bailey was no longer crowded. The barons were in residence, of course, for Parliament, but much of their various entourages were already on the road home, carrying with

them new tax schedules for the village wardens, letters of credit
and imperial orders, and probably more than a little gossip.

Two more days.

"Two more days," Jason Cullinane said, from near his left elbow. "Two more days until they make that bastard Miron the
baron."

"I hadn't heard you walk up," he said.

"Oh, I'm fairly good at walking silently," Jason said. "I had a
good teacher. Mother asked that you and Aiea make no plans for
tomorrow evening, other than to stop by her rooms for a private
goodbye." He looked out at the night. "It'll be good to be home—I
think I'll rush straight back."

Slovotsky smiled. "Oh, if Ellegon shows up in time, I bet he
can be persuaded to get you home."

Jason shook his head. "No, I don't think so. I think I'll ride
directly home—and maybe have an outrider or two, spotting for
me. I'd kind of like to have somebody try to kill me again. I can't
turn speculations and guesswork into proof—but maybe some
mouths can be persuaded to talk."

Walter Slovotsky shook his head. Only a Cullinane. Only a Cullinane would use himself as the bait in a trap by preference, rather
than necessity. Likely the breed was going to extinguish itself more
quickly than not.

"Well?" Jason looked up at him. "Do you have some problem
with that, Uncle Walter?"

"Nah. Not at all." There was a detachment of Cullinane troops
in the capital. A little early for them to be rotated home, what with
the Arondaelian replacements just having arrived, but it could be
arranged.

Somebody had to watch out for the kid.

Jason's face lit up in a huge smile. "He did it!" he shouted.
"They all did it."

It took a moment for Walter Slovotsky to realize what that had
to mean. Jason had always been more sensitive to the dragon's men-

tal voice than anybody else, perhaps from having first had contact
with Ellegon while Jason was still in the womb.

By then, the sound of leathery wings filled the air.

Ellegon?

°What gave it away?°

Did you—

°Well, yes and no. Can you keep a secret?°

Of course.

°So can I. Better wake up the barons and tell them that—a bit
dazed and confused, somewhat battered and bewildered, having
suffered greatly in his exertions over the years—Forinel is here.°

Yes. They had found Forinel, and they had brought him home
in time.

°Close enough. Sometimes, just sometimes, close enough will
have to do.°

High above the castle walls, a long gout of flame lit up the
night sky.